Praise for *The Ce.......*

"What a riveting, wonderfully intelligent novel! Karen Shepard's characters vibrate with desire and disappointment, so obdurately individual that a whole world springs to life around them and the past becomes completely present."

—**ANDREA BARRETT**, author of *Ship Fever* and *The Air We Breathe*

"Karen Shepard has created a novel so much of its time and place, the 1870s, New England, and yet so utterly relevant to our complex century and the wider world. Her vivid characters share our longings and yet can act only within the framework of their mores and politics. Or can they? This eloquent and suspenseful narrative deepens our understanding of love, loyalty, and the possibilities of transformation. A mesmerizing novel."

—**MARGOT LIVESEY**, author of *The Flight of Gemma Hardy*

"Shepard mines history for its facts and textures, its speech patterns and states of mind, its simmering prejudices and life-altering transgressions, and finds all that transcends history to enter the heart and lodge there forever. *The Celestials* works with the same primal heat as *The Scarlet Letter* and the same sympathetic scope as *The Poisonwood Bible*, and enchants and edifies in equal measure."

—**JOSHUA FERRIS**, author of *The Unnamed*

"A profound passion for a particular place at a particular time clearly inspired Karen Shepard's gorgeously crafted novel *The Celestials*. I have not read anything quite like this book before, though the story it tells—of good yet fallible people caught in the unforgiving riptide of history—is one we need to be told again and again. I love the way Shepard tells it with a cool, deliciously cinematic eye . . . yet a warm and generous heart. Her characters will haunt me for some time to come."

—**JULIA GLASS**, author of *Three Junes* and *The Widower's Tale*

The Celestials

The Celestials

a novel by Karen Shepard

Tin House Books

Portland, Oregon & Brooklyn, New York

Published by Tin House Books, Portland, Oregon, and Brooklyn, New York

Distributed to the trade by Publishers Group West, 1700 Fourth St., Berkeley, CA 94710, www.pgw.com

Library of Congress Cataloging-in-Publication Data

Shepard, Karen.
The Celestials : a novel / by Karen Shepard. — First U.S. edition.
    pages cm
ISBN 978-1-935639-55-8
1. Labor unions—Massachusetts—Fiction. 2. Chinese—Massachusetts—Fiction. 3. Identity (Psychology—Fiction. 4. North Adams (Mass.)—Fiction. 5. Massachusetts—History—19th century—Fiction. 6. Historical fiction. I. Title.
PS3569.H39388C45 2013
813'.54—dc23

                              2012050808

First U.S. edition 2013
Printed in the USA
Interior design by Jakob Vala
Interior photo credits: Anthony W. Lee and Private Collection
www.tinhouse.com

For my parents,
Sidney Glazier and Tang Yungmei

1870

Chapter One

In the blue of early morning, hours before the arrival of the Chinese boys, Julia Sampson felt her sleeping husband flush with heat and knew that he would stir. She left his body enough space and stroked his arm and chest. Sometimes this worked to cool him.

His head rocked against his pillow and he reached to swipe at his brow.

"Forgive me," he said thickly, taking her hand and holding it against his chest.

"For what?" she whispered, but he was still asleep.

When he woke, she would ask what was wrong. And he would answer that he didn't know.

Outside their bedroom window, dawn was the mildest suggestion. She felt as she always did at that hour. Their world was a world of two; whatever comfort and aid were to be found were to be found in each other. She wished once again for children, and then she shook her head, tucking herself against her husband so that when he did wake, he would wake to her.

Most of the Chinese strikebreakers had their foreheads pressed to the windows of the train's immigrant cars, their thirteen-day journey nearing an end. The childlike anticipation with which they had set out had been replaced by an anxiety from which all of them suffered and worked to restrain.

The roar of the fire-wheeled vehicle was relentless and deafening. The grit and grime were impossible to keep from their skin and clothes. The iron strips upon which the train shook and rattled, more than a few of them had agreed, looked like the character *gong*.

Some studied their phrase books: *He cheated me out of my wages. They were lying in ambush. He tried to kill me by assassination.*

Others tried again to develop a liking for coffee. The taste was like the odor of sheep. Several had refused the stew offered at the last station stop, their stomachs half starved from their continued fear of eating any of the provisions. How could they trust anything from the hands of these foreigners with the complexion of the shark's belly, whose men and women sat across from each other, their shoes touching?

One of them had seen a man pick up a thick book, brush it against his lips, and then hold it quietly in his lap.

A woman at the first stop had touched her hand to her mouth by way of greeting another descending from the train.

Most of them had been only days off the ship before signing on for this adventure to the east of this most unusual country. A mix of disoriented and weary, they were, however, grateful to have procured work so quickly. Those who had been in the country longer had spent their days well within the confines of San Francisco's Chinatown, some of them never hearing any language but their own.

Many of them believed that Americans walked in the formation of geese.

This continent, they knew, was divided into two lands: the northern one in the shape of a flying fish, the southern like the thigh of a man wearing a billowing trouser.

And now, headed all the way across this strange land, how would they fare? What would become of them?

With the train's deceleration, more of them crowded against the windows. *What can you see?* , they asked repeatedly, though no answers were offered. Their breath smoked the glass, and one of them reached up to wipe it clean with the wide sleeve of his blue tunic.

Their designated foreman remained in his seat, dating a new page in his journal: *6th month, 13th day.* He wrote in his labored English, *Bright and sunny; no cloud or rain.*

Had the train's route enabled a more elevated view of the town, the Celestials would have seen that North Adams had a peculiarly happy and peaceful look, as if a tea set were balanced in the hollow of God's large hand. Factories, hotels, and homes shared the roads and riverbanks with trees and hills, wildlife and rock. Great pines grew heavenward, the lowest branches as high as a high building. Even the long arms of a pair of the largest of men could not have met around the broad trunks. In spite of stubborn soil and the meddlesome disposition of the Hoosac River, East Hoosuck, later to be North Adams, had been laid out seven miles long from north to south and five miles broad from east to west. It was in shape a parallelogram, the only township in the county of regular geometric form.

To the north stood the Green Mountains of Vermont. To the east rose the Hoosac Range; to the west, the Taconic Range. Early settlers claimed it impossible to see the entire town from any one point of observation.

The southern and northern branches of the Hoosac River converged in the center of town; clear, rapid springs descending apace into deep, shady pools with gravelly beds. The trout populated them as plentifully as the workers occupied the tenement housing behind the mills. The first farmers, at laying eyes on this land, had said that the glorious beauty of a Berkshire summer and autumn would fill neither the granary nor the purse. But by 1870, farms cleared of trees and rocks and located near one of the many living streams shared borders with the thick and formidable forests, shelter to skunk, bear, and bobcat; moose, deer, and turkey; Canadian lynx, porcupine, and fox; loon, heron, black duck, and even, on occasion, the unduly adventurous seagull.

Mosquitoes and flies wandered in and out of M. S. Southwick's high-class millinery goods on the corner of Main and Ashland. Deerflies pestered the horses under the care of E. Vadnais, blacksmith at 66 Center Street. Bulb mites molested the gardens of Miss Fannie Burlingame on the corner of Summer and the high end of Church. Carpenter ants and wood-boring bees wreaked their havoc on porches of pine, alder, and ash. On the front pages of the newspaper, items concerning the best fertilizer for corn shared space with announcements of a village of vigor and enterprise where capital was not suffered to lie idle in the vaults of banks but was constantly in motion.

The hills were covered with greenwood of yellow birch, maple, and hemlock and crisscrossed with old roads and Indian paths and well watered with mountain brooks often breaking into waterfalls of unexpected charm. Rocks dripped with maidenhair and moss. There were orchids in the swamps. Limestone cobbles grew gardens of walking fern and purple cliff brake.

The town tended to vote Republican in both state and national elections, and was devoted in equal parts to the temperance movement and the nostalgia of a simpler past. The temperature had been known to change forty-four degrees in twenty-four hours. There was no month of the year that was not sometimes very pleasant and sometimes its disagreeable opposite. Floods and fires, illness and death were accepted as pages in God's large book, but so were the clouds settling on the summits and ridges of Mount Greylock, the tallest in the state, and the sharp yellow-greens of the trees' spring leaves, and the ash-purple blanket laid over the hills at twilight. On this thirteenth day of June, God's creative hand was renewing His original efforts to adorn the world with richness and splendor; the pastures were clothed with flocks, the valleys covered with fledgling corn, and the worms tunneled into the soft earth of early summer. All was wilderness and its contrary mate, and in the distance, the first whistle of the 4:15 from Troy vibrated rapidly against the thousands of eardrums attending to it.

There were an equal number of citizens not attending to the train's arrival, including Mr. Calvin T. Sampson's wife.

Julia watched her husband that morning as he readied to quit their well-appointed rooms on the highest floor of the eastern tower of the Wilson House.

He had mentioned history, as in history being made. She had not asked for clarification, as she knew he would offer it bidden or not, and he had been making this same point in one way or another for the last several weeks since his plan had commenced. He was in the prime of his life, the pioneer shoe manufacturer in North Adams. She handed him his hat and waited.

"Practically to a one, our nation's newspapers have sent representation to witness this event," he said. "These Celestials will transform American manufacture as we know it, and in their hearts those union hooligans know they are finished." He twisted the brim of his hat and she relieved his hands of it, placing it upon his head. "I did that," he said simply.

"So you did," she said with some careful pride.

He opened the apartment's door and turned again to face her. "You might reconsider your decision not to come," he said quietly.

She smiled and told him that perhaps she would, though she knew she would not. That he would now be even further disappointed when she did not make an appearance was a price she was willing to pay.

By June of that year, Julia Hayden Sampson was forty-three years old and had lost thirteen pregnancies. She did not think of herself as having experienced a common suffering. Each loss had been hers alone. She did not want to belong to that particular and unhappy community of women, and so she imagined herself an unpopulated island to which there was no bridge. A month prior, her woman's time had not arrived, and she had passed the weeks since occupying that terrible space constructed of the intricate mix of hope and dread.

It did not occur to her that in such a case even those she held dearest could not discover her. She did know that her husband was not a man to fail: since his boyhood, he had accomplished whatever he undertook, showing a power to execute as well as a mind to plan, together with much tenacity of purpose. The Asiatic boys heading their way were fresh proof of that. So the responsibility of the dark cloud over this life he'd built for the two of them was hers and hers alone. And for that reason, she had shared nothing of her latest anguish, planning to surprise him with good news, and dreading having to confess yet again to her utter failures as a woman and a wife. She would not be going to the factory today. Who knew what damage the atmosphere of a place like that could do? If this was history her husband was making, it was history that was at that moment of no concern to her.

Instead, she spent the next several hours before her dressing glass stripped to her skin, interrogating her body. Even when goose bumps raised themselves across her form, she did not stop. Surely, she thought, God would not do this to her again.

In 1870, the population in these United States was well over thirty-eight million. Ulysses S. Grant was president. The Civil War had been over since a bright Sunday afternoon five Aprils prior. The previous spring, Chinese and Irish crews had laid the last two rails joined with a tie of polished California laurel, and the final stake had been driven in the Transcontinental Railroad. Of 63,291 women in San Francisco, 1,452 were Chinese prostitutes. The Fifteenth Amendment was ratified on the first Thursday of February. New York was the largest city in the country, and North Adams the largest manufacturing center in the Berkshires, boasting thirty-eight factories and two hundred cotton mills. Or, in the words of a local historian, North Adams was the smartest village in the smartest nation in all creation: the concentrated essential oil of Yankeedom. Yet one-third of the town's inhabitants were foreigners—largely Irish, French Canadian, and Welsh—at work in the textile mills and tanneries, the paper factories, and on the formidable Hoosac Tunnel, which had been commenced in 1851 and which wouldn't host regular service until 1876, at a total cost of $20,241,842.31 and 195 lives.

Five languages were preached from the town's pulpits. And now another headed toward town: Cantonese, the language of the seventy-five Chinese male workers, most of whom had barely attained their majority, on the late train from Troy, and Omaha before that, and all the way back to their start, thirteen days prior, in Oakland, California.

The Celestials were coming. Denizens of a country so foreign that in America it was known as the Celestial Empire, inhabited by the alien and strange. *The Celestials were coming.* Two thousand citizens of North Adams awaited their arrival as they would the quiet but firm interruption of an opinionated dinner guest.

It was an unusually mild afternoon, a breeze from the north swaying the elms on the hill as nineteen-year-old Alfred Robinson worried the rock he had slipped into his pocket.

His fellow Crispins were three hundred strong on the south end of the passenger platform. They had been waiting for hours. The Order of the Knights of St. Crispin was a force to be reckoned with, the largest union in the country, forty thousand members in Massachusetts alone. And on this day they were joined by their brothers from five other local shoe factories, all staging sympathy strikes, refusing, among other things, to consent to a reduction from ten dollars a case to nine during the dull season. If Mr. Sampson had refused to recognize their strength so far, he wouldn't be able to ignore it for long.

On that thirteenth of June, Calvin T. Sampson was forty-three years old, married for just over twenty-one years to Julia Hayden Sampson, whom in her childlessness he conceived of as fragile, and his factory was one of the largest in

Massachusetts. He liked to say that from his establishment, or through his encouragement, every shoe factory operating in town had its origin. One of the leading citizens in enterprise and public spirit, he had plenty of money and knew how to make more and, as one New York paper put it, "in the democratic acceptation of the term, was a true and practical Christian, and a genuine, untarnished brick."

From the station at Troy, Sampson's superintendent, George W. Chase, who had arranged the Celestials' contract and traveled with them from California, wired his employer: *Just through Troy.*

Sampson stuffed six pistols into the pockets of his suit trousers and greatcoat, checked on the small army of constables he'd hired to meet the train, and took a carriage to Eagle Bridge, where he would climb aboard and ride with his new workers into North Adams.

He had blue eyes that Julia favored, a beard and a moustache already tinged with gray about which she was ambivalent, and stood five feet eight inches in his bare feet. He was the youngest son of Calvin Sampson and Polly Millard Sampson (dead at that point for twenty-four and sixteen years, respectively) and, with his eldest sister, Thankful, and nearest brother, Chester, was one of the three surviving children of the six his mother had been able to bring to term. For the last several years, Thankful had resided with Julia and Sampson, and she and Sampson had often spoken of how, while their mother remained alive, they had felt as if their job was to distract her from the three small ghosts always graying the room. Sampson had told his wife more than once that this experience gave him some understanding of her own losses. Her expression had disabused him of his certainty. And truth be told, he understood that the sadness that dogged her after each and every loss was a long, dark hallway to which he had no access. After the last pregnancy, he had reassured her that though he could not enter this corridor of her grief, he would be at its end awaiting her return. Her sobs had resumed and he had felt, as he often did when speaking of such things, that he had been asked to bottom a shoe with a hammer made of paper. He did not know what to do with his own sadness, and the one person he might've asked for aid in this regard was not available to him, and so he had determined simply to banish his distress and turn his attentions to hers.

He was no stranger to the flexibility of certitude, as he had claimed for some time to be connected by direct descent to the Pilgrim colonists, even to one of the company who crossed in the *Mayflower*. The absence of his ancestor's name on the compact had, he often explained, to do with his ancestor's not having attained his majority.

His grandfather had played a small but sure role in Shays' Rebellion, avoiding arrest by fleeing to the wilderness of Stamford, Vermont, and making the hard life of a farmer for himself and his family. Before transforming himself from farmer to businessman, Sampson had often found himself in one argument or another with the land, wondering what inducement this place could have offered, and always returning to his own troubled worrying that, though the rebellion had been worthy, hadn't there been something cowardly in his grandfather's avoidance of the consequences of his actions? Sampson believed in the value of making one's own way but he believed equally strongly that one's pigheadedness was one's own, not to be, at day's close, foisted upon someone else.

It was the trait of which he was the most proud and which he held most responsible for his current situation. For although he knew the newspapers and the politicians from West to East could argue that there were many logs that made up this particular labor bonfire, he had held the match to the pyre. What else could one do in the face of the bullying of a surplus of men professing to be shoemakers who knew nothing about it?

The disharmony between Sampson and his workers had existed for some time, and he kept a catalog of their offenses against him, which he took personally, as justification for his current course of action. In 1861, he had been the first in town to introduce the newly patented Wells pegging machine. His workers had left the shop, walked out in protest, declaring that skilled labor would be replaced by inhuman machines and unskilled operatives to man them. He had, he tried to assure his workers, their best interests at heart. Indeed, his interests and theirs were coupled. Labor and manufacturing were two parts of one scissors, useless without the other. Machinery would not *reduce* the need for labor, but *increase* it. The workers returned to their benches, but Sampson no longer regarded them as allies. He felt as he had during the first week of his one term at Drury Academy, when he had stood in the school cloakroom unbeknownst to the classmates whose conversation he overheard: "But did you see his jacket?" "I did," assured the other, "but I hear it is unlikely he will be here long." When he'd made his presence known, both young men had inclined their heads slightly, stepping back to let him pass. He found himself wondering if this was perhaps a version of what his mother and brother must have experienced when he'd announced he would not be continuing on the family farm. To alleviate his discomfort at the comparison, he took note of the fact that two-thirds of the workers who had struck had been French Canadians, foreigners not to be relied on to uphold or even understand the Christian American values by which he endeavored to live.

By 1863, Sampson had established his own store in Boston. By 1868, he no longer rented, but had purchased, the old tannery on Eagle Street and had added an eighty-square-foot addition, making the entire building 16,400 square feet, able to employ two hundred fifty hands. Sampson footwear was sold in Chicago, St. Louis, Louisville, Boston, and New York. On the fifth of March 1868, he became treasurer of the Baptist church; he would serve for ten years. Whatever talk there had been concerning his choices not to go to war and not to change his product from ladies' shoes and boots to brogans for solider and slave had ceased.

In April of 1868, the Knights of St. Crispin held their first annual meeting. By that May, all of Sampson's employees in the bottoming room, save two, were Crispins.

In mid-May, the foreman of the bottoming room made his way down to Sampson's office to inform his boss that there was a man upstairs whom the help did not like to have there.

Sampson stiffened slightly as if in preparation for an unpleasant medical examination. He knew already of which man the Crispins had complaint: St. John, an excellent man, who could make a very nice shoe. Sampson chose not to remember that St. John had worked for him previously, over a year ago, and had already been turned off once.

The foreman chose not to remind his boss that at that time, Sampson had sworn, in front of the other men, never to employ the man again, given as he was to drinking, gambling, and dissipation. So treacherous and deceitful was St. John that when the workers told the foreman they didn't want to work with him, the foreman had said he didn't know as he could blame them.

"What are the particulars of their complaints?" Sampson asked.

"He is a little light-fingered," the foreman answered. "He takes kit."

Sampson said nothing, and the foreman's nerves grew for no reason he could identify.

"The boys do not like to work with him," he finally added weakly.

Sampson made as to return to the papers on his desk. "I'm sure I don't know why that is of concern to me," he said.

The foreman did not like being in the office. Recognizing Sampson's tricks of intimidation as tricks did nothing to lessen their effect. Growing resentment, at his employer and at himself, was impossible to avoid.

"I believe the boys have an order called the Knights of St. Crispin, and that it was so constituted that they could not work with a man not belonging to it. I believe that St. John does not belong to it."

"That is nothing to me," Sampson replied. "I employ him, and I employ them. It is no matter to me what sort of alliances they do or do not make; what is of matter to me is that they remind themselves—that *you* remind them—of the larger roof under which they all huddle."

This particular comment, when reported verbatim to the bottomers, caused, not surprisingly, some ire. Sampson had intended it to do so, and he enjoyed therefore more delight than despair when the foreman assured him late that day that the Crispin workers would not return until St. John was turned off. Indeed, that evening over a late dinner out, Julia found her husband's high energy in recounting how he had bade them hustle their benches and kits out and pile them in front of the building somewhat alarming, and she shushed him so as not to attract the attention of the other diners.

He ran the factory for three weeks with only the feckless and morally troubled St. John staffing the bottoming room. The conclusion to Sampson's version of events was that, upon his absence from town one day, the Crispins whipped St. John while the man was on his way to dinner. Sampson and Chase had the persons who committed the violence bound over, and after the man got well he went missing, not to be seen or heard of since.

Thomas Healy, a cordwainer but not a Crispin, insisted to anyone who asked that St. John had no idea who whipped him and that where he had disappeared to was Albany, on his way to Montreal, with fifty of Sampson's dollars in his pocket, sent on a mission to find new hands to replace the still-striking Crispins. Healy didn't have any reason to doubt the tale St. John himself had told him, though he had every reason to doubt Sampson's, as the reason he himself had left Sampson's employ was on account of unfair treatment. In Healy's humble workingman's opinion, Sampson had never kept a single bargain he'd ever made.

On what happened next, there was little disagreement. Mr. Chase went to Maine, the foreman of the sewing rooms to Canada, the foreman of the bottoming room to Worcester County, all to find help that did not belong to the Order, extracting their pledges that they would not join.

And after some time, when they all did indeed join, Sampson had them sign another pledge, that they would ignore, this time in the presence of a justice of the peace. "This is to certify that I, _____ , have belonged to the Order of the Knights of St. Crispin, and have become satisfied that said order is of no practical benefit to its members, but a damage to them and their employers; and, also, that I have withdrawn from said order, and will not, in any way, directly or indirectly, aid in its support. To all of the above statement I do solemnly swear."

In February 1869, the *Workingman's Advocate* printed warnings about the possible recruitment of Chinese labor to the East from the West.

In May of the same year, the *Hide and Leather Interest*, a paper that spoke for industrial leaders, printed an article concerning the rash of Crispin strikes. An editorial called for a national organization of employers to fight the Crispins by importing Chinese and other strikebreakers.

In July, during a convention of Southern industrialists in Memphis, the possibility of importing Chinese as an alternative to slave labor was discussed. Most notable of the speakers was Mr. Cornelius Koopmanschap. Dutch-born and strong-willed, Koopmanschap specialized in procuring Chinese labor for interested industrialists. He fancied himself an expert on the Asiatics, and indeed, compared to the industrialists he addressed, he was. "Avoid the Chinese raised in the cities of the Orient," he cautioned them. "They are most vicious and degraded. Procure instead the peasants only recently migrated to the cities. They are easily managed, being patient, industrious, docile, tractable, and obedient."

Throughout the summer of 1869, editorials on John Chinaman, the Coming Man, ran in the *New York Times*, *Sun*, *Herald*, and *Tribune*, the *Springfield Republican*, and the *Boston Daily Evening Transcript*, all readily available in North Adams: "So fast do events move for America, in these latter days, that before the affairs of 'white man' and 'black man' are well settled, a new color comes upon the loom, to be woven into the mighty national fabric, and the 'yellow man' becomes the figure of the hour." "Accepted as a freeman, John Chinaman must eventually become a vote. Sambo must make up his mind to work or starve."

On October 2, 1869, Sampson signed the deed for a three-story brick building at the corner of Marshall Street

and the north branch of the Hoosac River. Known as
W. W. Freeman and Co., it was originally designed as a
cutlery works, but the enterprise had fallen through, and
Sampson made the building his for the reduced price of
$17,000. Julia, who had lost her thirteenth pregnancy the
week before, had had some concern about profiting off the
misfortunes of others, but Sampson had told her that she
was succumbing to superstition, which could do no good
to anyone. He had left her in the parlor, closing the door
to his study as a child would've done.

The renovated creation was the largest shoe factory in
North Adams, producing over fourteen thousand shoes per
week, employing one hundred fifty full-time workers, and
producing almost one hundred cases more per month than
the three nearest competitors.

But despite this growth, by spring of 1870, Sampson was
forced to call the bottomers into the receiving room, tell
them he had just come from market, which was rather dull,
and that he needed to pay them a dollar less per case, perhaps for six or eight weeks, and then he would put them
back to full pay. The Crispin lodge had then met and a committee was chosen to tell Mr. Sampson that if he did not
want to make shoes and would rather shut down, they were
perfectly willing to work again when business revived and
he could pay the old wages. He seemed very well pleased,
and the workers thought the situation settled. It was but a
few days before they heard of the recruited workers.

According to Sampson, the local Crispin louts waited
only for the recruits to step off the train before intimidating

them back from whence they had come. According to Frederick L. Wood, a cordwainer and Crispin who had never worked for Sampson, the recruits were sober Crispins all who stayed near a week, the local Crispins making a statement of the affair to them during four apparently very lively meetings over the course of four successive evenings, after which they went home.

With their anger and righteousness fueled, the local Crispins put aside their lapstones and their reason once again, asking for shorter hours (an eight-hour day), higher wages (a raise from $1.70 a day to $2.00), the right to dismiss workers who were delinquent on union dues, and access to the company books to inspect for profits in order to adjust wages to profits.

Sampson found the final demand the most outrageous and, when relating it to his wife, had needed to be reminded repeatedly to stop pacing in those idiotic little circles wearing out the rug she had recently placed on their bedroom floor. He had wondered again at the curiosity of his wife's inability to assert herself with anyone, it seemed, but her own husband. However, he had heeded her advice until she had suggested some understanding, some charity, on his part. God had been kind to the two of them; others were not as fortunate, and what was the good of having fortune unless one was willing to do good with it?

"I'm willing, indeed eager, to do good to those who do the same to me," he said, resuming his pacing, and then added, "And I would argue that in at least one arena, God has been anything but kind to us."

Julia's neck and face reddened as if struck. "That you can address these words to me, I cannot realize it. I am stupefied by it." Her voice was low and strong. "You humiliate me and injure the both of us," she went on, and his sister coughed lightly from the sitting room on the other side of the closed bedroom door. It was a comment he would always regret having uttered.

He wired Boston. New workers arrived. The Crispins dissuaded them from working. The new men returned to Boston. A committee of three Crispins met with Sampson, reiterating their demands, assuring him that they were looking forward to coming back to work for him.

"Boys, if you continue your idleness, you will never again work for me," he responded.

The youngest of the three, Alfred Robinson, said, "Why? Are you quittin' business?"

Alfred was a Southerner and had come to the Crispins only recently from tunnel work—two reasons to make his fellow brothers wary of him. But his sister was the recent victim of an unknown assailant on Pearl Street, and so when one of his companions told him not to be birdbrained, he did so more gently than he might have.

Sampson regarded Alfred, took note of the broken and reknotted laces on his boots, and then said, "If I am to fight an enemy, my batteries are masked and I keep them masked. It is for you to stay and work. I have made my last proposition, and shall do no more."

The Crispins had presented their ultimatum at ten in the morning. At quarter past, Sampson called Chase into his office, showed him a newspaper clipping from his desk drawer describing the successful use of Chinese labor in a San Francisco shoe factory, and asked if he could be ready for the afternoon train to the West. George W. Chase had joined the firm in 1865 as a bookkeeper and would retire from it as president when the Sampson company closed in 1901, perhaps the only colleague for whom Sampson had nothing but admiring words. If he was to send anyone west, it would be Chase.

Sampson swore to annihilate the Crispins in five years. He would do it in three, and there wouldn't be another union strike in North Adams in any industry for ten.

Chapter Two

The town's elite watched from the stationmaster's office above the depot. The eternally unmarried Fannie Burlingame, a distant cousin of Sampson's, was there in a frock of plain but well-cut black silk. Her uncle Anson had been the architect of the Burlingame Treaty, signed into effect a mere two years previous, admitting China to "the family of civilized nations." Pneumonia had claimed him in St. Petersburg, Russia, and his death had struck her such a blow that four months later it still seemed to her that her own lungs were constricted, never to operate as they had. She had woken before light, sure that she had heard his voice urging her to set an example as to how these Celestials deserved to be treated. She continued to find her father and her uncle the two men whom it was most important to impress, and she passed some of the time waiting in the overcrowded office by imagining how she might have described this day to her uncle. As it happened, she would describe this day not to him but to one of the Celestials. Lue Gim Gong would become her student, friend, surrogate son, and, some suggested, an intimate beyond the platonic, and when she died quietly at the age of seventy-four on a bright May Tuesday, the wall of her mind would be spread with an image of him. He enjoyed the story she told, and would often request it of her. "Tell me again," he would say. "Tell me again of my arrival."

The spectators below filled the passenger and freight platforms. They lined State Street and Main, blocking the doorways and first-floor windows of the Richmond House. They filled the street frontage of the H. Arnold & Co. Print Works and gathered at the newly built eight-foot fence around the C. T. Sampson Manufacturing Company.

They were ministers and farmers, mill workers and shopkeepers, cartmen and dentists, bank officers and reporters. Two well-dressed women in a buggy, their silks and cambrics lapping at each other like floodwater. The logger who had lost three toes to an ineptly wielded axe, his dog at his side. A traveling surgeon, short, dressed in a suit coat of light blue, black pants, and buffalo-hide boots, his saddlebag draped over his arm, a pipe in his mouth. A blacksmith, detected by the disproportionate size of his right hand over his left. A man gathering subscriptions for a religious newspaper in New York. A negro, well dressed and well mounted, drinking a glass of water like any other Christian. An inordinate number of children and dogs.

Daniel Luther passed Alfred a stumpy wooden bat. A fellow Crispin even younger than Alfred filled his pockets with gravel and dirt. There were rumors about the nature of the warnings issued to Sampson over the previous weeks.

Alfred had not been privy to the extension of those threats, but he knew who had, and had felt a stab of resentment at being passed over. He knew he hadn't been at the business of making shoes long, and at the business of unions even less so. He knew the Order's constitution read that a member must've been at the trade for two years or longer. He knew that an exception had been made, and he suspected it had less to do with his abilities and more to do with the attack against his sister. He knew, too, of the bitterness his membership had caused among some of the other members. The vote to allow him had, apparently, been the closest in the local lodge's history. But he'd been a quick learner, going from green hand to experienced worker in less time than many. And hadn't he struggled with the cost of flour and eggs and rent just as mightily as his brothers? And hadn't he understood the need for some band to which to belong?

Many of them, of course, were without their families. But that had been their choice. They looked forward to a family happiness that for orphaned Alfred and his sole sister, Lucy, no matter what kind of individual success they achieved, was too painful even to use as the stuff of fantasy. His brothers joined as a means to earn a better life. Alfred joined as a means to a life at all.

"We happy few, we band of brothers," his sister's closest friend, Ida, sometimes said when he was heading off to a lodge meeting. He knew neither whose words she spoke nor what intention she had, and he found himself, each time, unclear as to what his response should be.

Ida Virginia Wilburn was sixteen and already displaying the resolute density of the woman she would become. Her dress was practical, a gray muslin that wouldn't easily reveal wear. Her boots were black, purchased by her father in their hometown of Pine View, Virginia, several months back, yet they appeared as if just plucked by a salesman's clean hand from his store window. She stood across the street from the passenger depot at the side entrance to the Ballou House and could see Alfred, itchy with anticipation, growling and murmuring with those other boys.

Her mother had not been in favor of this trip. She had not been moved enough by the misfortune that dear Lucy Robinson, youngest daughter of neighbors and a friend for years and years, had suffered. Because, pray, what had Lucy expected? What had she imagined could have come of following that headstrong older brother of hers? (Alfred, Ida's mother insisted, had always had looks, but not much sense. Ida believed him to have neither, but Lucy adored him, so Ida tried to as well.) To work alongside foreigners in the wilds of that northern world, blasting their way through mountain rock that God had obviously not created for anything like a tunnel. It had been foolish.

But Ida's father had touched his beautiful wife with his farmer's hands and settled her as he would a horse, pointing out that Lucy and Alfred had taken the best option they'd had. There wasn't much else they could've done. No one had to mention the sad and threatening fact of the death of the Robinson parents the previous year. And Ida had remarked that Alfred wasn't working in the tunnel anymore; he was a cordwainer now, in one of the biggest factories in North Adams. That showed some sense, did it not? Though, now, watching the jostling and jockeying of his thick-armed union brothers, she thought perhaps he had merely traded one kind of danger for another.

"When we're tested," her father had said, "God hands us some of what we need, and it's up to us to mix up the rest."

And his wife had retorted that God handed us *all* we needed and more, but she had allowed her husband's agreement with his daughter, whose independence and will he much admired, secretly believing it made her somehow more *his*, that in this time of need, sending Ida up North to do what she could in tending to Lucy was the right and moral choice. None of them believed that Alfred was likely to be up to the task of doing what was necessary in the wake of the violence suffered upon his younger sister. Left unspoken was the small but welcome relief to both parents of the prospect of having only nine rather than ten mouths to feed.

So communication had been struck between the Baptist church of Pine View, Virginia, and its sister church on Eagle Street in North Adams. An appropriate traveling chaperone had been secured, a rooming situation with one of the church's elder sisters arranged. And Ida had left, her heart pounding in her chest like hooves on packed dirt.

She had not intended to witness the advent of the Celestials. She was not one to seek out violence. She would have preferred to remain in the stifling tenement apartment where Lucy, even several months after the attack, still lay on her single bed, sometimes working up the fortitude to cross the room and sit by the window. The diminishment of her friend filled Ida with impotent rage—at the man who had attacked her, at the inability of the sheriff to find him, at the other girls in town, who had stopped coming to visit and who seemed to Ida inadequate in every sense of the word.

But even this shadow version of Lucy was a joy with whom to share the days, and this caused Ida some considerable guilt. How did she gather such pleasure from being in the presence of one so clearly distressed? It struck an unforgiving blow to the image of herself that she hoped to hold. When Alfred had left that afternoon, secreting the rock he was sure neither girl had seen, Lucy had begged her to follow him. Who knew what would happen when the Celestials arrived? Keep him safe, Lucy had entreated, for me, and Ida had had no choice.

As the second whistle sounded, Ida stepped into the slant of shade provided by the porch of the Hoosac Tunnel offices. If Alfred or the others mixed in some unhappy business how was she to fulfill her promise to Lucy? Could she pull him from the crowd? She looked at her hands. They were broad and thick. One of her brothers had told her she looked as if she were wearing the mittens of Eskimos.

She wished for the shade and serenity of her father's workshop. She wished for the smell of his tobacco leaves in the rafters, the oil and sweat of his discarded work

gloves. She even wished for her brothers, paltry and defi-
cient versions of her father, all elbows and fists, ignorance
and temper. Even as a child she had understood that her
father was an exception to a rule. His refusal to share in
the temper of men was a rare and uncommon thing, and
she began, even then, to think of him more and more as a
species of one.

She had spent the war years in Virginia, daily astonished
less at the lengths of violence to which men seemed likely
to go and more at the relish with which they proceeded
there. Indeed, if she'd been asked, she would have been
obliged to say that the war had convinced her of a lurking
suspicion: that violence against their own was something
not that men avoided, but from which civilized society
kept them. Men were, one and all, always at the precipice
of a high cliff, waiting for an excuse to leap like savages
into the air.

Sampson stood on the bottom step of the train, his head
only inches above the tallest man in the crowd.

"Here it goes, friend," Daniel whispered to Alfred, both
of them trying to hold their ground against the surging of
the press behind them.

Sampson put his hand on his hip, pulling his greatcoat
aside to reveal the gold chain of a French-made pocket
watch, a gift one year prior from Julia on the occasion of
their twentieth anniversary, and the handles of three of the
six pistols. "Make way," he said, meeting Alfred's eye, holding it, and then moving on to Daniel and the rest of the boys.

The hired constables fanned out to his left and right. Behind the glass of the emigrant cars' windows, the Celestials
peered at the crowd.

"Rats!" someone yelled.

"Yellow scabs!" someone added.

But the sight of those faces had already had some effect,
their youth and utter strangeness taking even the angriest
by surprise. Even Mr. Jasper Davenport—who only days
prior had been assuring anyone who would listen in the
smoking room of the Wilson House that the trade of their
fair town would be ruined by the introduction of men with
little money to spend and little disposition to spend it, that
the community should be insulted and outraged by the importation of a nuisance such as this—was now quieted at
the sight of these smart, alert boys.

The youngest was fourteen. Sixty-eight were under
twenty. One of the oldest, at twenty-two, was the foreman,
an English-speaking Methodist, in this country for eight
years, having served his first five contract years faithfully
as a house servant and cook, and the most recent three by
some accounts as a miner in Weaverville, California, and
by others as a store owner in Nevada or a partner in one
of the large merchant houses of San Francisco. He was
known even in his native community by several appella-
tions, including his given name, Chung Den Sing, his common name, Chung Chung Bo, and others: Chung Tang
Sing, Ah Sing, Chung Ding Sing. He would be known in
North Adams as Charlie Sing. He stood behind Sampson,
the only Celestial of the seventy-five in the garments of

American civilization, from his sensible black cap and his walking suit down to a remarkably natty boot fitting his broad foot.

He had in his baggage a letter of credit from his San Francisco pastor to the clergyman in North Adams in the approved way. And he would, the following Sunday, relate his experiences as a new member of the Methodist Church to a full congregation. Despite his Western costume, the traditional queue the color and texture of Persian lamb hung heavily against his back, and he carried within his case for use on special occasions Chinese black silk shoes embroidered with peonies and dragons and a coat of sea-otter skin lined with blue silk, for which he had paid a prodigious duty upon entering California. His black cloth work shoes were rolled tightly in his work tunic, his whittling knife safely inside the toe of one of the shoes.

He would be, for the seventy-four men behind him, bookkeeper and purchaser of goods, interpreter and arbitrator, as well as administrator of shirts and socks, rice and justice, and the gold coins with which the boys were to be paid. For these caretaking duties, he would be paid the immense (for a Chinaman) salary of sixty dollars per month, nearly three times what the workmen and the two cooks would receive for the first year of their three-year contract. A discrepancy that would, in certain cases, prove to be the cause of some resentment.

Neither the whites before him nor the fellow Chinese behind him knew that he had been born in the Gow Low How village of the Hoiping district, South Canton, China,

December 11, 1847 (an unreliable date, as he was even at this point in his life known to lie repeatedly about his age). His father was Hou Hah (or Chung Som Doy, depending on which of the few documents in his descendents' possession were to be trusted), and his mother was Moo Ten.

Was his father killed as a lance guard captain in the Opium Wars? Was he descended from mandarins? "An Asian royal equivalent," Charlie would claim years later to his eldest son, "to a European duke." As he told it, his parents were slaughtered by rebels before his seven-year-old eyes, and he had been fostered by the missionaries John and Mary Singleton and taken under their care to California. He passed on to his children a rice-paper portrait done in colored inks of an elderly scholar who he insisted was his grandfather, Chung Gow Doy. More likely, Charlie was what most Chinese boys in California in the nineteenth century were: poor peasants who had risked what they could to travel around the world to Gold Mountain, hoping to earn enough to make it home again, wealthier, safer, happier.

Second Brother, Chung Ding Toy, remained in China and would precede Charlie in death by a year. Third Brother, Chung My, embarked with Charlie on the ship across the Pacific, but never disembarked, having fallen ill a week from port, as good as dead by the time the ship docked.

Just east of Omaha the train had been met with protesting onlookers, and an Irishman had mounted the car and stared at the Chinamen for several minutes. They had stared back. And Charlie had said, "What you doing?"

The Irishman had answered, "I come to look at the Chinamen."

"Well, look and go out," Charlie had said.

In the back of the car, some of the workers paused in their eating of square crackers and bologna sausages. Others continued to sip their tea. From the middle of the car, George Chase wondered how and when to intervene. His employer had given him no instructions regarding such a situation.

The Irishman took a step toward Charlie, who was tall for a Chinaman, just over six feet, but even so, the Irishman had half a foot on him. "I'll go out when I damn well please," he said.

Charlie said, "You will go."

The other workers watched as one would watch animals in a zoo, drawn by the drama of gesture.

"I will not," the Irishman said, presenting a revolver.

Chase stood, no less helpless than when seated, and thought how foolish his boss had been not to employ constables for the ride.

Charlie pulled his own revolver, and Chase watched him back the man out of the car as a boy playing Indians might back his surrendering father down a sloping front yard.

When the train was once again rattling along, he asked Charlie how he had been sure the man would withdraw, and Charlie replied that Americans always found it surprising to see an Asian man wielding a large gun. In those few seconds of surprise, much could be accomplished.

Yes, Chase agreed but, ever the pragmatist, added, "Yet it could've gone quite the other way."

Charlie had tapped his chopsticks against his bowl, dislodging grains of rice. "Of course," he said, not disrespectfully, and returned to his meal.

"Make way," Sampson again insisted. "These men are free to pass." He indicated the constables. "And these men are paid to make sure they do. They are being paid to use their weapons if need be."

He signaled to Chase, who in turn whispered to Charlie, who made his way through the two cars, speaking quietly to the boys within, and the group commenced to file off the train.

They were dressed in blue nankeen blouses, fastened by frogs and small brass buttons up to the throat. Blue trousers, narrowed at the ankle. Wooden travel shoes or black cloth work slippers, the sole an inch of white pressed wool. White stockings that seemed remarkably clean given the journey. Common soft hats of American manufacture, a purchase Mr. Chase had found himself obliged to provide before quitting San Francisco. The tops of their heads shaved and oiled, their queues shiny and long against their backs. The hairstyles were evidence of the care they had taken to maintain their habits despite the rigors of the crossing.

They each carried a tight, efficient roll of bed, blanket, and clothing over the shoulder on a bamboo pole that swayed and sprung like a conductor's baton with their quiet steps as they followed Sampson onto the platform.

Two rocks were thrown, one landing without damage on the shoulder of the smallest boy, and the two guilty French

Canadians were put in the lockup at once, nothing more to transpire from them. Although the Crispins wished all kinds of bad luck to Sampson, their hands remained in their pockets, fingering the small few coins left from their last pay, and the crowd parted, a mix of curiosity and disappointment already washing away the dangerous anticipation like river water receding from a floodplain, and Sampson and Chase, followed by the five state policemen and the seven private constables, led their modest band through the crowd. The boys moved along in pairs arm in arm, and Ida's first sight of Charlie was of a neat, intelligent-looking man with full lips and sparse eyebrows, his slight hand against the well-stitched blue cloth of his fellow worker's shirtsleeve. He passed within four feet of her and the sight of his hand, soft-looking and mildly doughy, like a child's on the verge of leaving infancy behind, filled her mind. She lost track of Alfred. She was sure that if she touched the man's hand, it would be as it was to touch the muzzle of a horse. She had a partner thought of Lucy in her bed, waiting.

"Why're you *blushing*?" asked Alfred, pushing at her shoulder with the heel of his hand.

He looked as she remembered him from his games with her older brothers: willing for the lessons they were about to deliver.

She shook her head, hoping to free the heat from her chest and neck. "I'm sure I don't know," she told him, taking solace in the fact that she was speaking the truth.

Julia Sampson heard the commotion of the crowd during its short time on Main Street. The white brick Wilson

House was to the right of the mob's turn, so even as she heard the crowd, it was already moving away from her.

She did not strain to make out the talk. She did not go to the window. She remained at her desk in the front room, her back to the windows and the street below. Before her was the writing slate she had used as a girl; she wet a fingertip dusted with chalk, wiped the slate clean, and made ready to mark some words across its surface.

The outside world alarmed her. She did not even like to leave windows open. Ailments of the head and the stomach plagued her. When she engaged in conversation of any kind, her fingers ticked quietly against her skirts. She was a tall woman, taller than her husband, a fact they colluded in hiding by way of smaller heels on her shoes and boots and one-inch risers in the heels of his, and the world was often surprised by the extent and persistence of her anxieties. And her husband, privy to the assertive and dismissive way she could have with him in the privacy of their own lives, felt somehow cheated of her delicacies. He had thought he was marrying an unassuming farm girl. They had been born within three days of each other, baptized on the same day in late March 1857, and would die within twenty-four hours of each other. He understood his love for her as part and parcel of his life's other ambitions. He would be a success for her and with her. But perhaps he had been too much of a success, creating a world of too much safety, a place where she felt strong and sure enough to vent the years of anger and resentment at her public frailties.

She imagined her husband at the head of that large crowd. She did not wonder what the Celestials looked like or in what manner they were dressed. Or how their strange words sounded coming out of their strange mouths.

In the bottom left corner of the slate, she wrote the word *husband*. In the bottom right, she wrote *child*.

A final cry from the crowd reached her ears, and then the world outside fell silent. At the top of the slate, she wrote *mother* and then drew the lines of an even triangle between the words. Without a child, she would never be at the head of her own humble crowd. Without a child, they would offend geometry; they would be a one-legged creature unable to stand or walk. The fierceness of her desire unnerved her. Dampness seeped through her dress under her arms. She wiped the slate clean with the side of her fist. It was not that she could not imagine losing this child. It was that she could imagine it too well. If she lost this one, something, finally, would break. She would become a stranger to herself. She understood this with a clarity that was equal parts dread and anticipation.

Two blocks away, Sampson was issuing more orders, this time to William P. Hurd, local photographer, who was setting up his glass-plate camera and heavy tripod on the factory's south lawn, making ready for a photograph for which Sampson had generated plans shortly after the Chinese had embarked from California. He stood in the evening sun, checking and rechecking the contents of his portable darkroom—chemicals, trays, and plates piled in the back of a covered wagon led by his astonishingly aged chestnut mare.

Once the Celestials had disappeared into the factory, the accompanying crowd had, save but one or two lingerers, dispersed, and these last few took no note of the man poking around in the back of his wagon. They did not attend to his positioning of his stereo camera—two plate cameras situated on a single mount—or to his worried checking of the falling afternoon sun. Yet the lingerers were rewarded for their loitering when Sampson ushered the seventy-five Celestials out the back door of the factory and spread them across the south wall of his formidable brick building.

The boys were baffled. They had not even had time to change out of their travel clothes or wash their faces. The tea water had been put on but not poured, and more than one of the boys fretted as he was arranged among his fellow travelers that the cooks had forgotten to remove the kettle and the water was, at that moment, boiling away.

The photographer had placed his camera too close, and the group had to wait as he retreated in order to accommodate the size of the gathering. Sampson muttered that he had paid Hurd to be ready, not to watch him make ready, and Hurd, burdened with tripod and camera, promised to be as quick as possible.

"What are they saying?" the youngest of the boys asked Charlie.

"They are fighting," Charlie answered. "It is not about us," he added, and the boy seemed reassured.

The low light meant that the exposure time was long. Sampson paced behind the camera, and Hurd agonized that the man's tread was making the camera tremble in minute but disastrous ways.

The photograph would be, as most of Hurd's work was, lacking, and the many magazines looking for images of the Chinese in the months following their arrival would not choose this one, a fact that bothered not only Hurd but Sampson as well. What was the point of having gone to this expense to show the world what he was up to if the world would not look? *But the world is looking,* Julia would remind her husband, fanning the illustrated newspapers before him. *Just not at your photo,* she told him. *Exactly,* he replied, closing the discussion.

But the Chinese boys, stiff and tired from their journey, hot against the American bricks in their dusty clothing, would remember the photograph more than they would remember anything else from that day. For most of them, it was the first time they had sat for a photograph. There was confusion and wariness about their new employer's reasoning. Was there to be a display on the factory walls?

Alfred, one of the few loiterers peering through gaps in the factory's fence, thought he knew just what Sampson was doing. The man was saying, as clear as if he had written a letter, "Take note, Crispins. See here what I have done to you and yours." A few weeks after the photograph, the caricaturists would agree. *Punchinello* would publish the cartoon "Yan-ki vs. Yan-kee," in which the Chinese swarm across a shoemaker's dinner table, taking his bread and cake, pulling a patty from his daughter's hand, stealing his pet dog.

As the years would pass, Ida would remember this day for Charlie's hands. Alfred would remember it as a symbol of all he was still yet to lose. Lucy as the first day in months she'd had an hour to herself. Charlie would remember it as yet another beginning, and Sampson would remember the weight of those pistols beneath his belt. And Julia, anxious blue-eyed Julia, would remember it as the day she lost her fourteenth child. And as the beginning of the small, hidden path to the fifteenth, the one who lived. And no matter where her mind traveled, it would always end in the same place: the smell of wet earth, the heft of something larger, the cousin sensation to the one she sometimes experienced in church. As if God's hand had reached down to lay itself across her brow. As if He were telling her to close her eyes, because He had for her a wonderful surprise.

Chapter Three

In 459 AD, five Buddhist priests arrived on the west coast of a country they called Fusang, planting as evidence of their presence seedlings of a particular species of cypress that some Californians still claim as indigenous.

On a chilly September morning in 1781, Los Angeles was founded with one Chinese inhabitant. Four years later, three Chinese sailors were stranded in Baltimore when the captain of their ship took off to wed his long-suffering fiancée. The sailors successfully petitioned Congress for the cost of their upkeep and lived for almost a year in the care of an American merchant in the China trade before returning home to report on the loneliness and isolation of American life.

From 1820 to 1830, three Chinese arrived in the United States. By 1850, their number was increased by forty. By the same year, North Adams had become the fourth-largest textile mill town in Massachusetts. It was a seven-mile ride through town.

In the 1860s, in some California industries, more than three-quarters of the workers were Chinese, and even the African American delegates at the first Colored National Labor Union convention in Washington, DC, in December of 1869 passed a resolution in favor of excluding the Chinese.

In early 1870, Charles Sumner, senator from Massachusetts, moved to amend a bill and allow the Chinese to be granted citizenship and voting rights. The legislation was defeated by a large majority.

The United States Census of 1870 would list 63,199 Chinese in America, 62,831 in the West and 368 in the East, which suggests that the seventy-five boys spending their first night behind the closed fence and doors of Sampson's shoe factory were nearly one-quarter of the Chinese east of the Mississippi. By 1875, there would be 201 Celestials in Sampson's employ, making North Adams home to the largest population of Chinese nationals outside of New York City in the eastern United States. By 1882, Congress would pass the Chinese Exclusion Act, the first exclusion act based on race to be passed in America. "He doesn't stand a Chinaman's chance" would become a commonplace saying.

But on the evening of the thirteenth of June, amid the unfamiliar smells of shoe production, Charlie was faced with quelling the anxieties of seventy-four boys still reeling from the news that they were strikebreakers. He appealed to their pragmatism and to their notions of duty—they had, he reminded them, signed a contract. He appealed to their lifelong training as good sons in the Confucian ways, and this was the most successful, since in the absence of a father, even a foreman who spoke the language of the white barbarians would suffice as the recipient of whatever filial piety the boys had to offer, and he convinced them to busy themselves with their choice of bunks and the arrangement of their personal belongings.

He himself chose the first-level bunk closest to the door, as when dining in public he'd select the table and chair closest to the wall for an unobstructed view of what might be coming his way, and, crossing his legs at the ankles, closed his eyes for what seemed like the first time in days, unexpectedly summoning a vision of Third Brother flying a kite on the hill behind their childhood home.

Before George Chase left for San Francisco, Sampson had extended to him three-quarters of an hour of instructions. Chase was to seek the counsel of a shoemaker of the name Battles, a man who already employed Chinamen in his factory. If he could not get men experienced in making shoes, he was to engage those who had a natural turn for mechanism.

Chase said, "I am going haphazard, and don't know whether I shall accomplish anything or not." To which Sampson replied, "Your time is paid, your expenses are paid, so go."

But upon his arrival in San Francisco, Chase, perhaps too filled with the surrogate power granted him by his employer, did not seek out Mr. Battles and attempted to secure the labor himself. He was thus forced to wire to Sampson: *There are not Chinese to be had.* Sampson wired back: *Don't question my instructions; follow them*, and Chase, confounded as to how his employer managed to know the things he did, swallowed his pride and sent his *carte de visite* to Mr. Battles, who introduced him to the house of Kwong, Chong, Wing & Co., which kept an intelligence office, sometimes known as an emigrant agency. Charlie Sing was a member of this house, and it was he with whom Chase initially met, a meeting about which Chase would have both fond and uncomfortable memories for years to come.

Charlie impressed him. His English was broken but clear, and he was already a Christian with a firm handshake. He was unusually tall, a fact that Chase hoped would not too much displease the short-statured Sampson, and his stare seemed to suggest both attention and a respect for privacy. Yet Chase was disconcerted. There was something blank about the man. Not a neutral blankness as one often saw in women of a certain kind, but something more fraught. Chase felt as if he were looking at a vast, uncultivated field, beneath which you might find resistant roots and formidable rocks.

Charlie would need to see Mr. Chase's letters of credit. The house was particular about where they sent their men. They meant to be sure that their men were going to get their pay and be treated as they should.

It did not escape Chase's notice that the sentiment of the Celestial's demand resembled nothing more than one of Mr. Sampson's.

Unbeknownst to Chase, two days were spent investigating the matter with the house's sources in the East before Charlie gave Mr. Chase any encouragement, but when he said he would furnish the men, he did so at once. The men could have been ready within twenty-four hours, but Chase did not want to hurry the thing up. Two or three times a day, he would go to the emigrant agency and watch the progress of events, passing judgment as he did on both Charlie and the men Charlie hired. A good many were drawn in by a notice on the door, in which the facts of the case were stated (save that hiring on meant hiring on as a strikebreaker), and when a man applied, Charlie took his name, and when a large number had been registered he selected out enough of the best to make the desired quota. Chase noted the reach of Charlie's hand in the situation and wondered at how long it would take this man to cross swords with the one waiting for him across the country.

It was a Thursday night when the bargain was closed. The contract read as follows:

San Francisco, Cal., May 26, 1870.

This contract, entered into by Ah Young and Ah Yan of San Francisco and Charles [sic] T. Sampson of North Adams, Mass., witnessed: That said Ah Young and Ah Yan, partners in business, agree to furnish C.T. Sampson with 75 steady, active, and intelligent Chinamen, such as are quick to learn a trade (1 foreman, 2 cooks, and 72 workmen), on the following terms and conditions: They receive $1 commission for procuring each man. Wages of foreman, $60 per month for overseeing 74 men; if more men are added, to receive 50 cents on each man per month. Workmen and cooks to receive

$23 per month for first year, $26 per month for second and third years, and for all time they stay after three years they receive $28 per month. Pay roll to be made up first of each month, and the amount paid over the 10th of the month for the month preceding, in United States gold coin or its equivalent. House wood and water furnished free to men. Two cooks to be employed for less than 90 men. Time, 11 hours per day from the 20th of March to the 20th of September, and 10 1-2 hours per day from the 20th of September to the 20th of March. Lost time to be deducted except when employer stops work for his own benefit, in which case men are to receive full pay. If stoppage of work occurs by accident for one or two days at a time the men are to receive 30 cents per day for board during the stoppage. Railroad passage over to be furnished free, and if men work satisfactorily for three years or more they are to have a free passage back. Should the men be discharged by inability of employer to give them work they are to have free passage back, and wages paid to time of stopping work. The employer is to receive $25 from the first six months' wages of each man as a security to him against a man's leaving before his time expires, the amount to be taken out of his monthly wages, viz., $2 the first month, $3 the second month, and $5 each of the next four months. Pay of men to commence when they begin work.

Witness, W.W. Battles. Ah Young.
Witness, Charles Sing. Ah Yan.
C.T. Sampson,
By George W. Chase.

The following Wednesday the men were on their way, each carrying between fifty and sixty of the maximum baggage allowance of one hundred pounds to a man. They had been placed in the charge of Charlie, and the first time Chase saw them all together was at the train station, where the new foreman introduced them informally, bowing his head gently in the direction of each of the seventy-four.

Charlie woke, as is customary for most insomniacs, between two and three in the morning, when the function of the liver shifts. If he had been in his home village, his mother might have prepared a bitter tea of root stems and tree bark to regulate the movement of the blood and the qi of the liver, but what he needed was not available, so he rose, slipped on his cloth shoes, and felt his way along the walls for a route into the factory's courtyard.

The moon was new and lent nothing but the palest light to the dirt courtyard. The night birds were not those with which Charlie was familiar. He had dressed for bed in a cotton tunic and drawstring pants, and he held his sleeve over his nose, trying to rebalance himself by way of a scent of home long since washed from the weave.

The courtyard was a hollow square of fifty feet, a giant's version of the courtyards of his native village. He sank to his knees and bent in the manner of prayer to press his nose against the earth, but his attempt to discover the familiar missed its mark, as the dirt yielded none of the rich humidity or smell of that saturated earth of home. Here, the land was grit and sand more than earth, and on his knees he could not see how something like this could support any kind of life.

He made his way to the Marshall Street entrance—two huge arched wooden doors, split across the middle like the doors of horse stalls he had seen in California. They were adorned only by two forged iron circular pulls and the fresh-cut two-by-four that nested solidly in the newly mounted brackets. The shavings from installation drilling still graced the dirt at the base like a dusting of snow, and he bent to finger them before sweeping them into the dirt with his foot.

As a boy, he and his brothers had played warlords, each designating a corner of their courtyard as his fiefdom, and battling with fists and wooden swords in the middle. Warlords commanded the most power, the most land and men, wives, and concubines. Their larders were filled, their kangs always heated. What boy would not have aspired to that life? Only the weak. *Or the scholarly*, Third Brother had suggested, drawing characters in the dirt. *Same thing*, Charlie had said, swiping his wooden sword across the back of his brother's knees, bringing him to the ground.

But then Charlie had had occasion to enter an actual warlord's house. His father had been unable to pay for a pig the warlord insisted had been killed by someone in the Sing household. It was an unlikelihood, but Charlie had been indentured out for several weeks in exchange, and upon entering the courtyard of the warlord's house had watched a houseboy rake the packed dirt into uneven rows, seen the concubines bundled into one corner of the garden, their babies at their feet, the wives, jealous and unhappy, in mismatched rosewood chairs, and had understood the warlord's power to be as much bluster as truth.

He had understood something similar about Sampson when his new employer boarded the train at Eagle Bridge. Erect, compact, and nervous, Sampson had introduced himself too loudly to the two cars of Chinamen and offered his hand only to Charlie. Charlie had noted the pistols, as had fourteen-year-old Long Ley Hin to Charlie's right. "*Six?*" the boy had asked incredulously. Charlie had said quietly, "Say nothing. They must be important to him."

Sampson had expressed gratitude for Charlie's role in securing the boys and hope for a long and prosperous relationship for them all. He sounded as if he were making a toast, and Charlie had added, "Yes. To luck," to which Sampson had replied, "Luck has nothing to do with anything. It's best you learn that now, and learn it well." As he spoke, he placed his hand on Charlie's shoulder and gave it a light shake, and Charlie had noted his easy, proprietary nature, as if everything in the world were to be handled and assessed like fruit in a seller's basket.

And so Charlie stood with his back to the entrance door, reminding himself never to forget that the world he now surveyed was that man's creation.

To his right were the packing room and offices, fifteen feet high, with white hard-finished walls. He made his way to the offices, Sampson's and Chase's, Charlie guessed, testing the locked knob of the first. Both locks yielded easily to the thin hair stick that had once belonged to his mother and that Charlie had had occasion to use several times before in this role. The offices were each handsomely furnished, especially the more private of the two. Chase's, Charlie guessed correctly again. But the Chinaman was more interested in the other office, Sampson's, with its wide views of both the street and the side yard. It had its own exterior entrance. He took in the lack of a reading lamp for either chair and the impractically small size of the bookshelf. The only adornment on the wall was a surveyor's map framed in bird's-eye maple by, Charlie correctly assumed, Sampson's wife. The overhead light was gas. There was a small woodstove in the far corner, a tidy stack of well-cut logs next to it, and despite the sparse and insistent practicality of the room, it was abundantly clear that this was where his new employer spent the most time and enjoyed the most happiness.

East of the packing room was the finishing room. To the other side of the factory's entrance was the sole-leather room, furnished with all the machinery, tools, and facilities necessary for the expeditious and economical cutting of the soles. Twelve non-union men were employed there, and he searched unsuccessfully for any sign of whether relations with these men would be defined by harmony or discord.

In the rear were engine and boiler rooms, coal house, and storerooms—all arranged and adapted for convenience, dispatch, and safety. An engine of twenty horsepower drove the machinery. The three stories were heated by steam, lighted by gas, and supplied with washrooms, cloakrooms, and advantages of every kind.

He climbed the wide stairs to the third, and top, story, leaving the second floor and the bottoming room for last. This level was divided into two vast rooms, both abundantly windowed and ventilated, again with white hard-finished walls. One was the stitching room, home to tables that stretched 115 in front of twenty-three windows.

The rear was the dominion of the sewing room foreman. East of this was the box room, where the boxes were made and stored.

Earlier that spring, Sampson had tilled some two acres in connection with the building, laid out walks, grass plots, flower beds, and trees, and although Charlie was too cautious to remove himself from inside the factory walls that June night, he did enjoy the scent of growth and greenery that made its way through the building's open upper windows.

The bottomers' room was on the second story, directly above the sole-leather room. Forty by eighty feet and eleven feet high. This was where the Celestials would work. Pushed against the walls, beneath and perpendicular to the windows, were a series of workbenches, destined within a matter of hours to be home to a team of three Chinamen per bench, one at the end and one on either side. Here, the teams would learn, through sign language and by example, how the parts of the shoes were to be put together. One foreman, an independent workman long in Sampson's employ, would go about his work unmolested. As for the other, a Mr. Robbins of Springfield, within an hour of his arrival and visit to the factory, he would be accosted in the street by one Crispin after another with mysterious and awful hints. Mr. Robbins, an entire stranger to North Adams, but a typical New Englander with a good deal of strength of character and firmness of purpose, would later say to a reporter, "I heard all they had to say, and then I did not encourage them to say more."

For both foremen, Charlie would do the translating, and the boys' wariness would grow. What could be said of someone who could stand, as Charlie could, with a foot in two lands, straddling the widest ocean of the world?

In the workers, the visitors to the factory would find the long slit eyes from their earliest remembered geographies. They would be struck with the general impression of extreme delicacy and effeminacy. The workmen would not to the American eye seem to be men. The breadth of their face and the fullness of their nose suggested what the Americans could describe only as an inscrutable expression, and many of them would leave ready to ask of their companions: *Is it the ignorance and prejudice of race or is it merely custom and familiarity which imparts such superior intelligence and sagacity to the American faces when compared to the foreign?*

That first night, Charlie read an inscription scrawled on the wall by the stairs: *No scabs or rats admitted here.* But there was good air for work, which Charlie was glad to note, as he knew that, before striking, the American workers had bottomed twelve hundred pairs of shoes a day, and he further understood that those numbers were not to be equaled but surpassed if this Chinese Experiment was to seem any kind of success.

Adjoining the bottomers' room to the south was a large room where the shoes were brought for inspection and temporary storage before going to the finishing room. Until the evening of June 13, the rooms east of and below this had been unoccupied, but now he made his way back to them, following the sounds of seventy-four men breathing and murmuring in their sleep, dreaming—happily, he hoped—in their native dialects.

Lucy Robinson passed yet again a difficult night, and yet again Ida had been summoned in the middle of the darkest hours from the Widow Allen's house to be her companion through it, Alfred awake and awkward on the other side of the thin curtain that separated the front half of the one room from the back.

Lucy did not like to speak of the attack during the bright light of day, and Ida had come to cherish these nights for the intimacy they allowed. The widow found Ida's tending to Miss Robinson both Christian and useful, as the Robinson girl's attack was still the central topic among the sewing circle and Temperance Society ladies, and her proximity to the victim herself—only once removed, really—lent the widow the attention and interest she had long felt lacking.

Ida had found the blankets in a twisted thicket at Lucy's feet and had remade the bed around her friend as she had once seen a nurse do in a Richmond hospital during the war, and then she had changed Lucy's damp nightdress, being respectful with eye and hand of the still-pink scars lacing her chest and side.

The man had been a stranger. Lucy had not been able to describe his face, and what she had been able to describe— a clean and pressed gray shirtsleeve, slight veins beneath the smooth back of a hand, the smell of a soap heavily laden with perfumes—had not been enough for anyone else to put details to person.

He had come up behind her on Pearl Street, an area of town overrun, as the local paper put it, "with hooligans and thugs not, it seems almost unnecessary to say, from local parts." He had guided her with such quiet insistence to the small space between the two O'Connell shops that several moments had passed before the idea of struggle had occurred to her. Once she had begun to twist away, he had produced the knife, and once she had understood the pain to be her own, she had abandoned her struggles. She did not speak of what happened after that, not even with Ida under cover of darkness. It shamed her more than she sometimes thought she could stand that the doctor knew as much as she herself did of the damages done to her person, inside and out. That unhappy mix of the private and the strange was one of the hardest burdens to bear. The doctor, the sheriff, the attacker himself, all of them unknown to her and her to them, until the wary bonding of violence. With her brother, of course, the opposite had occurred: the sister he had felt he'd known was in the stroke of a few minutes made forever strange. And now, months after the incident, she kept as still as possible, sometimes any movement at all causing the otherworldly pain to move through her with an extremity that sent the air out of her as if she were a bellows. It was one of the reasons she secretly hoped the man would not be found. If she could barely stand upright among friends, how could she possibly do so in the face of a stranger who had taken such liberties with her?

Ida resettled her on the fresh pillow, lay beside her on the narrow bed, placing a hand lightly on her friend's forehead, and it was unclear to which girl the gesture brought the most comfort.

"Oh, Ida," Lucy said, her eyes closed and dry. "There's no one going to want me."

Ida cradled her friend's hand in her own. "Don't be stupid," she said, as she always said to this, the inevitable worry. "They will be up and down the stairs for you," she said. "It will be like Penelope and her suitors. They will be eating your food, drinking your drink. Foolish men making fools of themselves, and though you could have your pick, you'll know your one love is out there, making his way to you."

Lucy smiled a little. "You're full of nonsense," she said. "Who knows where my one true love is."

Ida blushed. What she was feeling but wouldn't know how to say was, "*I* know."

What she said instead was: "Your Odysseus is coming even as we speak. I've always been better at books than you." It was a clumsy and inaccurate claim that she would continue to make about herself in relation to most people.

Outside, the stars were still visible as ghostly shadows. The earliest of morning birds sounded in the willows along the river, and the tenement began to come alive with the creaks and thumps of workers getting ready for another day. Upstairs, John Hardy stretched and pressed his thumbs into his eternally sore lower back. The Morgans' terrier barked at Joe St. Pierre in the hall, and Miss Carrie Gardner from downstairs let her latest beau out, her laughter an ungainly trespasser on the stairs. Throughout the town, the Celestials had invaded the sleep and minds of the natives. J. H. Adams, furniture dealer, reached for his wife across their youngest daughter, who was once again sharing their bed, and thought of the plaits of black hair swinging against the delicate backs of the newcomers like bellpulls in drawing rooms, the luxury of summoning help with a mere tug. Mrs. Tucker, milliner, washed her face at a porcelain basin decorated with the images of plump Chinese babies playing with lions and balls and felt, for the first time in the five years of owning the thing, an inexplicable embarrassment. J. W. Spear, recent widower and dry-goods merchant, used the precious minutes before the waking of his four children to sit in his nightclothes at his dear wife's writing table and pen the first draft of an advertisement he would run in next week's paper, entitled "The Chinese Have Come."

Some worried or ranted. Others argued with themselves or with spouses, boarders, or housemaids. Boys wondered what kind of mischief the Celestials could be made to get up to. Girls recalled the texture and shade of their skin.

Mothers reminded themselves to preach tolerance and kindness to their children at the breakfast table. Merchants hoped for a spirit of materialistic accumulation of all things American. Ministers prayed. The striking shoe workers slept in, their wives moving noisily around them, each gesture designed to say, *Bills, bills, bills.*

And the town entire marveled at the twists and turns in the roads God had laid for them. It was as if into the hands of seventy-five boys God had placed small mirrors, and as the Celestials walked the streets of North Adams, those mirrors captured the faces of the townspeople, suddenly new and unrecognizable. As the town slowly woke, the question filling minds was not only *What do we make of them?* but also *What do we make of ourselves?* The one question that crossed no one's mind was *What do they make of us?*

Alfred was awake, though not readying himself for work. He was not thinking much about the strike, his Crispin brothers, or the Order's plans to discuss what to do about these strikebreakers dropped from the heavens. Nights like these, with his sister and her friend behind that curtain, he did not sleep. He listened instead for the sounds of Lucy settling into Ida's care.

He had not given Ida Wilburn much thought in Virginia. She'd been merely his younger sister's friend, someone he often included in his play, but someone in and out of their home so often that he stopped hearing the sound of the back door when it was she tugging at its handle. But here everything, including Ida, was different. Here her face held in it his mother and father, boyhood friends and favorite dogs. And, maybe most importantly, his sister before the attack. So here, as far from his hometown as he'd ever imagined he'd be, her brisk countenance stopped him short every time and he felt as if he were riding a horse who had refused a fence. Each time, he had to find something to do with his hands, give himself enough time to gather the reins, circle his mount, and approach the fence anew.

The pain of the dead child dividing itself from Julia's body lasted through the night. With each cramp, she imagined herself not as a safe harbor, but as terrain that offered a child nothing of life and everything worth fleeing. She had felt this way so often that it had for some time been the way she felt about herself without child.

Sampson also did not sleep well, and she listened each time he woke, turning to her in midsentence as if their conversations carried on regardless of consciousness. The first time, he spoke of the tidy bundles of belongings the boys had carried, how they had reminded him of his own brown leather valise from nearly twenty years ago, when he was first starting out, carrying his goods from house to house. Did she remember how he had sold out his stock in less than ten days? How the gentlemen of Boston's Atherton, Stetson & Co. had been surprised to see him back so soon for another invoice of shoes?

That valise was still on the floor of her wardrobe, brushed daily by the low sweep of her dresses and petticoats. In it, she kept mementos of their early life together. Their baptismal letters from the church. The handkerchief she had held while speaking her vows. The first present he had made to her: a flat gray rock banded naturally by one white line, small enough to fit easily in her palm.

And, indeed, she did remember that twenty-fourth of April 1851, when he had left her for Boston. She remembered that her panic at being left was offset only by the joy of their reunion. She remembered the amount of credit: $117 for three months, and the condition that if it was paid in thirty days, he should be allowed a discount of three percent. He had paid it off, though not within ten days, not even within thirty, and they had had to appeal to his cousin George Millard for a small loan, which so bothered Sampson that as soon as it was paid back he promptly erased from his mind that it had ever existed.

She had learned long ago not to correct him on these adjustments to his life's stories, and did not do so this night, nor would she have even if not under great physical stress.

The second time he woke, he raised himself on his elbows and said only, "They don't drink coffee." And the third, he looked at her for several seconds, but said nothing.

His sleep was so fitful that when he finally did turn on his side and commence the breaths and thrums of real sleep, she worried that her own discomfort would wake him, so she repaired to her sister-in-law's room and bed, waking her to say, "I am losing another," and Thankful made space for her beneath her white sheets, helping her through the worst of it, changing the muslins between her legs, persuading her to sip from the multitude of medicines, tonics, and remedies she spent much time collecting and comparing, easing her, finally, into something like sleep. And although Julia had forbidden it, Thankful roused her brother, letting him know why it was necessary that now, in the early hours of the morning, he join his sad and sleeping wife. And he did, and Julia was glad, for she woke to her husband settling around her as a shoe with its mate in a box, placing his hand, dry and warm, on her head.

"Thankful never could hold her tongue," Julia said, already crying.

"Bless her for it," Sampson answered, wiping his wife's face with the heel of his hand.

"I'm sorry," Julia said.

"For what?" he asked.

She closed her eyes and held his hand over them with her own. "For everything," she said.

He made to move, and she knew what was coming: his request for her to open her eyes and believe him when he told her that he had nothing for which to forgive her. That she was, as she had been on the day they met, on the day they married, the one person in the world for him. That she was always and forever enough. Her moments of greatest loss would be in her mind always paired with the greatest evidence of her husband's love. It had the consequence of making the losses feel more enormous.

She pressed his hand harder to her face, curled her body more tightly against his. "Stay," she said. And he did.

Chapter Four

Wednesday the fifteenth of June saw the successful penetration of the factory by a Crispin spy, a Mr. George Fisk, from Boston. Sampson had vowed to close the factory against visitors and had begun a policy of keeping all entrances locked or guarded, but during a momentary absence on Wednesday of manufacturer, bookkeeper, and boy, one door had been left carelessly unfastened (the boy had already been relieved of his duties), and Mr. Fisk walked quietly in and found his way upstairs and into the bottomers' room. Each person who saw him supposed he had been introduced and vouched for by someone else, and so he spent an hour in clandestine inspection.

Despite his vow, Sampson had not been able to resist showing off his experiment to some privileged few, and already a manufacturer of shirts from New Jersey and several other shoe factory owners from around the state had been to look on at the enterprise. On Wednesday, the latest batch included two reverends and the owner of a textile mill from Pittsfield. The talk was of educating the Celestials. They watched the boys maneuver the pegging machine in its devious way around the shoes. Sampson passed around a shoe turned out and ready for market. It was as good as any you could pick out of a hundred cases downstairs that the Crispins had made, he said affectionately.

It was not the harm of Fisk's presence that upset Sampson, but the impudence in it. He perhaps would have let it pass—he had promised Julia he would try to behave against his instincts in matters involving confrontation—but Fisk returned later the same day, called for Sampson's presence, and informed one of the non-union cutters, before Sampson's face, that there was a better position waiting for him, and that he could make money by leaving the factory. Sampson felt himself entirely in the right when he pulled a gun on the spy and said, "If a man steps on my toes, I will have revenge on him, if it is not for years after."

Fisk responded, "I have not trodden on your toes."

Years later, when Charlie would introduce Sampson to the Chinese notion of losing face, Sampson would recall his exchange with Fisk, but at the time, he merely said, "Then I cannot say what is causing them to feel such an ache," and he informed the cutter that he best hope Fisk was true to his promise of employment, as that cutter would not find his livelihood there any longer.

That night at a pub near Greenfield where Fisk put up for the night on his return to Boston, he would tell the story to the barkeep and remark that he didn't really think Sampson intended to shoot him, but that he also thought the man so excited that he would not have known whether he had shot his weapon off or not.

Julia, hearing the tale from Sampson that evening, would have agreed. "It pains me," she said, watching her husband's shoulders as he poked at the container of ice meant to cool their rooms. "It was not merely an inhumane act, but a senseless one. The harm that could come from having discharged a man who'd presented you with no affront seems clear enough. The good you were after seems—" She broke off, trying to still her heart. "Well," she said finally. "The good seems not so clear."

Sampson hadn't turned around, still bent over the ice.

She went on. "I hear these stories one after another," she said. "Does my pain mean so little to you?" For a moment the only sounds between them were the settlings of ice.

When he finally did turn, his face was a child's. "How can you ask me such a thing?" he said. "You hurt *me*. I am hurt."

She wanted to apologize, to take him in her arms, and to feel him take her in his, yet she could not quit feeling wronged, so all she said was, "Then I have company." And they both stilled, neither able to comprehend her resolve.

There were as many Congregationalists, Episcopalians, and Baptists as Methodists at the Sunday services following the Celestials' arrival. The four churches stood a stone's throw from each other on what was commonly referred to as Church Hill, the intersections of Church, Main, and Monument Square. Just a little farther afield were the three Roman Catholic churches, but their congregations didn't have the history of mingling that the others did, preferring to keep to themselves.

The more curious filled the Methodist church's rough pews and stood three-deep in the back of the room, trying not to dirty their Sunday clothes against the walls.

On that hot morning, as Charlie spoke of arriving in San Francisco as a newly orphaned boy of eleven and working as a miner and merchant before meeting "the esteemable Mr. Chase," his audience had no way of knowing that sometimes he said he was thirteen when he arrived, that sometimes he was not a miner but a house servant, a storekeeper, or "a partner in one of the large merchant houses of San Francisco." He did not mention the Chinese joss house that was nearly or successfully burned down four times in the years he lived in Weaverville, each time by a different group, all of whom shared the common desire of ridding the town of its infestation. He did not note that short of the mines, the only prospect for a boy was working odd jobs in the shops. Although he mentioned several of the hardships of crossing the Sierras to get to Virginia City, Nevada—eating bark, twigs, and boiled hide, encountering surprise snow too deep for horses and mules—he did not dwell on what he considered the unnecessary details of the slightly unsavory means a boy in his position had to use to make the crossing a successful one: the bribes paid, the discreet rumors spread, all the small ways he had put himself ahead of the group. Who could say where the line between admirable and selfish opportunism lay? This was America. To succeed here, he would need to act like an American.

He also chose not to speak of the powerful miners' union he had encountered in Nevada, because he had already discovered that it was never a good idea to complain to one group of whites about another. It was instead best to alter one's story.

On that June Sunday, he spoke slowly and clearly, and if his sentences were incorrectly constructed, they were delivered with a near-perfect understanding of his audience. He was humble without being obsequious, vulnerable without excessive need. The men in the room, including Sampson, who had arrived to the service late and left early, were impressed with the narrative's adventure. The women with that as well as with the young man's ability to maintain his dignity even while faced with life's degradations. Most in the room would find it no hardship at all to agree with the correspondent from the *Boston Daily Advertiser* who would write of Charlie that he was as unassuming as the president.

Looking back, Ida would recognize his speech as the moment when she began to understand what the advantages of his perceptive abilities might be, a quality made all the more appealing by the apparent popularity they enjoyed among the other women present. The murmurings of approval lapped through the room well before his speech was over. It wasn't long after services were concluded that Ida and a small contingent of Baptist and Methodist women approached their respective reverends, suggesting in that way devout women have of making suggestions that it might be a good idea to instruct the new members of their community in the ways of a moral life. It seemed the Christian thing to do.

Later that day, Alfred was of a different mind, laying his knife and fork alongside the cold meat and cornmeal Lucy had plated for Sunday dinner. The ladies of the town were still offering food and services as if she were a charity case, permanently disabled. The three of them were eating better than they had in years, though the situation entire made Alfred somewhat ashamed, as he knew his striking Crispin brothers were having their suppers from the Order's treasury.

"Ida," he began, his head reeling at the prospect of disagreeing with her, "you know both me and Lucy appreciate all you've done for us, and I'm not in the habit of meddling in your business, but I can't ride this particular wagon with you."

Ida snorted. "What difference is it to me where you ride?"

Lucy placed her hands palm up in her lap and regarded them sadly.

Alfred said, "They've got different habits, different religion. Education, ideas of government. All different. They've got no patriotic love of this land."

Ida smiled. "Whose words are those, then?"

Alfred blushed. He did keep a notebook. It was easy to get mixed up at the meetings, and as a Southerner among Yankees, he felt it was important to keep things straight. Even the newspapers were filled with more speculation than resolve. The headlines swung from "The Asiatic Sons of Wax" to "The Crispins: Their Death Blow Predicted."

But no matter the headlines, they were all printing a version of the question the *New York Tribune* posed: What shall we do with John C. Chinaman?

Why me? Alfred thought, not for the first time since his parents had died. And if he were to be more truthful than he was at this point in his life capable of being, he would have to confess that it was a sentiment he'd been nursing for as long as he could remember. In his childhood, it had taken nothing more than his mother asking him to fetch water or his father asking him to light the candles to set his jaw in petulance and persuade him that no one had known suffering equal to his own. Realizing the childishness of the sentiment did not drain it of its power.

"You can't civilize them," he said now. "They've got no sentiments akin to ours. They're ready to work for nothing and accustomed to living on less."

Lucy started to speak and then fell silent again. In the tenement, children were being excused from dinner tables and given leave to do what they would for the rest of the daylight hours. Boots and shoes scraped on stairs. Shouts and hollers sounded beyond their door, everyone aware that Monday morning would be there before they knew it.

"Alfred Pell Robinson," Ida said, "that's the most ridiculous thing I've ever heard you say, and you've said a few. It wasn't so long ago that words like those were being spoken of those French Canadians you call brothers. 'The Chinese of the Eastern States,' wasn't it?"

He said nothing and just wondered grimly how it was that Ida knew what she knew.

"Of all people," she said, "the three of us need to do the right thing here. These Yankees are watching us. Use your head, Alfred. For once in your life."

He picked at a thumbnail. How was it that this short sixteen-year-old could take him like a surprise storm? How was it that her opinion had come to matter so much to him?

"There's nothing wrong with my head," he said. "Let 'em come single-handed is all I'm saying, like other emigrants. Let 'em come and take their chance. But they come banded together. That isn't right."

Ida was laughing. "*This* is the argument of a Crispin *brother*?" she said.

He tried to look unfazed, but she had already turned to Lucy as if he had vacated the room.

"Next Sunday," Ida said to her friend, "the church is giving out slates and primers. We'll sing hymns. We'll teach them letters and numbers from the Good Book. You've been sitting around this apartment long enough."

Alfred shook his head. "Aw, Ida, I don't know about Lucy. The doctor said—"

Neither of the girls looked at him. Lucy had discovered that if she stared long enough at her hands it was possible to feel as if they weren't hers. She flipped them back and forth against the cotton of her skirt.

"No one knows her better than I do," Ida said, reaching out to tent her own hands over Lucy's. Her best friend's hands continued to flip beneath hers like moths. "Even you know that," she said to Alfred, finally glancing his way.

In that instant, he understood what her arrival meant in terms of what her family and the rest of his hometown thought of him. And he remembered a time, years ago on the Wilburns' front porch, when Ida, three years his junior, had quizzed him on his multiplication facts, correcting his every wrong answer in her crisp, flat voice. She hadn't laughed or teased him. She had just laid out their differences in plain view. *Okay then*, she seemed to be saying. *Let's get on from here.* He had to admit that praise from her might have always carried more weight for him than kind words from other corners. It was always more powerful to be admired by critic than by friend.

Charlie lingered in the last pew, alone finally save the reverend's boy sweeping the center aisle. Sometimes, beneath a tree or in an open meadow, in the face of some extraordinary beauty, or sometimes in church, he could entice a stillness to enter his body, as if the divide between it and the world had been bridged. In church, the feeling was better. He considered the altar, the cross fashioned from what looked like the roof beams of a barn. The air was thick with a woolen heat. Outside, a small pool of boys waited. The reverend's boy raised his broom in their direction, glanced at Charlie, and left to join them. Silence returned.

The collar of his dress shirt was wilted. He could smell the damp worsted of his suit. Without moving his head, he took in the carved pulpit and the worn steps down to the wooden pews. He counted back to the row he himself occupied and, without turning, took in the open door, the sharp yellow sunlight beyond it. In a moment, he would stir himself to life, head back to the factory for the midday meal and a bowl of tea. There was laundry to do, and preparation for tomorrow's training. One of the boys was turning fifteen, and Charlie had suggested to the cooks that it not go unnoticed. Many things to think about, many responsibilities to others, when he himself had only the most tenuous purchase on this strange new place.

But, for now, he sat and looked without looking and waited. Sometimes, in church, the same bridge between earthly and heavenly could be forged, if he was patient enough. Here was terrestrial; here was celestial. And across that bridge always walked Third Brother, miracle and torment. Bringing water from the well, his bamboo pole bouncing like rubber as he walked. Spying on his older brother as Charlie unwound the red string holding the evenly braided hair of the neighbor girl. On the ship to Gold Mountain, sick with something Charlie didn't know how to fix. His eyes wide, as Charlie readied his own bundle for the descent down the gangplank. "Isn't he kin?" one of the seamen had inquired, indicating the barely breathing figure on the pallet.

Charlie had shaken his head and repeated what he had been told to recite by those from his village who had already been to Gold Mountain and returned successful and safe: "I not know anything. I not have anything."

The sympathy strikes at the other shoe factories in town were all but over. The owners had offered a return to work at a ten percent reduction, and having been refused, had said they would employ new help. With five days' successful work already under the Celestials' belts, there was no need for the owners to say more, and so their terms were accepted. By the Thursday following Charlie's speech, the only Crispins out of work were Sampson's Crispins.

Proprietor A. B. Wilson of the Wilson House had been told to expect perhaps two hundred workingmen at Thursday night's meeting. He had doubled his waitstaff, though he had forbidden the sale of spirits, as he believed this particular group of men never to have been improved by drink. Even small beer was off the menu. He tried not to dwell on the loss of revenue his decision entailed.

Despite having invented the Wheeler and Wilson Sewing Machine in 1849, despite having owned patents for the rotary hook shuttle and the four-motion feed, both devices used in modern machines, despite having built the imposing Wilson House in 1865 at the cost of $140,000, Mr. Wilson would die a poor man. In the words of one cousin speaking in confidence to another a week after the funeral: "Mr. Wilson was given great mechanical genius, but no more financiering genius than a child." But he was in 1870 the owner of the most elaborate building in Berkshire County, perhaps even in Western Massachusetts. As Washington Gladden, leading American Congregational pastor, would write: "Eight large stores, a fine Public Hall, a Masonic Hall, a Manufacturers' Club Room, and a Billiard Room are included within its walls; and besides its spacious offices, its ample dining-rooms, its large and well appointed kitchens, pantries, store-rooms, its excellent baths and its elegant parlors, it offers to guests a hundred airy and well-furnished chambers." Modern conveniences appeared on every floor, including gas, steam heat, and the best sanitary arrangements, and a first-class livery was close at hand. It was without a rival.

It was his philosophy to allow all members of the community to use the Wilson House's public spaces, which is how on Tuesday last, the Crispins had held their secret meeting in one room while Sampson and the other manufacturers had held theirs shortly afterward in another. The evening had passed without incident, as he had arranged for the Crispins to use the rear entrance. No one had been the wiser, and Mr. Wilson had found himself enjoying the sight of one class of man streaming out of one door and another passing through the other.

But now he was nervous, and he rarely grew nervous. It was only half past, the hall was already filled beyond capacity, and a glance out to the street indicated the arrival of even more. Chairs had been removed a quarter hour previous and still men were shoulder to shoulder.

He found Samuel P. Cummings on the hotel's front porch, greeting new arrivals. Cummings was of Danvers, Massachusetts, and not a French Canadian but of Irish/English descent. A shoemaker of twenty years' standing and one of the executive committee of the National Labor Union, by the following year he would be appointed grand scribe of the Order's International Grand Lodge, a position he would manage to hold on to for only a year.

It was Cummings, along with Alexander Troup of Troy, a national labor advocate, and Emma Lane of Boston, the mistress of Massachusetts labor women, who had been advertised to address the multitude, and Mr. Wilson knew, as all good proprietors did, that the way to bring problems to their quickest and quietest resolution was to place them at the feet of the most influential person in the room.

And so Wilson suggested to Cummings that the meeting be taken to open air, and the near four thousand workingmen from the county entire and as far afield as Troy didn't disperse from the head of Main Street until after ten that night, listening first to Cummings and then to Troup (Miss Lane failed to appear) brood over the coolie question from a rustic stand hastily improvised by Mr. Wilson. Alfred, having arrived only five minutes early, could barely turn the corner of Pearl onto Main and wondered why he had bothered to come at all.

Upstairs in their apartment at the Wilson House, Julia, Calvin, and Thankful faced each other warily around one of their favorite board games. A warning from the manufacturer pointed out the dangers of introducing dice into the family home, so the three used a totem instead. Thankful was ahead, having landed on both "The Assiduous Youth" and "Benevolent Man." Sampson had landed on "Dramatist," and was forced to begin the game again. The playing board, all three agreed, was beautiful, each of the eighty-four squares arranged in a spiral traveling from "Infancy" to "Dotage," and illustrated with images of vice or virtue. The rules were printed in an easily legible hand around the spiral. Julia, however, found herself oddly irked by the directions:

"Whoever possesses Piety, Honesty, Temperance, Gratitude, Prudence, Truth, Chastity, Sincerity is entitled to Advance six numbers toward the Mansion of Happiness. Whoever gets into a Passion must be taken to the water and have a ducking to cool him. Whoever possesses Audacity, Cruelty, Immodesty, or Ingratitude must return to his former situation till his turn comes to spin again."

Following their remarks about the game, the conversation was halting, Julia and Calvin still smarting from Wednesday night's disagreement, Thankful eyeing the both of them and thinking how difficult it was to have one's life tethered in full to another couple. How much easier, she thought, if she were moving to the ebb and sway of just a husband, rather than a husband and wife. How much easier, yet at her age, she thought sadly, how unlikely.

None of the three suggested ceasing, working as they were to keep the sounds of the meeting up the street at bay. The town's Crispins and their sympathizers gave vent to their feelings as their side of the question was advocated, and through the open windows came loud and frequent cheers, the periodic stamping of feet, and the clapping of four thousand pairs of hands. It was the laughter that seemed to disturb Calvin most, and his fingers thrummed the felt of the game table, their game pieces jittering. His agitation was so apparent that Julia took pity on him and placed her hand over his, settling his fingers and the game.

★

What to do? What to do? This was the question the meeting was meant to address and dispatch. Though he did not like to pollute his lips with Sampson's name any oftener than necessary, Cummings felt he must point out that of those who would test labor, Sampson was the champion. It was men such as he against whom the common laborer must protect himself as well as protect the Celestials, as they too were wronged by being forced to do work for fifty cents for which they ought to receive two dollars, and it was clear that John Chinaman was a gentleman far superior to Mr. Sampson.

So what to do? What to do to resist this innovation that threatened to ruin their organization and put them beneath the concern of the capitalist? Violence must not be resorted to under any circumstances. They must seize the power at the ballot boxes next fall. In the meantime, cooperation was the call of the day, among Crispins and between Crispin and Chinaman.

Alfred judged Cummings charismatic and compelling. He had pushed his way through the crowd to see a man strong-armed and sturdy-legged with a low center of gravity, as if when God had laid a hand to Cummings's head, He had put a little too much weight behind the gesture.

But as much as Alfred found himself wanting to believe, something kept him from handing over his full trust.

After Cummings closed the proceedings, and the crowd finally grew tired of itself and dispersed, Alfred discovered himself in a bar with friend and brother Daniel Luther, the same brother he had stood beside on the depot's platform ten days before, voicing what turned out to be mutual concerns, both of them knowing that they should keep their voices low.

"If violence is our enemy," Daniel wondered, "then whose suggestion were those rocks and bats? Were we meant to bang them together like a marching band?"

Alfred stared at his beer and thought, first, that this was a drink he couldn't afford and, second, that he must chew some mint on the way home.

Daniel went on. "And what about throwing the train from the tracks? Seems like violence to my mind."

Alfred felt as if someone had taken him into his own backyard, lifted a board in the fence, and shown him that behind the yard, the home, the street, the town he'd known his whole life, there was a mirror version, yet populated by all different people getting up to all different things.

"The train from what tracks?" he asked.

"Between Troy and here," Daniel said. "Some machinists in Troy and Eagle Bridge had organized, or been organized, to throw it at a dangerous point in the roadbed. Such of the Chinamen not killed or maimed were to be otherwise so disabled as to prevent them from engaging very actively in the shoemaking business."

Alfred's surprise and sadness at being left out yet again were magnified by the fact that his friend seemed to take Alfred's ignorance as utterly expected and, even worse, just.

"Where'd you hear tell of all this?" he asked, trying to keep his voice from sounding like a child's.

Daniel said the point was that someone's mouth was doing one thing while his hand another. Why was it that

Cummings encouraged the formation of cooperative ventures as a remedy to this botched-up situation, but Daniel had to hear about their own Order's co-op on the fly? And why cooperation in any case? You could say the only thing a course like that did was indicate that they'd given up all hope.

Alfred thought about pretending he knew what his friend was talking about but calculated that he would uncover more by being honest. "What did you hear?" he asked.

"A co-op is forming up Brooklyn Street," Daniel said. "A pistol shot from Sampson's."

"Smith and Company's place?" Alfred asked.

Daniel nodded. One question after another lined up in Alfred's mind. "What happened to the plan for the train?" he asked.

Daniel snorted. "It depends who you ask. Cummings and Troup say they frustrated it as soon as they heard of it. Jenny Gallagher says it was her brother what held up the telegram."

"Who's she?" Alfred asked.

"Just a girl," Daniel said, sliding his second glass back and forth, watching the beer rock against the sides.

Alfred hated that he had nothing but questions to offer. "Who's her brother?"

"Works in the telegraph office. She says it was him who got the message from the Troy machinists offering their services and him who held up delivery until the train was arrived."

Alfred went over the last couple of weeks. Had there been nothing but meetings secret only to him? "Where's Smith going?" he asked.

Daniel coughed. "Up the street even further. He and some-one else have formed to build another factory. Don't know where any of them think they're getting waterpower." The barkeep placed a third beer before Daniel and he lifted it in Alfred's direction before taking a large swallow. Alfred noted that his friend had not offered to buy him a second one.

"Who all's throwing in for the cooperative, then?" Alfred asked.

Daniel said he'd heard only a few names, twenty or thirty in all.

Alfred had spent and would spend much of his life look-ing for the person who would take him into account, who would sit up and take notice of the slimly built boy in the corner. Everyone so far had let him down in this regard. His family, the Hoosac Tunnel manager, Mr. Sampson, Ida, and now, perhaps, the Crispins.

"What do you suppose they're up to?" Alfred asked.

"Who?" Daniel responded.

Alfred tilted his head in the general direction of Mar-shall Street. "The China boys."

Daniel shrugged, both of them agreeing there was no real way of knowing.

The China boys were, at that moment, finishing up their dinner with their customary bowls of green tea. The two cooks were washing bowls and chopsticks in the makeshift kitchen. Some of the older boys lit pipes. Others fingered whittling projects in their pockets, trying to decide wheth-er to work on them. The talk was of their days so far and the strange ways and sounds of the pegging machines, the peculiar smell coming off Mr. Sampson's clothes, and the friendly girls in the sewing room with their strange hair and even stranger skin. When one called them White Devils, another responded, "White Devils I could get to know," and the older boys laughed while the younger ones glanced around, too wary to ask for clarification.

Charlie sat on a bench, his back against a wall. What had he been thinking, bringing these boys here? As consolation, he reminded himself that they would be living among whites in California as well. But he discovered little solace in this thought, since a small town such as this offered none of the anonymity or support of a city like San Francisco. He closed his eyes. What could come of this commingling of the races except for what his ancestors had warned?

The cooperating Crispins actually numbered thirty-one, two of whom Alfred would have counted as near friends. The Brooklyn Street factory would be up and running by the end of the month. It would not be the first, as Crispin cooperatives dotted the eastern states from New Brunswick to Baltimore. By August, the North Adams group had applied for and received a charter from the state and had $6,000 in capital.

The arrangement eliminated employers, and decisions on wages, hours, production levels, and other such matters would be collective ones. They employed women, all members of the Daughters of St. Crispin, though women were, by state law, forbidden to hold shares in their own names.

When the November late-season slump arrived, only Sampson and the co-op would remain in operation. By

December, newspapers throughout the Northeast would hail cooperation as the sure defense and protection of labor.

Alfred would borrow money from Lucy and Ida and become a shareholder and bottomer at the co-op two days before they commenced manufacture. For close to three years he would make less than the non-Crispins working in other factories, but more than Sampson's Celestials, and enjoy the risks and possibilities of self-employment. It would be the most satisfying time of his life.

That summer, when the doors to the co-op opened, the newly purchased and piled hides sending their animal odors through the building, the kits lined up against the walls like girls at a church dance, the first thing the cooperating cordwainers did was stand for a photograph. They did not stand against the wall of their own building. They walked, spilling into the dirt street, the women—many of them in their Sunday best for the occasion—stepping carefully between the ruts of wagon wheels, down Brooklyn Street, across River Street to the north wall of Sampson's factory. Word was that Sampson himself was in Boston and the only guard was posted to the office entrance on the south wall. A sewing girl, sister to one of the Crispin cooperators, leaned out the window, waving at her brother to indicate that she would be down in a minute to unbolt the gate.

One by one, men helping the women, the group of seventy made it through the fence and grouped themselves in front of Sampson's north wall, most of the original Crispins at the back entrance, the sewing girl hastily passing them a few wooden stools upon which to stand so their heads would be raised above the rest in the final image.

It was evening, the sun beginning to lower itself behind the hills with the grace of an elegant guest lowering herself into a front parlor's best chair. As Alfred was the only one among them who had witnessed the Chinese posing for their photograph, the workers arranged themselves according to his direction, which he offered in a manner he hoped would be understood as not filled with too much pride. It was he who insisted that the sewing girl who had signaled the all clear sit in the second-story window and that she secure a friend to join her. It had been that way, he remembered, in Sampson's photograph. In every way, the photograph mirrored Sampson's of the Celestials, the only difference being that the Chinese had been posed at the south wall and the cooperative at the north, as if one group had arrived only to push the other out the back. The photographer was William P. Hurd, using the same equipment he had used to document the arrival of the Celestials, all pulled in the same wagon by the same aged mare, who would manage to walk this earth for three more summers before folding her awkward legs and settling down for the last time in the far corner of her favorite pasture.

Chapter Five

Had Julia been at the Methodist church a week previous when Charlie had addressed the congregation, instead of still afraid to show her face, her failures painted there for all to see, she would have felt a kind of grace listening to his imperfect words, and she wouldn't have known whether to attribute it to his speech or to the man himself. Either way, despite being a devoted churchgoer, she would not have been part of the small posse of women suggesting further contact and interaction with these Chinese boys. For although she welcomed grace in all its forms, beneath the calm it brought was something fluttering and alive, something that would have made it difficult for her to rise to her feet. Had she been there, the line of churchgoers in her pew would've grown impatient waiting for the woman at the end of the row to open her eyes and make her way out.

So it was only at Sampson's insistence that Julia volunteered for the Celestial Sunday school. His consultation with the pastors of the village had resulted in the call for volunteer teachers.

It did not escape Julia that even before Sampson had laid eyes on them, the Chinese had seemed to transform her husband from the supremely pragmatic to the utterly paternal. He had never, as his peers had, offered his French Canadian employees schooling or stores, churches or homes. What he had wanted from them was hard work. What he gave in return was adequate pay. He had not felt they should expect his concern for their welfare to extend beyond that.

The contract with the Celestials, on the other hand, stipulated "house, wood, and water." *Free* house, wood, and water, Julia recalled, walking alongside her husband the day before Sunday school was to commence. He had asked her to accompany him on a stroll up the hill that George Chase and his wife had recently purchased. They were planning on making a home there, and Sampson hoped Julia might see the idea of home ownership as less frightening and more appealing. As lovely as the Wilson House was, Sampson had enough of the farmer left in him to value nothing more than land with a solid house upon it. He had always imagined himself on the wide porch of a sturdy structure, the land as far as his eye could see his own. Chase would end up building several structures, modest and grand, and the property, much to Sampson's annoyance, would quickly and forevermore become known as Chase Hill.

Sampson had already paid the Chinese workers' railroad passage there, and if they fulfilled their contracts he would provide passage back. If his business experienced a downturn, he was obligated to continue to supply full pay. The big wooden storage bins that had once been used to sort the spools of thread for sole stitching and the wooden molds for uppers now contained laundry. It was easy to feel these boys were in some way his own. Seventy-five, where before there had been none.

He was kind enough not to make this latter observation to his wife, though as they stopped at the crest of the hill to look back over the town and his factory, smoke pouring out of its central stack, he did suggest she might help them. A third of the Celestials had already completed their training and were at work. The cooperative, also visible from their vantage point, would be running in a matter of days. He must embark to Boston in the middle of the next week to meet with other manufacturers to discuss what course they would take to put an end to that Crispin enterprise. He held her elbow as they stood there. It seemed important that she feel about these boys as he did. Perhaps God intended for them to create what they could in this unusual way. "They are like children," he said, brushing at her eyebrow with the side of his thumb. "You can help them." And so she did.

Lucy and Ida arrived at the Chinese quarters early, having left a pouting Alfred behind in the apartment. He didn't see why they had to volunteer when from schoolchild to widow everyone else already had. "Be a Christian," Lucy had said, kissing him on the top of the head as their mother used to when he was a child.

The afternoon was clear, and the landscaping that Sampson had had laid in was in full health, and a few days later, when news of the previous day's earthquake in New York City finally reached North Adams, the two girls would comment how strange it was to look back on that Sunday weather and think that mere miles away a whole city was recovering from such a phenomenon. "Did you know," Lucy would ask, looking up from the newspaper, "that nausea is always experienced in earthquakes?" During the course of her recovery, she would develop a lifelong interest in natural disaster and extraordinary displays of wreckage. Ida would think it unhealthy, the focus on ruin rather than repair, but Lucy achieved solace from such stories, as if her own assault had been disaster to be sure, but natural nonetheless.

They made their way down the graveled walk to the building's rear, their conversation hushing as they entered the Chinese quarters, both of them aware this was not the sort of experience they would be having under any other circumstances. Ida thought of announcing to her mother that she was about to sit across from a foreigner who spoke not a word of God's English and found her neck warming as she crossed the threshold.

The Reverends Griffin, Sanford, Gladden, and Jennings were present. As was William Ingraham, Baptist Sunday school instructor of twenty years plus and Sampson's sewing room foreman, and, of course, Sampson himself. There was an air of mild panic among the men, and Ida found herself guiding Lucy by the elbow to the other side of the

room. Men in a state of unrest were in Ida's opinion to be
avoided. She had once, as a child, toured a gunpowder factory with her father. All the visitors had been obliged to
slip off their shoes and don paper slippers, the powder dust
on the floor too dangerous to come into contact with the
hard soles of street shoes. At the end of the tour, they had
disposed of their slippers in a wooden crate just inside the
factory's doors. She had yet to meet a man, other than her
father, whom she didn't believe to be the equivalent of flint
and shavings, liable at the slightest provocation to ignite.

It was to her surprise then that the large group of almond-
eyed creatures gathered at the wooden tables lined up on
each side of the room did not incite in her the usual response.
They were smaller of stature and slighter than they had appeared at the station, most of them clearly possessing no
more than her own sixteen years. None were very hardy-
looking, and she could not imagine them doing the heavy
work of farming and slating. Perhaps shoemaking, something she had always thought not particularly manly, would
suit them.

Their trousers looked excessively comfortable. As did
their black cloth shoes. Their hats, common felt ones of
black, hung above them on pegs situated in rows around
the room.

"Their heads are quite alarming," Lucy said.

Their pigtails were coiled around their crowns, putting to mind a fancy lady's chignon. Ida found the whole
thing charming. Their faces were plump and round and as
smooth and destitute of beard as a woman's.

Actually, Lucy found their shaved heads more than alarming. They were so smooth, so clean-shaven that she couldn't stop imagining what it would be like to touch one of them, slippery and viscous beneath her fingertips.

One looked at her and with a pleasant smile that narrowed his already oblique eyes said, "How do?"

Her attacker had bid her good afternoon as he had wrapped his arm around her from behind. The back of his hand had been hairless. She shook her head rapidly like a hound shaking a toy and the Chinese boy who had addressed her thought perhaps she suffered from the shaking disease he had seen in his grandmother. If so, she was harmless, he knew, and his heart warmed in her direction.

But Lucy refused to think her repulsion at the sight of the bevy of smooth scalps had only to do with her assault. Was she to be as simple as that for the rest of her life? And so she swallowed to ease her stomach and inclined her head toward the boy. "I'm well, thank you. And you?" she asked, expecting and receiving no response.

She would for the remainder of her life find her first and strongest reaction to the sight of human skin, especially male human skin, the same mix of unease and nausea that she experienced that first day of Celestial Sunday school. It would prove to be only one of the many ways that man had left his mark.

The mild panic of which the women had taken note had to do with the fact of Charlie's accident the previous day. Without debate was that Charlie's right thumb had been crushed in the cam of a pegging machine. He was currently laid up in a hastily thrown-together sickroom off the kitchen. Beyond that, there was some disagreement. Either the thumb had been crushed by the sudden starting of power by a green hand whom Charlie was instructing or Charlie had undertaken to manage one of the pegging machines, the most difficult and terrible of all the apparatus used in shoemaking, before he was ready for such an enterprise. In both versions, his thumb had hung by just a few threads, and a surgeon had been called and an amputation performed. If lockjaw did not follow, he would be able to resume work in a matter of a few weeks.

Ida had not realized at first that the man they spoke of was the same whose hand she had taken note of two Sundays before as he marched from train to factory. Once she did make this connection, she felt surprisingly sorrier about the situation, her sympathy compounded by her sense that it wasn't only the victim who had lost something when that pleasing hand was maimed.

The question for now was how to manage without their only interpreter. Perhaps they should desist for today and return when he was feeling more well?

Lucy spoke before realizing she was going to do so. She said, "But surely those doing the good work of God have faced problems larger than this. Not only can we manage quite well, I think, but we are obliged to see that we do."

The teachers and clergy were quick to agree, and she marked the instance as the moment when she realized that her attack had left her with more authority than she'd ever previously enjoyed.

She gathered a slate, a primer, and a Bible from the supplies laid out by the clergymen, and Sampson found himself impressed with her poise. He noted the unusual scarf worn high on her neck and tucked into her collar, and wondered at her name, which he wouldn't learn until several years later when he would seek out her identity from George Chase, who would utter the name quietly, reminding his employer of the Pearl Street attack.

Even on this first day, it didn't take long for the teachers and students to contribute to the growing noise of the venture. One or two boys per teacher, the earnestness of the whole group amounting almost to enthusiasm. Even Julia, sharing a table with Thankful and two boys, both aged seventeen, both, astonishingly enough, named Ah Ley, found herself carried away with the task at hand. In this equation, she held all the abilities. Lack and need sat securely on their side of the table. She pointed vigorously at the dimly burning candle before them. "Candle," she announced. "Candle." She wrote it on the slate between them and tapped it with her finger. Then she held the candle up with enough enthusiasm to cause one of the boys to startle. "What is it?" she demanded.

It took him a moment to comprehend. He would prove to be a trifle duller than Thankful's boy. He sat gazing with bovine patience upon the object, but then he ventured his own rendition of the word. She had him write his version beneath hers on the slate. He was rewarded with her genuine and earnest praise, punctuated, to her surprise, by her placing a hand on his shoulder.

Thankful raised her eyebrows at her sister-in-law, and Julia blushed, dropping her hand to her lap. The boy's shoulder had been small and round, softer than she would've guessed, and an image of cupping her hand beneath an infant's head came unhappily to her mind.

"These Americans," the boy would say to Charlie later that night, "they are always touching us."

"Try not to reveal your revulsion," Charlie would advise.

Ida and Lucy shared the table adjacent to the Sampson women and worked together to sketch and then recite the names of various simple objects.

"Cat," Lucy said, and Ida went to work at the tricky drawing of chalk on slate.

Lucy peered at the finished product. "That is not a breed I know," she said. "Is it missing a leg?"

The girls commenced with a laughter that left their pupils smiling politely at these most incomprehensible of instructors. But as the months passed, the attachment between teacher and student would become noteworthy, and it wouldn't be long before a Celestial would refuse to attend his lessons unless assured his teacher would be present.

Even so, the town's mildly patronizing stance toward this educational endeavor would keep anyone from even considering the charge struck between seventy-five young men of one race and fifty young women of another. For although the teachers were young and old, wealthy and not, the majority of the group were the young ladies of the village, or, as they would appear in the press, "the beautiful, refined, and intellectual" young ladies. The communal work of teaching and

learning, the shared space it required, was unprecedented for both American ladies and Celestial boys, and the unprecedented is almost always the certain spark to larger flame.

As if aware of this, during that first lesson, even under the influence of the morphine, Charlie fretted. From his sickroom, he strained to distinguish one line of conversation from another. He held his good hand to his head, the failings of his group lined like soldiers across the field of his mind. Quang Chung had an inability to keep quiet. Chim Kow had proven incapable of holding eye contact. Ley My had a habit of circling the outer edge of his lips with his tongue over and over, around and around.

Charlie knew that as a rule the Americans whose eyes came into focus as they landed on you were the ones toward whom the most caution should be displayed. He had been filled with skepticism about Sampson. It had taken much persuading by the company's other officers to convince him that the American was interested only in what he said he was interested in: fair work for fair pay. But Charlie found the man both appealing and mystifying in equal parts. How strange that the photo he had arranged of the Chinese on their arrival was displayed outside his office. How strange that he ended each day with an exchange with Charlie, inquiring after not the boys' work, but their welfare. Yet Charlie liked the swing of the man's gait as he patrolled the factory. He liked the midafternoon walk to the river that the man seemed to take every day. He liked that Sampson was a man in a three-piece suit throwing rocks like a boy.

But what could he expect from these Americans? And what did he want from them: to be one of them or to be taken care of by them?

His injured hand was propped atop an excess of pillows, as per the surgeon's instructions. The doctor had been blunt about the necessity of the amputation. Charlie was lucky, he had said. It was only a thumb. The tunnel workers were losing much more than that.

Charlie did not in general engage in fantasy, but lying there listening to the swell and break of the hubbub in the other room, he believed that if he were to unwrap those bandages, he would reveal his thumb, whole and intact.

The second week of Sunday school, Sampson asked Julia to check on his foreman during lessons. She protested that she was not a doctor, had no experience in the loss of limbs, had not even met the foreman, but Sampson ushered her out the apartment door telling her to stop being so silly. Introduce herself. Inquire as to the man's health. If he could not trust her opinion, whose could he trust?

Julia ventured into the sickroom during a break in the lessons. "Hello," she said. Charlie looked like a man who had spent the last week bedridden. Rumpled and limp as well-used sheets. She recognized the state all too easily. His mouth, she knew, would be sour and dry, his bones filled with ache. Yet his face was calm and smooth, his good hand quiet against the sheets. "Would you like me to read to you?" she asked.

Charlie was sitting up with his back against the wall, his feet crossed at the ankles. His bandaged hand was resting on a pillow in an eternal salutation. He regarded her. "Who are you?" he asked.

I am Mrs. Sampson, she thought, but did not say. Perhaps because she felt her life to be one of placation and compromise and perhaps because she wished, just for once, to get away with something brisk and startling if only to herself, she held out her hand and said, "I am Julia." And so, a secret, at least for the moment.

His eyes went from her hand to his own bandaged one and back again. He settled for a bow of his head. She reached over and took his left, healthy hand into a brief, firm shake, though because she'd taken him by surprise, and because his hand was at an awkward angle, the gesture was one of girlfriends rather than first-time acquaintances. He reacted the way he always reacted to surprise—as if inside his body the tide was on its way out.

"Oh," she said, taking note of how his face had gone still and away from her. "Apologies."

He barely knew this woman and she was already apologizing. Strange Americans with their strange ways.

It was his strangeness that would always allow the most uncharacteristic of behaviors from her. The sense she had that he wasn't quite of this world allowed her interactions with him to be unfettered by this world's rules. How else to account for her brazenness even on this, their first meeting?

Charlie closed his eyes. Perhaps when he opened them, she would be gone.

"Are you worn out?" she asked. "Being bedridden is harder work than it appears."

Perhaps it was his strangeness that also guaranteed her lifelong misreadings. She was not a stupid woman. If anything, she enjoyed healthier observational powers than most. About him she noted no less than usual, perhaps even more, but his foreignness meant that what she made of those observations was almost always determined by her own feelings and, therefore, almost always faulty in some crucial way.

"No," he said, opening his eyes.

She stood there.

"You want to read, then read," he said, without rudeness.

"Do *you* want me to?" she asked.

"I want nothing from you," he said. He had heard Sampson use that phrase the previous week when firing a white man and had filed it away. He depended, in terms of his use of the English language, on imitation. It made the imitated feel flattered and as though interacting with one of his own. Charlie would have been most proud to know that there would come a point in his life when his command of the language would no longer prompt surprise.

"Then I won't read," she said.

"Okay," he said, enjoying the roll of American slang in his Middle Kingdom mouth.

She held his eyes with her own. Later, they would tease each other about which of them had looked away first.

That second Sunday school session ended with what would become a tradition: the exchange of song.

Julia and Ida, Baptist church acquaintances, led the instructors in "There Is a Happy Land," "God Bless Our

Native Land," and a few other simple songs of that sort
and of equal relevance. Sampson, having arrived in time for
the end of lessons, beamed from the room's back corner:
once again, something he had put his hand to had come to
immediate success. He joined the singers with his own rich
baritone, happy to share his good mood.

Ida had taken Lucy by the hand to join the instructors at
the room's front, but Lucy had not been able to bring herself to sing, and even being up there beneath the gaze of so
many had caused her stomach to seize, and she was obliged
to drop Ida's hand and make her way to a side table, where
she sank thankfully to the worn wooden bench.

Ida tried not to see her friend's retreat as cowardice. She
had found herself wrestling with an impatience over Lucy's timidity. She wanted her old Lucy back, the girlfriend
of creek swims in their petticoats and horseback rides on
green-broke geldings their fathers had forbidden, skirts
torn on wire fences, and books and slates buried in secret
caves or forgotten in the long grass of the Robinsons' backyard. Happy as she was to have those late-night conversations lying beside each other in Lucy's narrow bed, she
wanted their old conversations once again, the future plans
of silly girls, all of them involving never being separated,
not by death or husband.

The instructors held the last note and there was silence
as the bemused Celestials regarded them. From his sickbed,
Charlie called out in Chinese, and the boys immediately
commenced a round of hearty applause and then gathered
to give a song of their own.

Back in their houses for Sunday dinner, the American instructors would tell their loved ones that the Asian air had been simple, monosyllables of all kinds mixed together in what was, they might venture to say, a rather lugubrious rhythm. The words, of course, made no sense at all, but neither, they would hasten to add, did much of the popular singing of their own language. To a household, all would conclude that the Celestials' song had indeed been peculiar, though not unpleasing.

Lucy, meanwhile, felt as if she might faint or throw up. She stared at the line where wall met floor the way one struck by seasickness stares at the smallest scrap of distant land. She could feel Ida's impatience like heat from a stove and it saddened her. One of her pupils, whose name she was ashamed to realize she could not recall, quit his singing and slid next to her on the bench and took her hand. She flinched, but he held it in a way that seemed drained of intimacy. He pointed to her head and stomach and then applied firm pressure to a spot on the inside of her wrist.

Her dizzy head righted itself; her stomach ceased its wavering. When she removed her eyes from the floor's seam, testing her newfound health, they fell on Ida's face, which wore an expression Lucy recognized easily from their childhood. It said: *You are making me sad*, but Lucy was so astonished to have the touch of a male bring solace rather than suffering that she could not rouse herself to remove her hand from the boy's, whose name she still could not remember, but against whose thumb her pulse beat like a small machine.

Chapter Six

The newspapers of Wednesday, June 29, reported that California produced three million pounds of quicksilver annually; St. Louis was to have a theological seminary for the colored; an old lady in Huntingdon County, Pennsylvania, had seventy pet cats; American girls were flirting too much in Paris; Thomas Keating, on a charge of second drunk, was fined seven dollars and costs; a lad named James W. Gray was arrested for being a stubborn and disobedient child; and a Crispin rally was held in Tremont Temple in Boston. That same day, several of the state's manufacturers also convened in that City of Notions.

By chance, Sampson took an early supper a mere two park benches away from Alfred, both of them having chosen the opportunity to get some air and time to themselves. They found the company of large groups unmanageable after extended periods. The feeling was exaggerated by the excesses of that particular city, which seemed somehow less American than others and left both men feeling anxious and grim, though in different ways and for different reasons.

Sampson had been to New York on but a few occasions and had found that city suggestive of everything to do with the future. He would have expected to feel a philosophical kinship with a city such as that, but had not. He had felt instead as if elbowed aside by some high-ranking officer of civilization, as if being reminded that in this march to further conquests he was merely a foot soldier.

In Boston, on the other hand, he felt not only the possibility of commerce but also the importance of his particular place in that endeavor. After all, his ancestor Myles Standish had been the first white man to land on the shore of what would be Boston Harbor. Or, at least, that was what was said. It was also said of Standish that he was broad in the shoulders, deep chested, with muscles and sinews of iron and had landed upon the peninsula partly to see the country, partly to make peace with the Indians, and partly to procure their truck. Apparently, his party had returned home with a good report of the place and a considerable quantity of beaver.

How could someone such as Sampson not like a city that would triple its physical size through land reclamation by filling in marshes, mudflats, and gaps between wharves along the waterfront? The city's irregular outline evoking its status as the foster child of rivers, creeks, bays, and inlets, its well-paved and long streets of handsome shops and fine blocks of commercial offices, all conspired to make him feel his rightful place was there, under the State House's high gilded dome, eating his dinner on a bench in the Common.

It was only the two hundred and fifty thousand citizens who disturbed these otherwise happy thoughts. Though the populace thronging the streets was well dressed, there were still far too many of them. Though the public vehicles were well appointed, they seemed to Sampson, and to Alfred, far inferior to a well-made carriage pulled by a single good horse. The men had, after all, both been farmers in what seemed to them now a long-ago and different life. For Alfred, though, Boston inspired what New York inspired in Sampson: a sense that the city and its populace entire were regarding him the way one might a stray cat that you fed on the front porch and that now stands at your door, crying for ingress. This was, of course, a familiar way for Alfred to feel. Fifteen years later, on his only trip to New York City, he would prefer the invisibility in which that city cloaked him, and would take Ida's hand, confident that no one they passed would take note or frown at the sight of one man cradling the hand of another's wife. And when she removed it, kindness flooding her eyes, he would remain equally confident that none passing them by had taken note of his humiliation.

Alfred turned his face to the early evening sun and chewed his apple and cheese with his eyes closed. Sampson sliced a wedge from the smoked sausage he'd brought from home with the buck knife he'd carried in his front pocket since he was a boy. Why pay city prices for country food? Two small pickles rested on the bench next to him, their juices seeping quietly through his cotton handkerchief.

He was not proud of the day's work, but pleased at its result. The leather dealers and boot and shoe jobbers had combined in the manufacturers' movement, and the arrangement had been made that the leather dealers would sell to the cooperative manufacturers only for cash down, and the jobbers and wholesale dealers would unite in refusing to buy their goods when made.

It tickled Sampson that a meeting such as this had proceeded beneath the dimwitted noses of those Crispins without their catching even a whiff of the goings-on. He was, of course, wrong about that, being guilty once again of underestimating those people whom it convenienced him to underestimate. For these reasons, he would have been unhappy, even angered, to learn that not only had the manufacturers' plans been laid on the table at the Crispins' afternoon session but also that the claim had been made by more than one brother that Sampson himself had been seen masquerading around town that very day, trying to know the content of this worthy gathering.

He would have been most bothered by the claim of "masquerading," with its overtones of the sneak and the coward. If he had desired to attend the meeting, attend the meeting he would have, unhatted. And had he been there, he would not have been angered to hear how often his name crossed the lips of the Crispin crowd. Mr. Sampson was to the working men what Judas was to Christianity, what Jeff Davis was to the freedom of slaves. His object was to change the whole civilization of Massachusetts into an Asiatic civilization, and since the blow of Mr. Sampson had been given with deadly intent, a blow of equal deadliness must be given in defense.

Sampson would have agreed with Alfred that these moments were practically the only moments of color in the entire afternoon's session. Alfred had grown tired of the motions and countermotions, the committees formed and the votes counted. Daniel had been right. You could not out of one side of your mouth decry apathy while out of the other deny the taking of violent action. By the time, late in the afternoon, when Mrs. Warner requested that a committee be appointed to request the gentleman in the corner who was talking to leave the hall, Alfred was ready to lay fists to his fellow brothers.

So distracted was he by his anger and frustration that he noticed not at all that he had eaten the apple complete, seeds and stem. His mother had always been able to calm these moods—his "states," she had called them—by forcing him down onto her lap, wrapping her arms around him, and holding him with a strength just short of discomfort. She had continued with this remedy long past the time when his body fit in her lap, and since her death he missed it so often that he sometimes wrapped himself in his own arms, which always left him with less comfort rather than more.

Given his state, it wasn't surprising that it was Sampson who noted the boy and not the reverse. He took the boy in. His hair was the color of straw and as unruly as a street child's. His brow sloped up and away from eyes the color of brackish water. Sampson felt he had known crowds of such boys growing up in Vermont, boys who had handled their from-dawn-to-dark farm chores with ease, whose definition of "future" had never ventured beyond the next meal, who were coddled by sister and mother, treated briskly by father. Boys whom Sampson's own father had on more than one occasion wished his youngest son more closely resembled. Sampson himself had wished the same even more vigorously, while protecting himself from the sting of their disregard by convincing himself that they were not a group to which a boy should want to belong. He had sworn to Julia shortly after they married that he would not make the mistakes with his son that his father had made with him. She had said that his father must have done something very right, and that all of their children would be lucky to have Sampson as a father. Any recollection of this exchange caused Sampson pain, and as the years passed, and being a father seemed less and less likely, he would have had to admit that all those boys, even the Crispin boys, shared more with him than not.

By Sampson's eye, Alfred was in his early twenties. His shoes were simple brogans, over five years old, it seemed to the shoemaker, but the leather was good and he guessed that Alfred's closet didn't hold footwear of any other kind. The boy appeared agitated, spitting onto the grass between his planted feet, ignorant of the sidelong looks of passing ladies. Partly due to his general good mood, but mostly because of his loneliness, Sampson approached the boy, laying a hand on his shoulder.

Alfred startled, knocking the hand away with a quick swing of his forearm.

Sampson laughed and put his hand back heavily, the way one does on the neck of a skittish horse. When Alfred recognized to whom the hand belonged, he ducked his shoulder away, standing to face him. It surprised Sampson, and he swallowed once again the bitter taste of exclusion by reminding himself that he held all the cards in this game. "A break between rabble-rousing sessions?" he asked.

Alfred looked around as if this might be some kind of test. He imagined what his father would have done in such a situation, and then he offered his hand and waited for the manufacturer to take it. It had been claimed that afternoon that the Chinamen would not make good shoemakers, nor would they make good mechanics in any industry. The machinery bothered them wonderfully, it was argued, and they never would encompass it entirely. Charlie Sing had had his thumb taken off, and several more thumbs would follow. If these claims were true, then the time when Crispins and Sampson would once again need to figure out how to negotiate with each other was not far off.

They shook hands slightly too firmly for slightly too long. Alfred said, "A break in capital's plotting to make life even harder for the workingman?"

Sampson laughed again and tried to remember if he knew the boy's name. "I know your face," he said, "but forgive me if I'm meant to know your name and have forgotten."

"Alfred Robinson. We met not long ago in your office."

Sampson remembered but to the boy presented a face full only of confusion. "I'm sorry." He shrugged.

Alfred shrugged back. And they stood there.

"Are you kin to Lucy Robinson?" he asked, surprising Alfred and himself.

"I am. Her brother." Since the attack, Alfred was used to people whom he didn't know knowing them.

Sampson said he'd never met her, but he seemed genuinely concerned about her well-being. But Alfred did not want to like him, even if he imagined having to work for him again, and he began a litany in his mind of the examples of the man's arrogance and posturing and unfair ways with the men Alfred called brothers. "She's doing much better, thank you," he said in a voice that he hoped communicated that any further travel down that road would result only in Sampson's having to return from whence he'd come.

"Well," Sampson said, seeming to have run out of things to say.

"Well," Alfred agreed.

And it didn't matter that they were about to part or that Alfred would not offer his hand again upon doing so. For all that Daniel Luther saw when he topped the rise of the park's far path was Alfred Robinson, newcomer to shoemaking, the North, and the Crispins, standing in the embrace of Calvin T. Sampson, the man who stood for everything Daniel and the other brothers stood against. Granted, Alfred was not returning the embrace and seemed, even to the sometimes dull-minded Daniel, excessively ill at ease, but it was surely an embrace, and although Alfred was uncomfortable he was also neither stepping away nor registering protest. So though Daniel's father would have said nothing good ever came of conclusions drawn from witnessing only parts of the whole story, Daniel had come to believe the opposite of his father's philosophy. People like him never got the whole story. His life depended always on being able to judge the depths of the hole from the fence post that stood in it. And he knew, standing there watching, that yes, Alfred was uneasy, but more than that looked grateful. His shoulders were curved into the embrace. His expression was almost sad. Had Daniel been in Alfred's shoes, he would have felt the same. They were, after all, practically boys, both of them still missing the tender regard of their mothers, not having found something similar anywhere else. So it wasn't the betrayal of the Order that saddened him most. He had for quite some time now counted Alfred as a friend, perhaps his closest, and had, until this moment, thought Alfred had done the same. So he pledged to keep quiet about what he'd seen, because when he had imagined them gathering comfort, he had always imagined it would be from each other.

If Ida had paid any attention to Alfred's comings and goings in the following weeks, she might have noted the coincidence of his absences with the growing number of incidents perpetuated against the Chinese. As it was, she and the rest of the town took note of the increased harassment but, because everyone believed the identities of the responsible parties to be clear in a general way, didn't feel the need to investigate the particulars. Each incident became, then, fresh evidence of the ignorance and troublemaking of the Order rather than the particular resentments and growing anger of certain members of that Order.

Ida would have been further surprised to know that it was behavior of her own that had contributed to that anger and resentment. On the Monday after Alfred's return from Boston, a small group of the Celestials had been taken to the Freeman printworks for a visit and a tour. This had been Ida's notion, backed up by the good women of the Baptist church. Alfred had listened, on Monday night, to her enthusiastic description of the Celestials' level of interest in anything toward which she directed their gaze. If she showed them a sign, they tried to read it; if she pointed out a flower, they bent to smell it. She wouldn't be surprised if after their one afternoon's visit to the printworks, they could be placed in charge of those machines. He remembered how much she'd teased him about the trouble he'd had mastering the pegging machine. He never had gotten the hang of the thing; his foreman had put him into the boxing room to see what damage he could do with hammer and nail.

Her opinion mattered to him even more than he had understood. He was coming to know this the way one comes to know by putting a hand to dry grass that the spring ground beneath is still wet. And so, on Tuesday, as the second group of interested Celestials made its way to Freeman's, bucketloads of water poured down on them from above accompanied by the stifled laughter of the factory girls wielding the buckets.

Town opinion was divided as to how seriously to take this incident. The Chinese had taken to drinking their after-dinner tea in the courtyard outside the entrance to their rooms, and that Tuesday evening the men spoke of little else from their haphazard circle of low stools. Several of the fifteen- and sixteen-year-olds argued that this had been an example of the brazenness of American women, a brazenness that secretly thrilled them, though they tried to keep the titillation out of their voices. They would've been chagrined to know that their attempts were unsuccessful.

The men weighed the implications of the water incident. All of them were old enough to know that one discovered more by silence than by speech, and silence had the suggestion of wisdom. Once they did let their opinions be known, the younger boys would be more likely swayed by them and less likely to dwell on the fact that there was but a few years' difference in age.

If indeed the women had been engaging in some kind of childish play, was that something to be celebrated or not? How astonishing, after all, that the eyes of the village girls had turned in their direction at all. A good sign, no doubt. Yet surely this news could be met with nothing but more resentment from the village boys and fear from the village elders? But some of the boys insisted that the girls had merely been vehicles for a man who had been seen in the shadows. Charlie hoped this to be the truth. It was dismaying, but expected and familiar, both of which were preferable to the opposite.

One of the cooks claimed that the children of such women would be redheaded devils whose knees didn't bend.

The other claimed they didn't bear children; they stole them. "There's nowhere to put your little thing," he pointed out.

Charlie colored. The cooks were the only two of the seventy-four whom he hadn't personally interviewed. He added their names to his growing list of reasons to do things oneself.

By the end of that week, the last of the Chinese were trained and hard at work in the bottoming room, and the town assumed that the further disgruntled and deflated Crispins were responsible for the delivery to the Celestials' entrance of two milk crates of dead rats that Saturday afternoon.

Charlie carried them himself to Sampson's office, bowed slightly, and said, "We have no use for these."

Sampson assured him that he also wanted nothing to do with the dirty things and suggested that he get one of the Celestials to dispose of them.

Charlie felt put off by this. Ignorant Americans seemed to be more Sampson's responsibility than his own. On his way back to the Celestial quarters, Charlie called over a newly hired office boy, not more than ten, loaded the two crates in the boy's thin arms, and said that Mr. Sampson had ordered the boy to discard them. "Work fast," he added conspiratorially. "Today, his mood is not so good."

It had taken Alfred hours to gather enough dead rats to fill even half of the first crate, but when his energy flagged, he had merely to conjure the image that had prompted him in the first place: Ida and one of her Celestial boys walking up the hill behind the factory carrying a kite of foreign design. He had heard that students and their teachers had begun these little outings, but he had not expected to see

Ida partaking in them. Why he had not, he didn't know.
The town was, for the most part, in favor of these jaunts,
seen as they were to be the harmless, happy games of children. And indeed, Alfred was witness merely to a man and
a woman walking up a hill. Perhaps it had been the ba-
nality of the image that had so bothered him. But it had
bothered him so severely that he had stood there and stood
there across the street, his eyes never leaving the top of the
rise over which they'd disappeared. And there he was when
they returned, an hour later, now more animated, though
not, he had to admit, more intimate, and the moment they
crested the hill, making their careful way down again, he
winced as if it were his knees bearing the weight of their
downhill strides, and he stood there feeling as if he were an
idiot or a dog, something other than himself.

So when, trudging through the muck of the riverbed or
slipping on the stacked wood in his neighbors' woodsheds,
a burlap bag tied around his waist with baling twine, he
thought he might just give it up, all he had to do was remind
himself of the way she'd made him feel, ambling slowly up
the hill with her Celestial, noting Alfred not at all.

What did he guess they'd been up to, he'd demanded of
Daniel.

"Flying a kite?" Daniel had suggested.

So he was left with his imagination, and it was then that
his rancor and rage began to rise in his throat like floodwater. And it was then that he got the idea of borrowing
Henry Bolt's terrier, which he set loose in the feed rooms of
a handful of barns while he stood against the closed door to

watch. The dog climbed walls, even made it partway across ceilings, grabbing the fleeing rats and dispatching them, his eyes already scanning for the next gray blur. Alfred was left more satisfied than he'd been in weeks. He asked Henry Bolt to set a price for the animal, but Henry called the creature to his side and said he wasn't for sale. And just like that, the warmth of satisfaction was gone from Alfred's chest, replaced by something he didn't know to call loneliness.

As the summer proceeded, more of the Chinese spent their free time out and about. They frequented the local stores, went to church and public lectures, marveled at traveling amusements. They flew more kites. They sat in the park, their faces to the sun.

Sunday school sessions became less formal and pinched. Laughter was more common than not. The exchange of gifts between teachers and students increased. Shoes of perfectly reasonable quality rolled out of Sampson's factory at two dollars a case less than they used to. The Crispins continued to hold their mass meetings, but by the second one at Tremont Temple, of the two hundred workingmen who convened the meeting, only fifty remained at the adjournment. Their half-hearted attempts to convince the Chinese to join their band of brothers had been unsuccessful, and by the end of July, all danger from them seemed, most of the town agreed, to be over. For a while, there were no new incidents.

And then Ah Ang Fook was accosted at the corner of Eagle and Main on his return to the factory. Small rocks hailed down on him from the rooftop of the Ballou Block. Several hit their mark and the following morning he dressed to conceal the bruises. The police were called to the scene, but by the time they had identified the roof and climbed the staircase, the perpetrators were long gone. Sampson denounced the act and out of his own pocket reimbursed Ang Fook for his purchase from the drugstore of the two bottles of Renne's Magic Oil that had been broken.

The week after that, Sunday school was extended to Wednesday evenings, and the women who had volunteered for extra duty turned in various directions outside the factory fence, calling their good-byes to each other in the cool summer twilight. Of course, Alfred had not intended for Mrs. Sampson herself to be any kind of a target, and Ida even less, but sometimes when one begins a boulder rolling down a hill it is impossible not only to stop it but also to keep it from gathering speed. He should have known there would have been other brothers equally unsatisfied with the Order's apathy in the face of the Celestial invasion, others secretly thrilling at each new revenge, but the thought had not entered his mind, largely because the Order's apathy was not central to his rage. The other brothers knew only that those coolie boys were partaking of a meal that belonged on a Crispin's table. Crispin hands had been tied by capital and the Order's own leadership, and they lashed out at those within reach.

They set upon the women from behind with volleys of stones and handfuls of gravel and saw only Mrs. Sampson's back as she fell to the ground, covering her

companion as best she could. Ida did not fall. She held
her primer as a shield before her face and began walking toward them. "Tom McLaughlin and Charlie Upham,"
she called. "What kind of cowards do you take us for?" she
asked loudly enough that several neighbors reported hearing her clear as a bell.

The boys dropped their stones and gravel, backing up as
they did so, and as she kept coming, their nerve, which had
been spontaneous and rash to begin with, fizzled entirely
and they fled, cutting across Freeman's lot until sure she
hadn't pursued them.

Julia suffered a cut at the back of her neck, just above the
collar, and Nancy Harding, the girl she had tried to shield,
had to pick the dirt and chips of stone from the heels of her
hands with a sewing needle, she had fallen so hard against
the road, but other than that, the women were unharmed,
though Julia was still so flushed, her eyes so bright, upon
her return to the Wilson House that Sampson would not
be convinced by her assurances until she allowed the doctor
to be summoned and he pronounced her level of agitation
to be completely normal given the circumstances.

Tom McLaughlin and Charlie Upham were dispatched
to the county jail, paid their fine, and within a month had
found their separate ways out of town for good. Still, there
was no doubt now amid the town that the problem had
not disappeared. For the most pessimistic it was a sign that
the early success of Sampson's Experiment was over. In the
days following the episode, Julia found she could set her
heart to similar racing with ease. And as those effects of

the attack receded, she felt a vague sadness and impatience with all that was settled and sure.

Having heard about the incident, and the injury inflicted upon his employer's wife, Charlie made his way to the Wilson House, explaining to Sampson when he opened the apartment door that he was there to pay his respects and offer a gift of good health.

Sampson, surprised but not unpleasantly so, widened the door and stepped back, beckoning his foreman to enter.

Julia was seated on a chair by the window, a blanket covering her lap. Their eyes met, hers alive with tiny movements of alarm. Charlie bowed, lowering his gaze, his face still and blank.

He offered his hope that her health would be improved as quickly as possible. He placed a small carving of a dragon on the table before her, apologizing for its hasty and rough construction. He explained that the dragon was a symbol of blessing and fortune, as it was the only animal to unite heaven and earth. He politely refused Sampson's offers of food and drink and made his exit, wondering all the way back to the factory at the behavior of this strange American lady.

Had Alfred known that the photos of the Celestials had been Julia's idea, it is hard to know whether he would have felt better or worse about the attack against her. She had argued to her husband that they would remind the town that these boys were here, genuine people with genuine needs and responsibilities, and remind the Celestials of the same things. Both walk down the street, both eat and drink, both are made of flesh and blood in the image of God.

Even as she was making these claims, she knew she did not really believe them. Each Sunday, she could not have felt herself to be more different from the pupils across from her. That feeling, since it both shamed and excited her, was why she was so insistent on the execution of her idea. It was as if she were seeking to pin those boys to paper herself.

Julia had never wanted her own portrait taken, though Sampson had suggested it on more than one signal occasion. It had been too nervous-making, the idea of a likeness of herself set onto card stock, held in a frame, slid into an album. What if she could not control her expressions? What if her portrait revealed something about herself she wished not to see? But while making her arguments to her husband, she found herself imagining a portrait with, to her surprise, Charlie Sing.

After his visit to the Wilson House, she had begun reading to him from time to time at the end of lessons. It was a way, she had told him, to improve his already strong command of the language. Sometimes he read to her, but not for long, instead passing the open book back to her, his finger marking the spot where she should take over. She never objected, partially because she enjoyed reading aloud and did not find opportunity to do so very often, and partially, though she would not know to articulate it this way, because there was something about his quiet and calm to which she was drawn. They never spoke of the fact that she had not identified herself as his employer's wife.

She had not thought she put him before any other Celestial in her mind, yet there they were in her imagination, the two of them framed in card stock. The unbidden nature of the image made her feel as she used to when Sampson would catch her unawares, placing a hand above her hip bone, sending small charges through her as if he were flint, she the tinder. The opposite of quiet and calm. She knew not to make these thoughts part of her arguments.

"Would it make you happy?" he asked.

She was so surprised at this question that she asked, "Would what make me happy?"

"Exactly," he said, perplexing her even further.

She warmed beneath his gaze. Attention had always had this effect, as if a lighthouse beacon had suddenly fixed on her, picking her out from a shoreline of gray rocks.

He granted permission for her plan. Out of love, Thankful would tell her later, and she knew her sister-in-law to be speaking the truth, and over the following months and years this would be one of the many things for which she felt shame.

When Alfred found himself one Saturday evening sitting next to Ida and Lucy on a green picnic blanket, cutting thick slices of Lucy's homemade bread, all he knew was that he was sitting close enough to Ida to feel her warmth and smell the odor of camphor peculiar to her skin. When had she come to mean what it was clear to him she now meant? He knew not. What he did know was that she had rolled her dress sleeves to her elbows, and her forearms, bare in the sun, rendered him without words.

She had plenty of words. He'd done nothing but bow his head under the hailstorm of her speech for the last two days. She sat cross-legged on the blanket and pelted him with questions. Had he really had no inkling of the mischief of those fool brothers of his? Either he'd been part of their idiocy—and didn't he like to claim proudly that the brothers always acted as one?—and should be more ashamed of himself than usual, or he hadn't, and the loyalty of his tribe wasn't what he'd thought it to be. The impulse to add that if that were the case, then he'd lost another family rose in her throat and she was so taken aback at the cruel journeying of her own mind that she took an abrupt and oversized bite of bread to keep herself from speaking any further.

But it was too late; Lucy, who had been sitting at the blanket's far corner silently eating grape after grape, was weeping. They drew around her, though as he was asking his younger sister what was wrong he was also aware that the length of his kneeling thigh was pressed against the length of Ida's own. If not for the cloth of his pants and her skirts, he thought. And then he thought he should at least try and behave as a better person would and moved away to draw Lucy into his embrace.

"You are too hard on each other," she said, wiping her eyes with the back of her hand like a child. Speaking her mind seemed to make her crying more vigorous.

Alfred had one arm around her; Ida another.

"We have only each other," she said. She was willing to receive their embraces, but she kept her own hands to herself.

"I'm sorry," Alfred said. What he meant was he would cease from making the Celestial boys his targets and would encourage others to do the same. He would turn his attention to his sister and he would keep it there. It was the thing his family and their friends had expected him to be unable to maintain—close and careful watch over his sister. Kneeling there uncomfortably, he swore to himself that this time he would not live up to their diminished expectations. Yet even as he took his oath, he knew that he took it for Ida.

As for Ida, she said nothing, only thought that what her friend had said wasn't true, at least not for her. Lucy and Alfred had each other. What Ida had was a picnic blanket that might as well have been an ocean, Ida on one far shore, Lucy on another.

Chapter Seven

By the eighteenth of August 1870, the thermometer in North Adams had been averaging for the prior four weeks upward of eighty degrees. The cooperative shoe company had orders for over three hundred cases ahead, and over one hundred seventy hands more than had worked at Sampson's were now employed at the Crispins' venture. That morning's *Transcript* published the text of the contract between Sampson and the Chinamen in full, and in the same issue, Julia read of the suicide of a Mr. Adolphus Wells, a man of intelligence and industry, exemplary in all his life. A carpenter of superlative workmanship, he had been in poor health for several years, and after losing a job the previous spring, he feared that he should never work again. His domestic relations had been happy, and to all appearance, his life had seemed more free from trouble than the lives of others. How dreadful were appearances, thought Julia. How little we know of the hidden lives of those about us. She winced at the public display of a situation so private.

The prior Sunday, a meteor had passed over the village. It had been nearly midnight and she had been awake and at the bedroom window. The meteor was sufficiently brilliant to light up the landscape despite the moon being at its height. She had wanted to wake Sampson, but not turn from the window. She had thought of calling out, but had not wanted to disturb the night, and so she let him sleep on, pretending in the morning that she, too, had missed the thing entire. But now, the image of Mr. Wells facedown in river water shared her mind's space with the meteor's flash, skyrocket without the noise.

On August 18, she accompanied the initial group of Celestials to the first of their photographic sittings. Standing there in William P. Hurd's studio, the August air as thick outside as in, Charlie hushed and herded the first group of five boys. It had not been difficult to persuade them, though he had been able to offer no clear explanation of their employer's motivations. No one could say why husband and wife Sampson wanted all seventy-five of them to sit for individual *cartes de visite*. It was impossible to imagine to whom they could conceivably offer such cards. But once they'd been assured that the almost two-dollar sitting fee—more than twice their daily earnings—would be paid by the Sampsons, they had agreed that it seemed prudent to give the man upon whom their livelihoods depended what he seemed to want.

There was no distinguishing between Sampson's desires and those of his wife. Mrs. Sampson had been in the last week more and more of a presence, insisting that Charlie impress upon the boys that they were to dress in their favorite clothes and bring with them an assortment of their possessions. Perhaps a favorite book or keepsake. She had seemed to have not the slightest idea what those things might be. Charlie concluded that although it had been Mrs. Sampson who had come to the factory to make the request, she was acting as an emissary for her husband, who perhaps hadn't had the time to do so himself. The notion that the photographs were an idea hatched from her own mind was an even more baffling one and Charlie naturally turned away from the complicated, choosing, if he could, the path of least confusion, although he found himself unable to ignore all consideration of her. She was, he was coming to feel, a bewildering figure. Why had she appeared in his sickroom to read to him? Why had she continued to do so? Why had she not introduced herself as Mrs. Sampson? And why, perhaps most confusing to him, did these uncertainties not make him retreat to a self-protective distance?

But in Mr. Hurd's studio, he noted that Sampson in no way seemed to be part of the endeavor. Mrs. Sampson expressed an enthusiasm for the objects the Chinese had brought that he found startling. She picked up Ah Har's rice paper letter and asked Charlie if it was a letter from the boy's family. She wanted to know if Chung Him Teak had carried the scarf with him on this whole long journey from home. If Sam Toy had carved the dragon himself. If many of them were talented in this way.

Charlie shrugged politely. Usually, this kind of hysteria made him shut down, close as many of his watertight doors as possible, but in Mrs. Sampson, he realized with some mystification, it made him want to coo at her until she stilled and calmed.

She teased him gently about falling short of his responsibilities. "Do you know them not at all, Mr. Foreman?" she asked, turning back to the treasures before her.

He had grasped enough of overheard conversations at church and Sunday school and the factory to know that the town's opinion was that Mrs. Sampson was delicate and shy, so he remained without speech, set off-balance by her apparent self-confidence. He would never know anyone to go from anxiety to sureness as quickly and as often as he would come to learn that she did.

Even then, he was beginning to understand that she was, as he was, willing to offer others what they most wanted to see. He would never fully grasp that this was not something held in common only between them, but a trait shared the world over.

She was right, he thought on that August afternoon. He knew none of the boys' stories. He was not even confident of all their names. He could not have listed their home villages. Was this something he should be working to remedy? It had never occurred to him. Because, of course, Charlie shared the guilt of everyone who had ever referred to the boys as Sampson's workers, the Boys, the Chinese, the Celestials. How wrongheaded to think that seventy-five individuals could be defined by one or two words. And how much of that wrongheadedness had been encouraged by that first stereograph Sampson had commissioned. Every visitor to the factory who passed by the outer wall to Sampson's office also passed by that stereograph: a mass of dark-haired boys dressed in dark clothing and topped by dark hats. Perhaps Charlie was thinking of that image and feeling the wince of self-recrimination as he recalled his role in arranging the boys into their lines and in reassuring them that nothing of note would come from this. For whatever reason, as Hurd welcomed him into the portrait chair and gave him simple instructions, Charlie glanced up at Julia standing with the five boys behind the camera, not smiling, simply watching, and as he met her eyes with his own, he had the terrifying impulse to tell her about himself. Not the version he had given to the Methodist congregation, or to Mr. Chase, or to the immigration officer years and years prior, but everything he knew about himself and his life thus far, everything he understood, as plainly and clearly as he knew how to tell it.

As Hurd finished his instructions, and the small sounds of the Celestial boys around her ceased, their attentions turned to their foreman in these peculiar circumstances, Julia felt an unfamiliar anticipation. It suddenly seemed to her the most intimate of situations, to be here on one side of the camera viewing someone on the other. She felt as if she and Charlie were sitting for some larger portrait, as if they occupied an upstairs room of an intricate dollhouse and an unseen camera peered at them through the tiniest of windows. A small tremor passed beneath her skin.

Hurd told Charlie to hold still and assume a pleasant expression. Julia noted his attempts to follow these instructions, and for the six seconds that Hurd removed the cap from the lens, she and Charlie held each other's gaze, neither of them feeling as if they should look away.

As it turned out, that first excursion to Hurd's studio would prove to be the lip of the gorge over which Charlie and Julia would allow themselves to fall. In the following weeks, as the rest of the boys were photographed, Julia and the foreman became more and more at ease with each other, and although it was she who made it her duty to educate him, it was he who made it his duty to receive those lessons. It was she who first led him to the Natural Bridge, reading Hawthorne's description of the place as they strolled, and it was she who demonstrated how one was meant to walk backward up Bethel Street to avoid infection of the lungs, or so said the town's widows, with no argument from its physicians or pharmacists.

Extended Sunday school hours meant that many teachers and students were spending Sunday and Wednesday evenings after lessons engaged in informal activities, and on several occasions, Charlie and Julia's excursions were joined by other Celestials and their teachers, Fannie Burlingame and her by-then-favorite student, Lue Gim Gong, among them. Charlie served as translator, though Fannie had learned a few Chinese words. "Tell them," Julia would instruct, "that here is where the settlers held their own against the Indians." "Tell them that this is a parsnip; this a beet." And if he had had any hopes as to the focus of her attentions being particular in any way, they were stilled. Fannie often teased Julia, telling her that if her lessons were to be this dull, she would drive these boys back across the ocean. She should, Fannie advised, let the boys do some of the talking. They had remarkable talents and stories to share, she assured her cousin. All one needed to do was ask and listen. And Charlie began lining up possible talents and stories in his mind so as not to be caught unawares if Julia's inquiries commenced.

Four months after his arrival, on a mild fall day, they were a group of a half dozen when they sojourned to the Mohawk Trail, winding its way over Hoosac Mountain, and Charlie had a most difficult time with the signs at the foot and summit. WALK UP, IF YOU PLEASE, read the first. RIDE DOWN, IF YOU DARE, the second. Julia laughed like a girl at his stuttering attempts at translation and explanation, and when she quieted he noted with some surprise that he wished for her laughter to return. And the next time he saw her, when they had finished their reading, he pulled from the pocket of his smock his mother's hairpin. She felt it too large a gift. He insisted, and told her that if she liked, he could demonstrate how one was to maneuver the pin so that it would not fall out. She held it in her lap and looked down at it, assuring him that if she could not manage it herself, she would be sure to avail herself of his offer. She told him it was a most beautiful object. He said that it was the woman who gave the object its beauty. She stood and tilted her head slightly as if to get a better view of him. She told him that his mother must, then, be a beautiful woman, and then she took her leave.

But by the following spring, despite the time spent in each other's company and their enjoyment taken with that company, they would share equal surprise when, on an excursion to the Notch Brook and the Cascade, the brook's marvelous descent to the river, she took his hand to aid his crossing of water infamous for its peculiar coldness, and found herself reluctant to release it. As they stood on the brook's banks, shadowed by baby Christmas trees, a blanket of the tiniest of wildflowers soft and crushed beneath their wet and chilled feet, they both felt as though they had made the difficult ascent only to pour over the precipice like the water itself, descending a thousand feet in one liquid rush.

Sampson was quite delighted with the assortment of *cartes de visite* and tintype portraits with which his wife presented him on a warm night in October of 1870. Of the seven copies of each printed by Hurd, she gave each Chinaman six and then, knowing it would please her husband, collected one copy each in the most expensive album Mr. Hurd had in his display. It was of handsome burgundy leather with relief work of a pattern of fleur-de-lis on front and back, the edges of the pages embossed in gold, the spine hinged in brass, the whole treasure box snapped shut with an elaborate and fussy lock.

Sampson would tend to leaf through that album much less than would his wife. Perhaps because Julia's own world

was so inward-turned, she found herself much more interested than her husband in the world outside their own.
But that night he set aside his after-dinner cup of hot milk
to further examine her gift. No matter the weather or his
physical condition, Sampson finished each evening with
a cup of hot milk. It was a habit that Julia had initially
found charming but now, standing by the chair in which
he sat, watching the milk's surface cool into a gray skin, her
stomach turned and she removed the cup and saucer to the
mantle, out of her line of vision.

Thankful joined her at his chair and the two women
watched him browse the album. Julia reached down to
demonstrate how the cards could be removed from the
heavy card stock leaves. In this way, she explained, her husband could order and reorder the pictures at his whim.

All of the prints were of head and shoulders circled in an
oval window. Most of the boys wore traditional Chinese
clothing, the same nankeen blouses from their first day in
town. One, whom Sampson did not recognize, wore a quilt-
ed jacket with brass frog buttons at the throat and collarbone.
The boys seemed to be sharing the same mandarin hat. With
a small exclamation of surprise, he noted that several of them
had signed Sampson beneath their images. Julia told him
that the boys had agreed it was a sign of necessary respect.

"Well," he said, "that really is most pleasing."

He could not have named a one of them save for his
foreman, who he noted had not signed Sampson's name
to his card. And as Julia pointed to one and then another,
telling him some small thing about the boy's family, likes

or dislikes, and aspirations, it was as if she were telling him that it had been discovered that crows had hopes and desires. One might marvel at the surprise of such a thing, at the mysteries of the animal world, but one would not run out into the meadow trying to ascertain the particulars. He was glad she was doing so. He was glad she seemed to be pleased at her activities. He felt as a good shepherding dog must at the end of a day's work: all his charges safe and sound for the night.

Thankful made a small sound. "Having them all together there," she said, wrinkling her nose slightly. "It is unpleasant, don't you find?"

"I do not," said her brother, running his hand over the bumps and ridges of the album's cover. "I like it completely," he said, reaching over to rub Julia's hand as he had rubbed the album. "Thanks to my dear wife for collecting them here for me to have and see. And further, for working hard to make these boys feel as if our streets are theirs to be traveled."

Thankful was unconvinced. "All together they are most like some kind of *swarm*," she said, more to herself than to her brother. She gave her shoulders a mild shake. "I suppose, though, a little discomfort is worth the financial sense they make. What European or Canadian do we know who can live on ten cents a day?"

Silence hung in the room for a moment, husband and wife acutely aware that Thankful received the benefits of her brother's business enterprises without taking any of the risks.

"I think," Julia said kindly, "that the ten-cents-a-day theory is but a theory fabricated by anti-Chinese alarmists. I'm sure they endeavor to make their tomorrows better than their todays. As do we all," she added equally kindly.

"Well, if that is the case, dear sister, then my brother best take care. Whatever they have been compelled to endure in overpopulated China, they must have no intention of repeating here. It won't be long, if you are right about their *goals*—and for sure you must know more about that than I—before they learn to demand higher wages."

If Sampson had allowed the conversation to continue, Julia would have tried to conceal her fluster by arguing that any good Christian would be in complete and utter support of labor justly compensated.

Sampson, however, having the male distaste for a disagreement between women he loved, and having noted himself on some level those same implications, patted them both on the hand and declared that Thankful had no cause for worry. No good, he understood in some vague way, could come of continuing this line of conversation. So he told the women that it was clear from this very gift how happy these boys were to be here, housed and fed and working under his protection. When looking through this album, he saw a passel of happy boys. Like schoolboys. Or family, he added, touching Julia on the arm again, and she found herself on the edge of tears and wondered whether her husband brought her there with or without thought, and which was worse.

The task of those initial photographic sittings proved to be overwhelming for Julia, and she had been obliged to recruit the help of her Baptist sisters. Young Ida Wilburn, though not a village native, had always struck Julia as capable and sure. Whom else did Julia know who at that girl's tender age had had the courage to travel so far from all she knew and loved? Ida had been only too happy to grant help. Julia had also appealed to shy Clara Cuddebank and sweet Pauline Horner, and of course to Fannie Burlingame, whose support of the Chinese carried perhaps the greatest weight among the town's women. The citizens of North Adams grew familiar with the sight of these odd flocks making their way in and out of the studios, communicating with each other in broken English and enthusiastic gestures. The most withdrawn of the village girls seemed in particular to flourish with the Celestials, the boys' shyness and reserve somehow sparing the girls the usual problems they feared encountering with large groups of boys. It was as if they had been asked to tend to a herd of well-behaved farm animals.

During the ten years that North Adams would be home to the Celestials, the boys would return of their own accord, supported by their own pockets, to the studios of Henry Ward and William P. Hurd. They made presentations of copies of the photographs to "their girls," as they had come to speak of them in the privacy of their sleeping quarters. But beyond that first album, the images for which they paid dearly served not to reinforce their sameness but to highlight their differences, not only from the town's opinion of them but also from each other and from what they had been and what they now were.

The boys' uniforms of pegging smocks and black felt work hats were left on the hooks by their bunks in the factory sleeping quarters, as were their South Chinese peasant tunics and trousers. In the prints, hymnals, Sunday school primers, and other books began to appear on knees. In one, a gold ring and gold trimmings on mandarin slippers were painted on after the fact, as was a red pom-pom the size of a penny plug of taffy on top of a skullcap of black silk.

Head-and-shoulders bust portraits gave way to full views. They sat with their legs spread in the way of mandarin aristocratic power, or relaxed casually against the back of uncomfortable chairs. Legs began to cross ankle to knee. Heads began to tilt; hands draped casually across laps; mouths remained, with one exception, set in sober lines.

In October, Alfred noted a portrait of Ida with four of the Celestials and Charlie propped on the front table. A gift for Lucy, apparently, from Ida.

"Why would she figure you'd want this?" he demanded of his sister as he studied the full lips, the wide noses, the large ears of the image in his hand.

Lucy looked up from the sock she was mending. "They're our pupils," she said.

"This one's not," he said, pointing to Charlie.

She went back to the sock. "Mr. Sing is the foreman, their leader. It's like he's everyone's pupil," she said.

He glanced around the room and wondered at further surprises that the innards of drawers and cupboards, lockboxes and closets might hold. His sister regarded him and then asked him to pass her the scissors.

"Is this it, then?" he asked. "No others?"

She snipped the thread and turned the sock right side out, stretching it, testing her handiwork. "Do you wish she had given me *more?*" she asked. "You seem riled enough as it is."

"I don't care," he said, though his eyes continued to glance here and there.

Lucy rolled the socks into a ball. She looked at her brother. "You're all red," she said.

"No," he said.

"Yes," she said.

"So what?" he said.

She took a breath to try and gentle her emotionally tongue-tied older brother into being a little easier in the world, but by the time she had exhaled she realized she no longer had any patience with the particular obstacles her brother was negotiating. It did not make her feel unkindly or impatient, just weary and removed, and when she stood, she patted him gently on the cheek before silently retiring to her room.

Did it not bother his fellow Crispins? Alfred demanded of Daniel Luther later that night. Daniel answered that he imagined Alfred's fellow brothers had larger worries. Alfred had felt a certain coldness from his friend for the past several months. Alfred worried that pursuing the problem in any direct manner would further decrease the time and attention

Daniel was expending on him, and so he took note of the distance and tried to pretend he had not.

As the months passed through fall and winter, class sessions expanded. Village families were now inviting individual students to their homes for private lessons or, even more disturbing, supper. Girls everywhere were doing nothing but balancing gifts in their small hands. Ida and Lucy had so many that they appealed to Alfred to build them a corner shelf for the display of the carvings, boxes, inkstones, and teacups. And didn't he think they might be able to hang the kite somehow from the ceiling? It was, he noted, the kite he had seen Ida carrying with the Celestial boy all those months ago.

"I will," he told her, "for trade."

She was so immediately wary that Lucy laughed and said, "You should see your face."

"What're you after?" Ida asked him.

He found it hard to speak and realized that he had no answer in mind. What *did* he want?

Lucy was tickled by his awkwardness. Perhaps, she thought, there would be happiness enough after all.

"A photograph," he managed.

Ida caught Lucy's eye and raised an eyebrow at her. "Of what?" she said.

Alfred knew what she was doing, and he hated her for it. "Never mind," he said, lifting his hat from the peg by the door. "I'll make your shelf." And he was gone, his footsteps echoing behind the closed door.

"Oh, Ida," Lucy said. "Don't be cruel. It's sweet what he wants."

Ida stared at her, her most lovely, generous friend.

"Go on," Lucy said. "Go after him."

And Ida rolled her eyes, sighed, gathered her bonnet, and went quickly down the stairs.

Their photograph was a strange affair: Alfred on the left, his gaze like an arm across Ida, whose eyes held the camera defiantly, as if registering her protest with it. Neither looked particularly happy. Ida's hair had been misbehaving that morning, and she had solved the problem by wetting it severely against her head.

They left the studio with three prints, one of which they gave to Lucy, who framed it and kept it, wherever she lived, on her bedside table. Alfred never framed his copy, and over the years its corners frayed, the image suffered from stains, and the card stock eventually thinned, collapsing this way and that whenever he handled it. Ida put her copy in her travel trunk, where it remained until, in 1897, the undiagnosed pain in her side growing more and more vast, she was moved to sift through her trunk's contents, a display of the same instinct that had moved her before the birth of her first child, though this time, she knew, the nesting was in preparation not for arrival, but for departure. So a week before her death, she found herself holding the print and was grateful for Lucy's stubborn insistence, because it was nice after her complicated, though not unhappy, life to see an image of two people who matched in simple, easy ways. It was nice to feel as if the life she'd had had been her choice, and not merely the only option available.

The photographer, Mr. Ward, felt the portrait more than adequately displayed many of the effects his studio could produce, and he chose it as part of his window display for several weeks at Christmastime. It was in this way that Alfred's Crispin brothers came to the desire to sit for their own photographs. Perhaps the brothers speculated that if the rat eaters and young Alfred could do it, then why not the rest of them? Perhaps those of a more generous mind toward Alfred thought, too, that he had done a good and smart thing by sitting for a photo with one of the most active volunteers of the village. He might, some of them may have thought, be leading the way in reclaiming the proprietary hold on the village girls that the Chinamen seemed intent on maintaining.

And so, before the year's end, the Crispins too were making their way to the town's two studios, sitting for their own photographs, saying with their own images what the Chinamen and Sampson were saying with theirs: *See here. Look sharp. Take note of what we are made.*

By November's end, all shoe factories in the village, with the exception of Sampson's and the cooperative, would suspend operations until January, when the trade would open up once again.

At the October 1870 fair in Pittsfield, the fruit display would be uncommonly large and fine.

On a Wednesday evening in early November, when unseasonably warm weather had taken off the last of the previous Saturday's fall of snow, the American Bible Society would present to the Chinese at its headquarters copies of the New Testament in the Chinese language. Charles Sing responded on behalf of his countrymen very happily, and all present seemed much pleased.

For Thanksgiving, Charlie would order turkeys for each of the Chinese pupils to present to his Sunday school teachers. He would not, until the following Thanksgiving, think of including other prominent and influential members of the community on the list of those to receive the poulterer's best birds.

By year's end, one half of the slate pencils used in the world would come from Vermont, and the same state would have a man with a beard seven feet long.

The new year of 1871 would arrive and would, for the most part, be greeted with a certain wary optimism. The citizens were, by and large, willing to grant the peaceful incorporation of Sampson's Celestials into the town's workings. Alfred felt his position with his brothers, if not to have improved, then certainly not to have worsened. Ida felt Lucy to be sturdier and more capable every day and her mind turned, with some trepidation, toward her own inevitable return to Virginia. Charlie felt confident that the boys were doing what they had been brought there to do. The boys themselves, even the most homesick of them, felt that with seven months of contract labor under their belts, they could manage two and a half years more without much damage. Soon enough they would be home, enjoying their families' congratulations and gratitude. Sampson felt he could now perhaps breathe easier, and could even afford generous thought to be sent the way of the cooperating Crispins. He said as much to Julia, who complimented him on his Christian spirit and said, meaning it, that she was much pleased by his change of heart.

And in the following year, on a late winter day, Charlie would tell Julia about Third Brother. In return, Julia told Charlie that she had lost fourteen children, something she had confessed aloud to no one save Sampson.

He regarded her for so long and so well that she feared she had not made her meaning clear. *Poor, unhappy children*, he finally told her, his arms useless by his sides.

1873

Chapter Eight

The year was 1873. The final day of July. An oppressive ninety degrees in Sampson's office, even with both window and shade pulled against the sun. Sampson had to twice be reminded to lay his work aside and make ready to meet the 4:15 from Troy. Chase was gentle in his prompting, successful at keeping impatience from his voice, equally successful at instilling a sense of urgency. Mrs. Sampson had been at her sister's in Michigan for nearly six months, and before that with her husband vacationing in Florida for several weeks. She hadn't been in residence in North Adams since early January.

The town had thought it strange enough that the Sampsons had taken that unprecedented trip south; it was unlike him to leave the business in anyone's hands but his own, and unlike her to venture outside the village lines, let alone to the wild and unfamiliar Florida. The quiet speculating had continued when, in February, husband had returned without wife. This had not, the Baptist sisters assured each other, been the original plan. They tried to imagine the Julia they knew traveling by herself the rest of the long way to Michigan and announced that they could do no such thing. The fact that they knew her not well at all did not enter their minds.

In the strong current of whispers such as these, Chase thought it neither appropriate nor kind for the woman to descend from the train only to find herself alone on the platform. He understood her to be one of the two most important women in Sampson's life. Miss Thankful Sampson had been the other, and Chase had spent much of the week previous imagining the shock that it must have been for Sampson to discover his sister's still body Monday morning last. It was his task, Chase had felt and would often feel, during the years of his employ to Sampson, to allow the man's best foot to come forward, to encourage somehow his employer's true heart and mind to reveal themselves in his behavior, and so now, for the second time in the hour, he bent at the waist and reminded Sampson that he would be wanting to meet Mrs. Sampson at the train.

Sampson looked up from the spread of papers on his desk, and Chase had the distinct sense that the man did not at first recognize to whom the face he encountered belonged.

Although there had been much to celebrate in the years since the Celestials' arrival, there had also been some difficulties and it was not yet clear which way the scales would tip. Gilbert and Sullivan had collaborated for the first time; the first typewriters had been mass produced; and in North

Adams, G. W. Nottingham had collected the births for 1872 and discovered some three hundred, bringing the local population to upward of fourteen thousand. The North Adams Gas Light Company was building another gasholder, with a capacity of thirty-three thousand cubic feet, and the strawberry festival at the Methodist church had netted thirty dollars. Sampson had added two more stories to his factory's rear and had refurbished his already handsome offices. He had contracted two additional groups of Chinese workers, the first of forty-eight and the second of twenty-two, and their assimilation was proceeding without unhappiness and with a yearly savings of forty thousand dollars. Some of them had taken Sampson's name. Copies of their portraits all went into a second handsome leather album with brass hinges that sat with the first on a shelf in Sampson's Wilson House study.

But in August of the previous year, one Celestial had died of consumption, and in February of the current one, another had succumbed to typhoid fever after two months of illness, and not all of the boys agreed with Charlie's decision to inter the latest unlucky soul in lot 507 of the Hillside Cemetery, which he had purchased upon his own decision at a cost of thirty dollars, and several of them had voiced their opinions forcefully. None of them had been much reassured or swayed by his explanation that it was best, when in America, to do as the Americans did. Surely, one of the cooks pointed out, the foreman had not forgotten that none of them were, in fact, American?

And although Grant's reelection had been handily won, the Republican Party had split, resulting in the defection of many liberal Republicans to Grant's opponent, *New York Tribune* editor Horace Greeley, who died before the electoral college could cast its votes. His party's platform opened with "First, we recognize the equality of all men."

By 1872, the number of Crispin lodges had fallen to a mere fifty-two. And when the sixth Grand Lodge met in Philadelphia the following year, the few delegates who managed to be present attended, as Brother Frank Foster put it, "the funeral of the K.O.S.C."

Jimmy O'Brien had just sold out the Tweed Ring in New York City. The Chicago fire had left ninety-eight thousand people homeless, two hundred fifty dead, and more than seventeen thousand buildings destroyed, and Catherine O'Leary would spend years trying to refute the rumor that it was her cow that kicked over the lantern that began the blaze. The Chinese joss house in Weaverville, California, that had brought young Charlie such comfort when he had been a resident in that forsaken place had burned down yet again, but this time there seemed no one interested enough to oversee its rebuilding, so it would remain a ruin for decades until the local historical society would raise the funds to resurrect it as a museum, of interest to only the most comprehensive of tourists.

And despite acceptance of the Celestials by most of the villagers, including their attendance of a grand and festive celebration of the Chinese New Year for two consecutive years, there had also been some scattered violence, mostly in response to Sampson's April 1871 decision to replace his white overseer in the bottoming room with Charlie Sing.

Sampson had refused to acknowledge the violence, insisting that Mr. Sing was the better man for the job and that anyone who said otherwise could not call himself a Christian, but Charlie had made certain to include some of the more outspoken objectors on his Thanksgiving turkey list both that year and the following one, and had suggested to Sampson that he abstain from his desire to begin hiring white men to mix in with the Chinese workers on the bottoming floor. Sampson had held off, but only until midsummer of the present year, when, he said, he could resist no longer. The expected grumblings about his decision came not from the white laborers but from the Chinese themselves. They already had so little, they protested to Charlie. He was their foreman. It was their interests for which he was meant to care. Did he think it fair that the already small place they could call their own was to be invaded even further?

By March of 1873, the cooperative shoe factory was advertised for rent and would never again appear in the city directory, and Charlie steeled himself for the display of further resentments against his kind.

And so, by the day Mrs. Sampson was to return from her long stay away, the mood in the town and factory was not a stable one. Things were going to happen, though nobody could guess what. Even Lucy Robinson, in the scar tissue of her healed wounds, could feel a change in weather coming.

Eleven days previous, Ida had delivered the mail to the Chinese boys at the start of their lesson. She handed Charlie the letter postmarked from Michigan and said too evenly, "More news from the Midwest," then watched his reaction with care.

She had told no one that the foreman had received three letters from Michigan in Julia Sampson's absence, but letters passed through many hands and by that point, only a year into the postman's tenure, everyone knew that this postman's indiscretion would keep him from rising any higher than the position he currently held.

Charlie avoided her eyes with a small bow and slid the letter into his work tunic's inner pocket, where it kept company with Julia's previous missives, the corners of all four envelopes poking occasionally at his chest. It did not escape Ida's notice that he was already moving toward the door before the final hymn had been sung, and when Alfred met her at the factory's gate to walk her home, she made small fun of him, her voice filled with mockery and impatience and nothing like good nature.

Ida had, over the last three years, taken much note of Charlie and his ways with his charges and the townsfolk. He had proved to be all that she had thought he might and more. He was calm and deliberate, a careful worker and a thoughtful speaker. He reminded her of her father, though she would not share that with him for years.

Charlie walked, as he did almost every evening now, to Natural Bridge, the latest letter humming against his chest. He had not argued with Julia when she had told him in late December that the trip was a necessity and that it would be, of course, unwise for him to contact her while she was away, but his center had felt as it had when he was a boy making

his careful way across the bridge that spanned his hometown river. The woven rope bridge had given and swayed
beneath his cupped feet, sending his heart into the air and
down again. When her first letter had ended with the news
that she would be extending her trip indefinitely by going
to Michigan, he had sunk to the snow-covered ground, not
rising until his pants were soaked through.

None of her letters had offered anything resembling full
explanations for her behavior, and he had found it difficult
not to think of her trip as flight. He had tried as their intimacy had developed to keep his dignity and reserve, but
sometimes during their moments together he had not been
able to keep the force from his embrace, and he had felt her
brace herself as if against a strong wind.

Her letters were long, and he read them so often that
he had committed them to memory. If, as a child, she had
complained of cold, her mother would say, "But it doesn't
make you any warmer to complain of it." She had loved
for her father to carry her "pickaback." Charlie had not an
inkling of the word's meaning, but loved it nevertheless.
Raisins and peppermints had been her favorites, though
she was happy to settle for sticks of striped barley candy or
something called the "Salem Gibraltar," which she would
have to explain more fully when she saw him next. Her
family's farm had been in a valley where, in winter, the
sun set at four and the snow sometimes drifted so that
they could not see their nearest neighbor for weeks, but
she and her sisters had had an unused shed as their castle,
music had been made by rain on the roof, and abandoned

plows had been transformed into litters carried by servants dressed in satin. Her favorite tales had included *Jack the Giant Killer*, *Aladdin*, and *Red Riding Hood*. Her sister had several of them still, and one of the many pleasures of her stay had been the surprise of rediscovery.

By the time Charlie reached the mouth of the path to the small gorge, it was growing dark. His impatience prevented him from climbing the full way to the bridge, and he settled behind the large boulders. It was unlikely anyone would be coming this way at this hour, but in that event, he wanted to be out of sight.

The letter was disappointingly thin, but the sight of her small, tidy penmanship thrilled him and the slow speed at which he had to read bothered him not at all.

My Celestial,

The weather here is too unbearable for me to write much—the letter paper dampens almost immediately, the pen nib works not a whit—so just an inadequate note to assure you that I am thinking of you and I trust you are thinking of me. Although I miss so much of our village, there has been something quiet and lovely about my stay here. I never cared much for machinery, and so much of North Adams seems like one giant, buzzing factory. (Remember the view we had of all those smokestacks from the north hill?) I did, of course, out of necessity accustom myself to the noise so that it became like a silence to me, but now that I am here, where the factories have been replaced with the sounds of hog farms

*and chicken coops, it is hard not to feel that all that machin-
ery is like some overgrown, spoilt child. I am sure I am not
making myself clear. No matter. Suffice it to say that I would
rather sit under the trees and hear the birds sing than have
a whole handful of gold or silver. I have read in a fairy-tale
book of people who could understand what the birds were
saying. Wouldn't that be wonderful?*

*My reasons for coming here in the first place and stay-
ing as long as I have seem to be drawing to an end and I
imagine I will be home before too long. You will be nearly
the first I arrange to see upon my arrival. Until then, I am
Your Julia.*

Charlie read the letter several times in the failing light, following her words with his finger, still dirty from his day's
work. The mosquitoes took pity on him. The cicadas loud-
ened, as if to make thought a blessed impossibility. He told
himself that the silence the factory noise had become to her
also included Sampson, and not himself. He believed her
memory of the view from the north hill to be a fond one.
He felt sure that her desire to listen to the birds was a wish
that included his presence. He tried to disregard her continued refusal to explain why she had departed and could
now return. He tried to ignore the pain that the "nearly"
at the letter's close caused him, its implications spread out
like broad hands leaning heavily on his chest.

Sampson buttoned his vest, repocketed his watch, and
shrugged his jacket onto his shoulders. He wished, briefly,

that he had a glass in which to check his figure, but satisfied himself with brisk tugs at his waistcoat and coat sleeves.

His telegram to Julia the previous week had been concise and plainspoken. He had not wanted to upset his wife unduly, but neither had he wanted to evade the gravity of the situation. *Thankful is passed. The services are held until your return. CS.*

The degree of his self-protection had kept him from acknowledging the largest of his own fears: that even this news would not be enough to bring his wife back and that without her he would not be able to surmount the monumental sadness incited by his sister's death. If he had been capable of utter self-honesty and a different literary style, he would have written a letter, not a telegram, and in the letter he would have said, "Without you, I am a man alone at the bottom of a vast mountain, my face lifted to the sheer expanse above me. Without you, I am this man for time eternal." But he wrote none of these thoughts, and it was only because Julia had known him for so long and so well that she was able to hold that telegram in her shaking fingers and know the sadness that the words contained.

He had lost so many of his siblings that he had spent his adult life always expecting to lose more. So this news, she understood, was being greeted not with surprise but with the more devastating sadness of the arrival of what one already believes to be one's fate. She telegrammed back: *I arrive 31st, 4:15. My heart breaks for you.*

Later, he would berate her for all she had not told him, in that telegram and in her letters from her months away, but even knowing all that she had omitted, he would reread that telegram and feel as cared for as he had when he first received it. Indeed, he was carrying it in his jacket pocket as he strode toward the depot, and he moved his fingers over it the way a child might a pocketful of marbles.

It had, against all likelihood, been Ida who told Charlie about the time and date of Mrs. Sampson's return, though she was not clear about why she had done such a thing. They were just beginning their private Thursday lesson, which had become over the last six months both her justification for extending her stay in North Adams and her favorite event of the week. With Julia gone, Charlie had found himself without a teacher. He was too tortured by her absence to care at all about filling it, but Fannie Burlingame took it upon herself to suggest to Ida that she offer her teaching services. Fannie herself had become very close to one of the other Celestials, and she felt that setting town tongues wagging any more than they already were was to be avoided when possible. The idea was to demonstrate how much these boys deserved to be accepted, not how much danger there was in doing so. But, Fannie had thought, if tongues were to wag, then better they wag about Ida Wilburn, an outsider, than about Julia Sampson.

Ida enjoyed these lessons so much that after a few months of them, she invited Charlie to dinner at the Widow Allen's. The dinner table had been excruciating, the widow chattering on, caught between thrill and alarm at having a *China-man* at her table. But Charlie had handled the hysteria as if tending to a panicked chicken, and then, after dinner, when the widow retired to the living room with her after-dinner sherry (purely medicinal), he offered to help Ida with the dishes. She stood at the dry sink regarding him. "Well," she said. "Knock me over with a feather."

He looked at her blankly.

She smiled and handed him a wet plate. "Just means I'm surprised, is all," she said. "Which doesn't happen very often," she added.

"Why not?" he asked, placing the well-dried plate in the rack and reaching for the next one.

She shrugged. "I'm just usually the one with the most common sense in the room," she said. "Hard to be surprised when you're the practical one."

"That is sad," he said simply.

She stopped washing for a moment and looked at her hands beneath the dirty water in the basin. It *was* sad, she thought.

"I am surprised all the time," he said.

She looked at him and thought, *That's sad too.* They had given each other small smiles and finished the dishes listening to the sounds of evening birds.

So when, at the start of the lesson that July day, Ida had, with some hurt, taken note of Charlie's distracted mind, she had inquired after his health, and he had assured her that he was fine. The whole conversation might've ended there, had he not then looked at her, the expressions of decision making crisscrossing his countenance. He was expecting, he finally offered, news of a friend who had been away a long while.

She knew of whom he spoke, and it should've made her nothing but grim, but instead of desolation or woe, she felt flattered and moved that he had taken her into his confidence. Her instinct was to give something in return, and so she offered what she felt he would most like. Fannie Burlingame had shared the information with her on their way to lessons: Mrs. Sampson would be arriving that afternoon on the 4:15 from Troy.

His face, filled with gratitude and surprise, was an image that would never fade from the bank of her mind. Years later, dying, her children around her, she would conjure that face. She had made him happy, she would remember.

If Sampson had not been so delayed, he might have seen Charlie making his own way to the depot. As it was, Charlie had the time to slip behind the station unobserved by anyone save Ida, who had followed him at her own safe distance. He stood in the copse of elms and birches on the hill, his dark-blue-clad figure dappled in shade. Ida stood a stone's throw from the corner of Chestnut Street and took her concealment behind the farthest outbuilding of the freight station.

Had she not been wearing the crimson scarf that Charlie had given her the previous Christmas—each Sunday school teacher had received one from him—Alfred probably would have missed her as he took the ridge shortcut to Tim Crawley's place on the south end of town. As it was, he did not miss her, and so he too was crouching on the hill above the depot when the 4:15 made its shrill call, when it eased into the station, coming to a slow and gasping stop at the passenger platform. And all four attendees—Sampson, Charlie, Ida, and Alfred—had a clear view of Mrs. Julia Sampson descending the train's two steps, an infant child in her arms.

Chapter Nine

The infant girl was a sensible and sober thing, making not a sound from depot to Wilson House. Her hair was of darkest black, and her eyes were the shape of almonds and the color of rosewood. She regarded her mother from her bassinet until her heavy eyelids grew heavier, rising and dipping in that sleepy way until they remained closed, her tiny chest rising and falling like a panting puppy's. One arm was cocked to her turned head and the other stretched straight in the manner of a fencer poised to parry.

On the other side of the closed bedroom door, Julia's husband waited. It sounded as if he were moving furniture. Beyond her bedroom wall was the emptiness of her sister-in-law's room. It would make a good nursery, Julia thought before she could stop herself.

Years ago, she had read in *Godey's Lady's Book* that motherhood was the most striking and beautiful aspect of the female character. Only motherhood could provide the fulfillment of a woman's physiological and moral destiny.

Her husband would want an explanation. Charlie would want an explanation. By now, she was sure, word was moving through town like river water. The whole town would want an explanation. She felt as if any story she offered could not be the entire tale. Who knew how this baby had found her? Who knew why she had kept the infant to herself for so long? Who knew what fear kept one from doing? Who knew why this time her hope had been addressed?

It had been a Sunday in October, their first time lying together, and it strangely pleased her to think of God on His day of rest having seen them hiking up to Balance Rock, and heard their quiet voices, breathless with their exertion. When they arrived at the top, Charlie took Julia's hand, and they stood there in fear and astonishment, wondering how it could be that their hearts reached after this particular other. They prayed for guidance. Julia thought, *I shall be better for knowing him*. Charlie saw an image of the two of them reading side by side in a room, one of her hands on his, the other turning the pages of history. They were still touching.

"Do people come this way?" he asked quietly.

"Often," she said, and he dropped her hand to reach for her face. She did the same. Their noses, when they finally kissed, nestled above each other's upper lip. They inhaled.

From that day forward, seeing Charlie in her mind's eye meant seeing them both from above, as if watching a couple of whom she had no understanding or knowledge.

And that day in late October 1872 when she had found her tired self in the embrace of that kind, careful Celestial, both of them bathed in the shadow of the impossibly balanced stone, and his body found its way inside hers, she was undone. Because no matter the regard in which she knew her husband held her, in his eyes were sadness and disappointment. Though he sought to convince her that the desire for children was more strongly held by her than by him, what was a farmer or businessman without an heir? In her Celestial's eyes there was nothing but astonished pleasure. "Let's keep our eyes open," she said, shocking herself, and they did. Her eyes watered with the strain of it. It felt to her as if God had reached down, taken her between finger and thumb, and placed her on top of that precarious rock, where He set her to spinning with a gentle push.

He kept their mouths close and spoke, his lips moving against hers like the sign language of tiny animals. "You are the most mysterious thing," he said, and she thought he was right. They were mysteries to themselves.

She had lost so many babies that the moment this girl arrived Julia had been steeled for her departure. She had read too much of the consolation literature surrounding grief and the mourning of the death of children. She was tired of its emphasis on the joyous afterlife. Although she would always be a believer, and never felt calmer than in the face of something she recognized as God's grace, those lost babies had caused her to believe that a woman's highest duty was in fact to suffer and be still. She had learned in her bones the useful lesson of doing without.

It had seemed to her that Life had stood before her telling her that she must learn to like him in the form in which she found him before he could offer himself to her in any other aspect. And then had come Charlie and it was as if he had taken her by the chin and tilted her head up and then down, allowing her to view the world above and below her own small one. And if life with Charlie had been the teetering, the arrival of her baby girl had been the push over the edge. But after falling, she had bobbed softly back up, as if floating on deeply salted water. Life was neither what it had been nor what she had thought it could be. There was no way of knowing what would happen next. What she would tell Sampson when she joined him in the other room was what she felt: that it was quite something to have won the privilege of going on.

Long after the Sampsons quit the depot, Ida stood watching Charlie on his hillside perch. She had planned to follow him, to discuss the extraordinary sight they had both seen, but the longer he stood there, the more his body, leaning against the slightest of maples, told her that the sight of Julia with babe in arms had in some way undone him. Her feelings for him were so well intentioned that she began to believe it did him an injustice to watch him unseen in this way, and so she sent him good wishes in her mind and turned quickly to go the long way round to Lucy and Alfred's, where she was expected for supper and where she would not reveal what she had witnessed.

★

In 1881, no fewer than eleven bills would be submitted calling for Chinese exclusion. Senator John Miller would exhort Washington to "secure the American Anglo Saxon civilization without contamination or adulteration."

This would be about the sanctity of the American home, about protecting it from a race that cared nothing for marriage or family. George Frisbie Hoar, the senator from Massachusetts, would lead the argument in defense of the Chinese. He would be considered by his opponents a doddering fool, mocked for not facing up to the realities of the present and the dangers of introducing the alien to the pure.

But on this moonless July night in 1873, Charlie remained as Ida had seen him through the fall of darkness. He stood as one of the trees around him, his movements like theirs, minor and cadenced, the play of a natural kind of rhythm.

He knew the baby was his, and it was as if the sight of Julia with their own small child had drained his body of all its agitation, replacing it with a serenity he was not sure he had ever felt. He was a basin drained of dirty water. He was a breeze-filled room. He was a father caught up short by the sight of his first child. Through his mind, a phrase ran round and round: *We* made *this thing*.

His mind filled with an exhibition of memories, and for hours he did what was for him the unusual: allowed it to go where it would. A millet pillow that his mother had made with four characters embroidered on it: *May Everything Go Well*. The tiny pigtails, firecracker queues, one behind each ear, that young boys wore before their hair grew long enough for one big plait. His mother grinding rice into flour. One of his brothers in a child's bamboo chair made level with stones.

The lustrous brown cow with short black horns and a woman's lashes who shared his grandfather's room. The sounds of the ocean from the bottom of the ship. The first signs of Third Brother's fever. His face as Charlie descended the gangplank.

He had lied about it to his parents, but word about what had passed on that ship had, in its winding way, gotten back to his village. His mother and father had written to him that he had not followed his duties. He had not cared for his brother well enough. He had sacrificed his brother for himself. He had shamed them. Peace and prosperity would not follow. But Charlie knew that the Chinese way was to find truth in several religions, and to the teachings of Confucius he had also been instructed to add Buddhism and Taoism, and once in America, he had further learned, or decided to believe, that Jesus was also a great sage. The best way, Charlie had long ago decided, was to take truth where you could find it. In this manner, families, even those scattered across oceans, stayed together, worked in harmony. American families, he had felt for some time, were like horses on a carousel: always in motion but never coming together.

The Chinese Imperial Government would forever define him as a self-exile, a felon. An individual has a supreme duty to the collective. But which collective? Could there be a collective of two? He wanted to puzzle out the answer

with Julia, the two of them on a blanket beneath Balance
Rock, in full light, the smell of cut hay, fledgling corn, and
her damp skin all around them. He tried to imagine her
answer, and he could see her beautiful mouth forming
words slowly, as she knew he had made a habit of watching
mouths closely in order to be sure of comprehending. He
felt the weight of her leg across his, the callus on the tip of
her sewing finger as she traced the curve of his ear.

He had heard much about the foreigners before he had
confronted them himself. They had suns that made darkness like day, their noses were shaped like sharp beaks, they
lifted their feet like prancing Manchu ponies, their men
and women were shameless enough to walk down the
street arm in arm.

Julia, too, had sought to know something of his country
through their conversations, and then through books, and
then through their conversations about those books. Much
of what she gathered made little sense to her but found
lodging in her mind nonetheless. She failed to grasp almost all of a mention she had come across of a thirteenth-
century mathematician's methods for explaining how to
fashion equations involving a triangle and a circle, but the
equations involved something called *the celestial unknown*,
a phrase she liked and remembered.

She had not, out of kindness, shared all that she had read,
although she had, out of a lifelong respect for authority, believed some part of it. The Chinese were from one of the
primitive cradles of human culture—credited with the in-
vention of gunpowder, compass, inoculation—yet for ages

they had made no advancement. Pride, fear, and cunning were the chief elements of their character. Their men were a little larger than the average American woman. Their feet were small. They did not reason; they had no original ideas; they did a thing because they saw it modeled by someone smarter than they. Their religious ceremonies appeared to be an effort to guess the future by the tossing or burning of little sticks. The Chinaman was always on time, was not thievish, and did not clamor for privileges. The Irishman hit at random and wasted his strength; the Chinaman did not.

Upon unplaiting his queue for the first time and combing her fingers through the thick black hair, Julia had told him that she had read that their queues were greatly prized. She asked him if it were true that the loss of the plait was a loss of such magnitude that many men killed themselves if it was cut.

Sometimes, Charlie had managed to murmur, her hands in his hair. His hair spread across her lap like a second skirt.

He had not told her what he thought now: that without his queue, returning home would be an impossibility.

He closed his eyes and asked for wisdom. He saw only Julia and the child. Might it have been better to have stayed where one began, gone nowhere new, encountered nothing unfamiliar? Who knew how or why one docked at certain ports? Who knew where one was traveling, or how one would get there? He knew only that to question good fortune was to watch it slip away. Which was why he drew from his pocket the small knife his father had made for him, and in a few awkward strokes cut his thick braid as close to his skull as he could manage. It fell to the ground and he gathered it up and secreted it in his tunic pocket, already making plans for where and when he would present it to Julia, making clear to her his desires and the lengths to which he was willing to go to achieve them.

Sampson considered himself a patient man, though most who knew him did not. His characteristic patience, he felt, had been on display for the larger part of the last several hours. He had not raised his voice; he had not risen from his chair in the front room, taken when Julia had come, finally, from the bedroom, the infant child apparently secure enough in her sleep. Subterfuge and betrayal are, of course, most easily perpetrated by the innocent. It was one of the many ironies with which he and Julia would soon be acquainted. He had fallen in love with what he saw as her innocence and fragility. He had for some time resisted sharing the multitude of questions and hurt feelings tumbling through his body like thrown dice. Yet now, the clock on the verge of striking midnight, the gas lights flickering bravely in their glass globes, he was no closer to understanding the extraordinary sight of his wife debarking the train carrying an infant girl.

"It is our own sweet child," she insisted. It was what she had been saying in one form or another for hours, and although he understood the words, there must have been something in his reaction that suggested to her the necessity of repetition. And she herself had only the dimmest sense of how she was going to explain. She had had months and months to do nothing but contemplate the growing life within her and its implications. But the more she had tried to attend to the explanation for the thing she found happening to her, the more she had thought only of the thing itself.

When she had understood that this baby had taken solid hold, she had encouraged Sampson to take an unprecedented vacation. They stayed in Florida for several weeks, and it had been, to her surprise, a lovely time, the consequences and difficulties ahead still deep within her belly. Husband and wife relaxed for the first time in a long while, and shedding outer layers of clothes, walking the beach, and reading in sea-worn wooden chairs beneath the rocking shade of tall palms had been like breaking the surface after a long time underwater. She could imagine that her husband next to her was first and foremost her friend, as he had been when they fell in love, and as such would greet her news with joy.

Why not just tell him there on the beach? She knew her time of remaining silent was slipping away, but it was in many ways a lovely silence, and betrayal and secrets lead to more of the same, and she hadn't been able to tell him anything, and it wasn't long before she found herself suggesting that instead of returning with him to North Adams as planned, she might travel to Cassopolis, Michigan, and enjoy a visit with her sister. It had been so long since they had seen each other.

Her sister, of course, had assumed the baby's paternity was not an issue, and had been all too happy to marvel with her at the daily changes in her body and mind. They had opened their blue eyes wide at the growing size of her belly, had expressed similar disgust at the ugly way pregnancy had with one's navel. They had giggled at her growing bosom, had wrapped her breasts with strips of linen to keep the tenderness at bay. So it had been easy for her to imagine that her sister's response would be the world's. In the meantime, she enjoyed the tiny silver stretch marks across the underside of her belly and the tops of her thighs that made her feel shiny and scaled. The spread of her feet. The ache behind her knees. The pleasurable waves between pubis, womb, and breast. The way she could conjure the baby's movements inside her. When she closed down thought, she was rewarded by that quiver that seems like the first touch of a stranger who has singled you out in the crowd.

Of course, once the girl had made her way without fuss into the world, Julia's sister had taken note of what the rest would also observe. But a semblance of cozy calm can be maintained by an unspoken agreement to deny the facts. Her sister did not ask her to explain, and Julia did not offer. And now, with her husband in the formerly childless quarters they had shared for years, she hoped for the same thing. She had not asked for much in their twenty-four years of marriage. She had managed with what he saw fit to offer. They were two people who had lived through those years of turmoil before and during the Civil War, a time when, as his sister used to say, people ate it up, wore it out, or made it do. And so, she told her husband that she hoped he would forgive her for wanting to be sure this child would arrive in the world safe and whole before announcing its presence to him. It was her fervent wish that he share her wonder at being granted this blessing. All children were strange things, weren't they? Otherworldly. As if closer to God than the rest of us. Who knew, she said, why the Lord had seen fit to provide them with so much hardship on the way to this child. It was not their job to question the road they had traveled to get there. It was their duty to accept whatever they should find in the Lord's provisions with such grace as they could.

Because she believed that despite the many differences between herself and her husband they were, at bottom, bred of the same stock, she believed that her entreaties would hit their mark. She believed that he would enter into that agreement with her, would agree to forget and then forget he had forgotten. He would keep no lists.

But he crossed the room and took her slim shoulders in his wide hands. He did not shake her. His grip was not uncomfortably firm. It was tender, but clear. He called her his darling. He told her he loved her more than he thought it possible to love someone. But this child was not his child.

Chapter Ten

Ida's growing interest in the Celestial foreman had not gone unnoticed by Lucy, yet she reminded herself that she enjoyed no exclusive right to Ida's attentions and so kept her silence, maintaining an outward placidity that pretended to have noticed nothing at all. Her interior, however, was a creek swollen with spring melt and each time Ida quit the apartment to instruct him in yet more English, or to host him for another meal at the Widow Allen's table, it was all Lucy could do to keep herself from expelling a brief cry. Ida had spent over three years tending to her in large and small ways, and didn't that imply something about what Lucy could expect from her best friend?

Although she had in many respects overcome the horrors of the attack, and had been for some time making her own modest living in the world by sewing ladies' underclothes of the type sold in the best shops of New York and Boston,

she felt most of the time, and knew that Ida understood this, that her life was a waiting life, lived in the antechamber to life's vast central hall.

Her assailant was, the sheriff had assured her with impatience, likely to be long gone and never to return. The sheriff wasn't an unkind man. He had done his best, but his best had proved to be not good enough, and his impatience was born of shame at his failure. Lucy blamed him not at all, partly because it was not her nature to assign blame, and partly because she had always thought of the unknown man as *her* assailant, something in her possession. The smell of his laundered clothes and strong soap lined her nostrils still. *My assailant*, she might whisper to herself when no one was around, the way children in their beds at night holding a precious object aloft might whisper, *My toy*. She thought that somewhere, wherever he had put in, he thought of her in this same manner. The intimacy, although terrible, was awesome, and who wouldn't want in some way to return to it? So she found herself playacting her own life until his inevitable return, when her life, one way or the other, could begin again. It was as if that day in the alley he had set her at the head of a wide, lonely path, and without him, she could never advance any farther down it.

It was why Ida was still with her even after three years' time, sending letter after letter to her family in Virginia explaining Lucy's continued state. It was why Alfred and Lucy remained in North Adams, though the cooperative, after three years of success, had been put up for rent over four months prior, advertising in the same issue of the

Transcript that quoted Sampson as declaring that he was refurnishing his office "in a very elegant and tasty manner and putting in a new boiler." Alfred had in that time been employed at nothing but odd jobs fewer and farther between. Success for a cooperative had not meant the same thing as it did for a private manufacturer. Those banded brothers did not have the liquid assets to weather dips and dives in the market. So it was as if not just Lucy's life but also the lives of those who cared for her were on hold, each of them faced with a closed door, waiting for someone else to open it and usher them through.

Until recently, however, Lucy would have said she was comforted and contained by her sense that Ida was standing beside her, and they were holding hands, each keeping the other from the unknown chambers ahead. So as she had begun to feel Ida's grip loosening, she had been surprised and invigorated by the extremity of her entitlement. *How dare you?* she found herself thinking more and more often. *How dare you?*

Indeed, tonight, Alfred full of delighted speculation about the sight he had witnessed at the depot, she found herself unable to focus on his energetic gossiping. Instead, she couldn't help but feel that what was important about this news was Ida's reaction to it. Her friend had stayed after dinner even though Lucy felt sure this was supposed to have been a lesson night with Mr. Sing. But having announced that she was staying, Ida then had nothing to say. She didn't chide Alfred for his interest in things having nothing to do with him. She didn't even appear to be listening. She'd eaten her food, downed her milk, wiped her mouth, and sat back, her knife and fork, like a long-married couple, placed across her plate.

Alfred was asking them to comment on the baby. Didn't they find it odd that Sampson's wife had disappeared for months only to come back with a child? Didn't that seem like a somewhat unusual way of going about the business of birth?

The women's responses had not seemed necessary to the progress of his talk, but he was growing impatient with the sound of his own voice. He was someone, after all, who wanted nothing more than to belong to a chorus.

"Well?" he said, tapping at his tin plate with his knife.

Lucy's insides startled: even still, the sudden sound of any kind of knife going about any kind of business brought back those minutes in the alley.

"I imagine," she said, "that for Mrs. Sampson, the business of birth has long been unhappy and strange."

Everyone knew about the Sampsons' trouble. It was why, it was said, they hadn't moved into a grand house on a hill. Who could blame that poor woman? Who wanted to be surrounded by empty rooms meant for children healthy and alive?

Alfred said, "I don't know about that, but Sampson himself looked like I might knock him over with a spoon. There's no way you're telling me he knew."

"I'm not arguing with you," Lucy said.

"Well," Alfred said, looking as if she had been doing just that.

Ida stood with such force that the table shook. "Feather," she said to Alfred. "Knock him over with a feather. Not a spoon."

Her two friends stared at her.

"Does it seem to the two of you that we've been sitting at this table our whole lives?" she demanded, her voice louder than she'd anticipated.

Brother and sister looked at each other, and then their plates, and then back at Ida.

"Because it seems to me that we do nothing but eat meal after meal at this table." She indicated the empty plates and cups, then shook her hands like a waterbird drying its wings. "Mercy," she said. "At least someone is out there living." She looked from one confounded friend to the other. They said nothing.

The light was almost gone from the room. No one moved to the lamps.

Ida felt as if she might strike something. She thought of Charlie's kind, plain face and childlike hands. Her heart calmed. Staring at Lucy, she saw the infant's black hair, its warm-toned skin against the white blanket. *Charlie*, she thought. Surprising her again.

Lucy said softly, "I'm sorry if I've kept you from what you've wanted."

Ida took a step back, pushing her chair away from the table, and it tipped backward with a clatter. "Everyone keeps me from everything," she said. And then she left before having to see the hurt she had caused spread across her best friend's face.

★

The following morning was the first of a new month, and the work at the pegging berths couldn't have been going any slower, and there was no foreman to make it otherwise. He had not come home until dawn, and more alarming than that, Ley My had told the others he was sure Charlie's queue was missing.

The white workers, recently recruited to mix in with the Chinese on the bottoming floor, kept at their berths, though their hands remained idle.

From the back, Quan Tuch announced that yesterday had been payday, and he had seen Mr. Chase hand the bundle of gold coins to Charlie, but was it necessary to note that none of them had seen any coins since?

In this room, where the sound of the machines was usually as relentless as a hard rain, the muffled sounds of work elsewhere came through the floor and wallboards. Vibrations made their way through the men's shoes. The room was already warmed by the growing heat of the day. They had spent years in this room, and now they were ready to think the worst of this man who seemed to sacrifice the least but reap the most. Change was coming, and they welcomed it, the way some villagers in their hometowns welcomed demons. The terrible might result in advantage or its opposite, but either way you wanted to be there to see it.

None of the white men could understand Chinese, but just the sight of the Celestials clumped at one end of the room was enough. Their work together these last few weeks had been excessively polite, the civility of executioner and condemned, and neither group had been as yet able to determine which was which.

It seemed to the white men that the tenor of the conversation at the other end of the room was shifting into something more worrisome. Had they had grasp of the language, they would have heard a litany of complaints against the foreman: He made more money, yet worked less. He had total acquaintance with and power over their bills. He determined what they needed from the market and when they needed it. He read and wrote their mail. He received and distributed their pay, deducting what they owed without offering an accounting. He was their hands and eyes in dealing with the town, and for years had persuaded them to pool extra money that none of them could afford and buy Thanksgiving turkeys for key figures, a list of whom he himself drew up. And only he seemed to be singled out as worthy of the town's gratitude and good wishes.

This last spring, they felt he had capitulated too quickly when renegotiating their contract with Sampson. They were now receiving less pay. They were now required to pay part of their heating costs. They understood times were hard, but at whose doorstep did he lay his loyalty?

And most disturbingly, he seemed to be bent on burying their dead in the local cemetery with Methodist ritual. It had become clear that the dead were not likely to be exhumed and their remains sent back to China.

This was the worst thing. Without attention to rituals, there was no way to resolve what was doubtful, receive the spirits, or distinguish humanness from righteousness.

Their foreman was a spirit of disorder. He stood for anarchy and individual gain.

There was silence again when the group came to the end of its complaints.

Ah Chung glanced at the berths of white workers. Homer Handley smiled and held his cutters up in a wave as if interrupting his usual work. Ah Chung gave him a small nod without gathering the attention of his fellow workers, and then both men dropped their eyes back to their previous concerns.

When Lucius Hurd arrived at his South Adams studio to open up shop on that overcast August 1, the Chinese foreman was standing by the door, waiting. Mr. Hurd had on one or two occasions been visited by the Chinese, but his studio was smaller and less convenient than that of his older brother, William, and situated in the decidedly more rural South Adams, and Lucius Hurd prided himself on what he would describe as a more dignified approach to promoting his work. His wife found this streak of passivity to be his tragic flaw, the source of all their unhappiness and continued struggle. Too good for his own good, she told their eldest daughter. Certainly for mine, she often added.

And so the sight of the Chinaman, worn and bedraggled as he was, was a welcome one, and Lucius attempted to convey as much in his cheerful greeting.

The Chinaman seemed not to notice, and Lucius had the distinct sense that if he had never succeeded in unlocking the door, the man would've expressed nothing but contentment at standing outside the building for the rest of the day. About this, Lucius Hurd would have been wrong. Charlie's insides were at war. His only chance at not falling to the ground in pieces was to make his outer body a lacquered shell within which the inner tumult could be contained. He knew this photographer not at all, yet he'd seen the portraiture he had made of a few of the boys. He knew of what kinds of transformations the photographer was capable with what had seemed to Charlie nothing more than the turn of two ankles, the confident spread of knees, a hymnal, and a silk fan. One or two of the boys, Charlie knew, had given copies of the photographs to their Sunday school teachers. Charlie had teased one boy about the gift, but the boy would not be teased. With an utter seriousness, he had said, "I give her a ghost image of myself so that she can remember the form from which the ghost comes." He had indicated his body with a gesture of such fluidity that Charlie had been seized with shame and had teased him no more.

Lucius kept the curtains drawn and lit the lamp on his front counter. The Chinaman looked as if he'd slept outside, and clearly his hair had had an unsuccessful encounter with dull blades.

Charlie noticed him regarding his hair. "You can shave and trim?" he asked, pulling from beneath his tunic a small towel, which he opened on the counter, revealing a razor, some soap, a comb, and a pair of work scissors.

For Lucius Hurd this was proving to be a most remarkable day. He told the Chinaman that it wasn't his usual trade, but he didn't see why he couldn't offer him a decent shave and cut. As long as the man wanted nothing fancy.

Charlie frowned. "Nothing fancy," he repeated. He reached under his tunic and produced a small money bag from which he pulled one gold coin. "Best American portrait," he said, putting the coin on the counter between them.

So Lucius Hurd would give this man a shave and a haircut. He would dress him in his finest costume suit. Perhaps even a hat. He would take the portrait. And then he would pass the rest of the day as he had expected to pass it. In the evening, he would close up shop and retrace his morning steps back to his home and his family, where he was sure that not even his wife could object to a hard gold coin placed in her small, beautiful hand.

Almost as alarming to Homer Handley as the strange behavior of the Chinese was the fact that Mr. Sampson seemed not to have made an appearance at the factory that day. Midmorning, an errand boy had found his way to the bottoming room after having had no success in locating Mr. Sampson downstairs. And sometime after the midday meal, Mr. Chase had leaned into the room, scanned it, and gone out again.

Homer knew what his Crispin friends said about Sampson—that he made a lot of promises and never kept them, that he told everyone what they wanted to hear, that his interests were only for himself and his wife. That he was so selfish that he didn't even want to share his fortune with offspring. But to him Sampson had been nothing but fair, and what Homer admired the most about the man was his dogged discipline. His sense of responsibility to this world he had built for himself. Homer, too, believed that if you built something, you took care of it. Weekly oilings of woodwork; periodic tightening of table joints; cleaning windows with strong vinegar; repainting house and barn.

Someone whom Homer had come to admire for his consistency of purpose acting in unfamiliar ways was distracting enough that once they had recommenced work, he made several careless errors that afternoon about which Emmett Fletcher, usually the one to make mistakes, teased him with much gratitude and little mercy.

Had Homer learned, as Mr. Chase had upon inquiring at the Wilson House's front desk, that Mr. Sampson was indeed in his apartment, but had left instructions not to be disturbed, he would have assumed, as Mr. Chase did, illness. For what else could keep a man such as Mr. Sampson at home on a workday?

The imagination of neither man was broad enough to include a romantic reunion with Mrs. Sampson. Though both men would've said that the marriage was a strong one, the best example of what marriage ought to be, neither would've thought it a place of romance. Formidable, fair, and upright were the words that came to mind when the Sampson union was discussed, if it was discussed at all.

Sampson had spent the day, as many people do when they believe themselves betrayed by loved ones, feeling hurt and inflicting hurt. He had not been able to move his wife from her insistence that the child was his. He had spent the morning trying to catalog the one hundred fifty boys in the factory and realizing that he was acquainted with their faces almost not at all and their names even less. He found himself by the late afternoon a creature pacing a wall of bars.

Could he interview the boys one by one? Could he look at them and know? He examined the infant girl in her various states of quietude and squall. Would her features be apparent in her maker's?

He had, by the time Homer was pegging the same shoe for the third time, struck upon an idea that he felt held promise, and he spread before Julia the photo albums of Sampson's Boys on the card table, eliminating the twenty-two boys who had arrived most recently.

He realized with embarrassment that he disguised as anger that he had not a clue which of these boys were her students. And that her teaching of them had been his idea in the first place. He insisted that it was her duty to him and to God to tell him all that she knew.

The more her husband spoke, the more Julia wept.

She held the baby up to him. "She's my child," she said. "After all these years, *my* child."

He could barely understand her, her crying was so violent.

She pressed the infant bundle against his belly. "Please," she said again. "Can't you love her for that?"

It seemed to him that no matter how he answered, there would be his life before this day and his life after, and he knew not how to reconcile the two.

Old and in need of the support of two grandsons, who were youthful and impatient on each side of their fragile grandfather, Homer Handley would be one of the many attendees at the Sampson funeral on a Sunday afternoon in October 1893, though he would not attend the reception. He had not, of course, been invited, but even if he had, he would have instructed his grandsons to take him home. His purpose was to honor the man by seeing him laid to rest, not to share the passing with others. Who knew why he'd felt so attached to this man for so long? And when his grandsons had delivered him home, and his wife teased him gently by asking if all had gone well at the funeral of his dear friend, all he would say in response was that he had thought it pleasing to see so many folks of so many stripes. His wife would cup his cheek as she had been doing for some thirty-plus years, and he would reach up to return the gesture.

But by the end of that working day, the thunder and lightning had begun and Emmett Fletcher was predicting hail. It had been a long and anxious day, and the hot storm wind, the flip-flopping of the leaves, revealing their silvery undersides like thrashing fish, and the smell of water in the air made Homer long for home and his wife. They would drink cold lemonade and watch the storm from their porch, counting the seconds from lightning to thunder to know how far they were from the eye.

And then he glanced to the Chinamen's side of the room and noted that the foreman was back, wearing Western work clothes and sporting a new haircut of the oddest design. The other workers were gathered around him in a mass alive with fear and ignorance, righteousness and anger. Homer felt as he imagined his terrier to feel on the days when the dog watched the humans pack up for an outing: *Who knows how long this may last, but nothing good can come of it.*

Chapter Eleven

It seemed to Charlie that he did nothing in the days following
Julia's return home but negotiate and mollify. Even for a man
with his abilities, the demands he encountered were a challenge. When had he ever imagined himself having to explain a
situation such as this one? He professed ignorance. He promised investigation. He counseled patience and loyalty and suggested that idle speculation could do no good. On his return
from the South Adams studio he had had to field dismay and
upset about his haircut, and to put an end to their sense of
betrayal, he had doled out their salaries, adding a little extra
for each man from his own share, telling them it was a bonus
from Sampson himself. He had charged them with living up
to the high regard in which their employer held them.

Sampson didn't return to the factory for the remainder
of that week, and Charlie was glad of it. His growing intimacy with Julia had not meant a change in the opinions he

held of Sampson. He never spoke ill of the man to others, never thought ill of him in his own mind. In fact, it was rare for him to think of Julia as another man's wife; she seemed so much her own person, and his relationship with her so much its own place, inhabited only by the two of them. He had felt, falling in love with her, as if they had discovered a door in the familiar earth leading to another country where nothing was anything they knew.

She, he knew, did not always feel this way. And it was by way of her sadness at her betrayal of her husband that Charlie found his own guilt. Her heavy heart filled his with the same weight. He came to think of it as more evidence of their love. Now he saw Sampson not just as a model for his aspirations, but as Julia's husband, someone who would care a great deal about Charlie's feelings for his wife. He understood this so acutely that he marveled that he had not felt it before. He hadn't even seen with any clarity the sort of future they might have together.

Presently, however, their years ahead were his only concern. Even the unrest among the workers could not take his mind from its one task: a life with Julia and their baby. And why not? Why couldn't anyone's life be his own?

And so as soon as the factory's machines had been quieted for the week and as soon as he could extricate himself from his charges, he headed to the Wilson House, the portrait in its stiff envelope in his breast pocket like armor for the heart.

His hair was slick with Macassar oil, his recently purchased navy-blue worsted suit was pressed, his collar starched, and his tie pinned with a delicate clip of jade and gold. In a small sack, he carried offerings for the baby. He had no idea what Americans brought as gifts for the newly born, so he relied on Chinese tradition. He was ignorant of the child's name. He didn't even know if it was a boy or a girl. A wavelet of sadness broke across his chest.

As he walked, he fingered the items in his pocket: For a rich, healthy life, coins tied together with red string. For protection against the demons who steal young children to reinforce the foundations of bridges, a tiny arrow he had carved from wood. To give the baby's head a proper shape, a little pillow filled with rice. His stitching was clumsy, but he had used a piece of silk from a head scarf of his mother's, and he hoped that Julia would forgive the handiwork in favor of the sentiment behind it.

He nearly collided with Sampson on the way through the Wilson House's front doors.

Sampson's jacket was unbuttoned, his collar askew, yet even so, the man was better dressed than Charlie could ever be. Sampson's face registered no recognition and then he looked as if he might laugh. Charlie thought that if he did, he would strike him. But Sampson only grasped him by the shoulders and pulled him into the front hall. "Sing," he said. "Just the man. Do you have a minute?"

Charlie thought about saying no. He remembered years ago, as a child, what a revelation it had been to realize that when his parents summoned him, he need not answer.

"Of course," Charlie said, allowing himself to be led to one of the reading rooms off the lobby. For this man he would always have a minute.

They seated themselves in armchairs that promised more comfort than they delivered. Other than Morris Kronick, the hotel's thirteen-year-old Jewish errand boy, they were alone, and the boy was asleep, his hands tucked under his arms as if for warmth.

Sampson modulated his voice not at all. He had two things to ask. Perhaps Charlie had already heard the news of Mrs. Sampson's return. Perhaps he had heard more. It was actually of no mind what Charlie had heard or from whom, since it should have been clear to the foreman by now that the only version of events that mattered was Sampson's own. Here was the situation as he understood it, and as he hoped Charlie would as well: his wife had brought with her from Michigan an infant girl.

A girl, Charlie thought. He felt no disappointment that the child was not a boy. *Our daughter*, he thought.

Despite her protestations to the contrary, Sampson went on, it was clear to him, and would be to Charlie, that the girl was some share Celestial. He needed Charlie's help.

At this, Charlie's heart rippled like a cloth spread across a wide table. He had always had this reaction to men of power asking for aid. There was something lovely and exciting about their petitions, like a praying mantis bowing before his mate.

Sampson seemed to hold no embarrassment at making this request, and though the foreman would have liked to believe that what accounted for this was Sampson's belief that they were equals, he knew the opposite to be the more likely explanation.

"I must have the father's name," Sampson said. "And I must have your help to achieve it."

Charlie had a vision of pulling his calling card from his breast pocket and handing it to Sampson with a bow.

What did American men like Sampson do when so extremely confronted? Charlie's life had been devoted to nudging and ushering Americans into the positions he desired them to take, as if trying to push a bead of water across a table. The idea of direct confrontation was so foreign it was like the woods on the far bank of the river that had run along his hometown's edge.

Morris Kronick woke with a start, rearranged his limbs, and regarded them dully.

"I am here to help," Charlie said, feeling the deception even more than usual. Had everything he had ever uttered been a lie?

Sampson appeared relieved. "I need you, of course, to think of your men, to think of anyone who . . ." Here he faltered, uneasy. His sad eyes swept the room. "Well, anyone with whom you think I might want to speak."

"Yes, of course," Charlie said, already filing through his workers' faces and names as though, if he looked carefully enough, another father would appear before him.

Sampson also needed his foreman, if it was not too forward a request, to speak to Mrs. Sampson. She had always liked Charlie. Perhaps even if she would not speak direct about the recent events, she would somehow allow Charlie access to rooms that she had so far kept hidden. At least from him, he added quietly, and Charlie had the urge to cup the man's shoulder. He pushed at the sack of gifts for his daughter with his booted toe and assured his employer that he would do what he could. He would call on Mrs. Sampson at this very time.

"Oh, no," Sampson said. "Not now. She is resting with the baby and says they are not to be disturbed."

He looked as if he would speak further, and Charlie waited.

Sampson looked at the boy asleep again in the chair across the room. The sight seemed to sadden him anew. "She is changed since her return," he said.

Charlie's gut flipped with worry and possibility. "I would think so," he finally offered.

Sampson glanced up at him as if unsure whether the Celestial was, against all odds, employing humor. "No," he said. "Not in the obvious ways. She is somehow more . . ." He appealed to Charlie helplessly.

Charlie had never seen him at such a loss. He found the situation unpleasant. "In China, they say new mothers are as the tiger."

It was unclear whether Sampson understood what he meant. He again turned his face to Charlie. "I've really never seen anything like it," he said.

And Charlie nodded as if his boss had unrolled before him a map to his wife's inner workings, a tidy scale in one corner, a compass indicating true north in another.

"What is the child's name?" Charlie asked quietly.

Sampson regarded him as if from a distance. He said nothing, unable, even in the context of this unprecedented intimacy, to admit that it had not occurred to him to ask, or to her to offer.

Ida kept from Lucy and Alfred until the following Saturday evening, embarrassed at her outburst. Since Thursday last, she had felt her self to be the breaking wall of a dam. She'd been able to manage her days and restrain herself from speaking too loudly to shopkeepers or losing patience with children in the street. But her body had grown heavier each day as if, with full petticoats and skirt, she was wading farther into deep mud.

She tried to sort out what she knew from what she only thought she knew. Charlie and Mrs. Sampson were indeed faithful friends. Beyond that, she reminded herself, she knew nothing. She had no right to feel betrayed, and yet she did, her feelings sneaky trespassers on grounds she had thought well fenced. So she found herself climbing the front stairs of the Pearl Street tenement, hoping that the sight of her friend would deny any further mortification.

Lucy and Alfred sat on the small bench they used as a sofa, reading together a letter on the paper Ida recognized as belonging to the oldest Robinson cousin, still in their Virginia hometown. Neither of them seemed to have heard Ida's entry.

They laughed, leaning into each other's shoulders with an ease and affinity before they looked up.

"Oh, Ida," Lucy said, her face filled with affection. "Now I am happy."

Ida knew her to be speaking the truth, but had also seen what she'd seen: the reliable constant of family warmth. She knew her sentiments made no sense. She understood that she herself had more family to return to than Lucy or Alfred had in this world entire, but that was of no matter. She understood that things as they had been in this faraway town could not go on forever. She could not remain forever sitting across a large room from Lucy, four hands held in two laps.

"What's the matter with you?" Alfred asked.

"Not a thing," Ida said. "What's the matter with you?"

Alfred blushed, and Ida gave him a quick smile as she made her way to the chair.

Lucy stared at her queerly, and Ida allowed her friend's open countenance to loosen her heart like kind, working fingers unlacing a boot.

"What's the news?" Ida asked, indicating the letter, hoping that they would not require her to speak of her outburst.

"It's good," Lucy said, but glanced at her feet as she spoke, so Ida braced for whatever was coming next. The cousin was to marry. Her husband needed a reliable hand in his lumber mill. The town was in need of a primary school teacher.

So, here it is, Ida thought. Here is the gate in the wall. A life waited easily for the Robinsons on the other side of that wall. From her own vantage point, the news was jubilation's opposite, so she was surprised that when she closed her eyes against the worried countenance of her best friend, the face that came into focus was the broad, full one of the Celestial foreman.

"We are not yet decided," Lucy said. "What is your mind? Should we go?"

Ida kept her eyes closed. "Do you want to go?"

Had her eyes been open, she might have been witness to the pain spread across Lucy's face.

"I'm only curious what you think," Lucy said. She understood, looking at her dear Ida, that they were in a trap of their own making. She wished that she could free them as one freed the hem of a poorly made dress, one stitch at a time, the thread coming easier with each snip and tug.

Even Alfred felt the sad mix of desperation and resignation in the room, and a mild panic spread across his chest, believing as he did that nothing good could come of a woman's unhappiness. When Ida remained silent, continuing to sit there with her eyes closed, he said, perhaps a little too rudely, his own mixed feelings about leaving Ida at war within him, "It isn't her life."

"Alfred," Lucy said. "Ssh."

Ida said he was right.

Lucy said, "If we go, you must come home with us." She held a hand to her chest as if to soothe its heat. "I cannot think of a day spent without you in it," she said finally.

Ida opened her eyes. They were the words she had been waiting to hear, but she understood that her friend uttered them now only because she *could* imagine such a day.

Ida would never grasp how fully she had misunderstood this moment and her friend's emotions in it. She would never be able to see Lucy's need for her as any kind of match for her need for Lucy. She would always make sense of Lucy's kindnesses and generosities as those of someone on the verge of departure.

"Maybe I will come," she said. She kept her inner eyes on her conjured image of Charlie and wondered at the release of a heavy weight, as if she were a sandbag being poured empty. It did not occur to her to worry at the ease with which her reliance on one person had seemed to translate into reliance on another. She did not ask of herself, as someone else might have asked of her, whether she wanted to be the sort of woman who was in such need of care and attention that she could discover it in any corner of any room.

Julia opened the windows in the bedroom and the front parlor as wide as could be managed. The August heat was breaking and an evening wind had found its way through the street. The sounds of Saturday rode through on the wind's back.

She did not worry: the baby had already proved herself a champion sleeper.

She lowered herself onto her side next to her infant. The chest rose and fell in the movement of rapids over river rocks. Normal, Julia's sister had said. Julia still barely believed it.

Outside, the sun lowered, and evening blanketed the town. The hoots of children subsided. The whip-poor-wills and grosbeaks began. Somewhere, someone was cooking something delicious. Somewhere else, fertilizer was being spread.

Her senses were like no previous acquaintance. They were the ropewalker's cable she had been witness to as a child, high and taut beneath the canvas roof of a circus tent. She

tucked her hands beneath her cheek and continued to regard her girl. *I could stay here for all time,* she thought. She
understood herself to be free of exaggeration's grip. Her
world was now her body, the girl's, and the circle they fashioned together. These were her feelings, simple and plain.

Chapter Twelve

Julia had insisted on returning to her regular teaching commitments despite her husband's protestations. The more adamant he became, the more sure she was of her decision. In the few days she'd been home, she had found this to be the case more and more, and she was not yet recovered from the surprise. Whereas she had spent the first night and day unable to slow the rapid pacing of her mind, unable to keep possible solutions and entreaties from turning over like a factory's waterwheel, she now imagined her mind as an ancient Greek column, her life an edifice with that column at the center of a great roof. Her husband was welcome to join her, but the shelter was not dependent upon him. For the first time she imagined herself as advocate and adversary. It was not a completely logical way to feel, since in most ways, the shelter over her head did surely depend on the presence of her husband, and she was in many ways anything but his equal.

It was as if she had been given clear knowledge of God's large purpose. So when she pulled on her gloves and gathered the handles of the baby's wicker basket, hefting it against her hip, her husband merely stood there. And when she reminded him that he was not to come to the lessons, not to meddle where he had no business meddling, he only nodded and wished her a good day.

He spent the afternoon sitting in his favorite armchair, and upon her return several hours later, he would be unable to answer her inquiries as to how he had passed his time.

Even before her arrival in the classroom, the teachers were engaged in speculation and debate. Mrs. Hollings revealed that she certainly wouldn't have accepted Mr. Sing's purchase of Thanksgiving turkeys if she had known what kind of degradation those boys were bent on practicing. Miss Cowley advocated caution, arguing that judgment should, as always, be reserved until the full situation had been made clear. Not to mention, Mrs. Brighton added, Mrs. Sampson's impeccable record as a woman of dignity and moral activity. Mrs. Hollings granted them what she could, but argued that there was a baby who came from somewhere, was there not? And what was to be done about it now? Clearly this mixing of the races had come to the most distressing of situations. Somebody, they all agreed, must take up the reins of responsibility. None of them noted the irony of having this conversation within the Celestial classroom, the Celestials themselves politely awaiting these very same volunteers to commence their usual lessons.

The minds in the classroom were not entirely turned to the Celestial child. There was happy news of Mr. Robert Kingsley, engineer on the Hoosac Tunnel project, who had been so badly injured at the recent east end accident. It had been supposed that he would be rendered blind, but the news today was that the sight of one eye proved not to be wholly lost. The party of Gipsies that had lingered on Main Street since Tuesday last had finally seen fit to continue on its way. Several of the volunteer teachers were still speaking of their picnicking on Mount Greylock the week previous. Before the spread was laid, the rain had begun to pour and they had found themselves in the very home of the clouds.

There was talk of the boiler recently installed at the Sampson factory and fully suitable for driving a forty-horsepower engine. And of the peach crop, and the Hoosac Tunnel, which had been advanced 288 feet during the month of July, with less than 1,500 feet of rock remaining to be pierced.

The previous month, in the *Transcript* of July 10, 1873, the Chinamen had made the following appearance in an account by a press excursion party from Boston:

Sampson's Chinamen

We were of the few who early the next morning visited the famed shoe factory of Mr. Sampson, the introducer of "Chinese cheap labor" into Massachusetts. We were in the main workshop when the Chinamen came up-stairs to their work, six-and-a-half-o'clock. Such a merry sight we never saw in

a Yankee factory. Laughing, jumping, slapping their com-
panions on the back, tickling their ears, and other pranks,
their eyes glistening with roguery and sport, they poured
up the narrow staircase into the room, one hundred and
eleven strong, as though they were going to an all-day frolic.
Rapidly they passed to their respective benches or machines,
quickly donned aprons and hats, and soon were at their
work—all respectful, all industrious, and all seemingly
happy. The best commentary on the success of the experi-
ment is that last Monday the first three years' contract for
their labor expired, and the whole original force renewed
the same cheerfully and willingly. Two additions have been
made to the original number, engaged in San Francisco,
and but a few have left from causes independent of the
labor and compensation. We could not help asking ourselves,
where else can we find factory hands who go to their work
laughing and hilarious, or work so long and willingly
without desire of change? These Chinamen seem to grow
in strength and vigor the longer they are in this climate, as
the growth of beards indicates; and if they could marry and
fully adopt Western customs we have no doubt they would
easily become assimilated with the great American compos-
ite of nationality, which in time will graft African, Indian
and Mongolian upon the Caucasian tree.

On July 10, everyone in the schoolroom had read and concurred with the article's final claim; to react any other way
had not crossed the mind of a one of them. But on this day,
less than a month later, as white and Chinese alike turned

to see Mrs. Sampson cross the threshold of her husband's factory with a new wicker basket on her arm like a scale, the human noise of the room subsided. Perhaps the China-men's growth had been too strong, too vigorous, thought the native volunteers. And even the most progressive of the Chinamen, faced with the sight of their employer's wife and the child's Celestial eyes, felt that assimilation was not the goal toward which they should have been striving.

Julia was not so lost in the new definitions of her world that she neglected to detect the awkwardness, and a flick-er of disquiet about Charlie's ability to be totally discreet passed through her, but her attentions were to her daughter as the needle of a compass to true north, so why should this not be the case for all others?

This was perhaps explanation for why, as she stood there searching out her usual table and students, she took note of the room's quiet but did not necessarily assign herself as its cause. The absence of the courtesies that usually greeted her arrival could be the unease of reunion, she told herself. She had, after all, been absent for several months. And men did tend to discover even more clumsy versions of themselves around babies.

Sitting across the room, Fannie Burlingame, Julia's cousin by marriage, fellow volunteer teacher, supporter of all things Chinese, took note of the room's tempera-ture. Given how much of a supporter she had been of this Chinese Experiment of Sampson's, she would have shown her public endorsement for these boys no matter what her personal feelings about them, but she had been gladly surprised by the extent to which she had come to care about Lue Gim Gong. She had discovered in him a talent for horticulture and she and her orchards had been much pleased by his attentions. She felt about him the way an unmarried woman of a certain age feels about most younger men: a kind, vaguely maternal regard. Indeed, she would before long formally and officially adopt him, and in the end, bequeath to him an orange grove in Florida and a sizeable part of her formidable estate, treating him in death as she had in life: as the son she never had. So, of all people in the room, she understood how a white American woman, even a white American woman of a certain class, could come to find herself engaged and delighted with one of these Celestial visitors, but engaged and delighted was one thing, the picture of mother and babe across the room quite another. It was, she felt, an unhappymaking situation all around, and a further misfortune that she must call the woman in question cousin. Her face expressed such worry that one of her students fetched her some cold water and insisted she drink.

It was young Lucy Robinson who stepped forward, breaking the stillness to stride across the room and bend at the waist to peer happily into the basket. The attack against her had been such an affront to the regulations of social interaction that she had found herself since that day able to cross those boundaries with more ease. It was as if having had the rim of a cup broken, she had discovered one could drink from it nonetheless. And an infant was an infant, and Lucy a nineteen-year-old lady. Her vision of the future was a warm, grassy meadow flocked with babies. It had always been thus. The attack had made these hopes more desperate, not less, and she tried to keep the sharpness of her need out of her speech as she relieved Mrs. Sampson of the basket, advising her to sit. She took the child expertly from its nest, cradling the tiny head against her shoulder, her body finding a rocking rhythm as easy and natural as the gait of a well-trained pony.

"Oh, Mrs. Sampson," she said, taking in the oaty smell of the child's head, "she is a beauty."

"Yes," Julia said, as if congratulating her on having noted something all others had missed. "She is extraordinary."

The straightforwardness with which Mrs. Sampson made this statement filled Lucy with envy and then shame. When would other people's joys cease to inspire in her their opposite?

Julia did not like to watch her child in someone else's arms, but she understood this was the sort of maternal extremity to be avoided, and so she resisted the urge to return the child to her own embrace. Still, she stood there feeling as she imagined a schoolmistress must, having given a very young pupil something delicate and fragile to examine, hoping that care will take precedence and the experience will prove to be one of discovery rather than destruction.

"Her eyes are quite exotic, aren't they?" Lucy said.

Julia could not ascertain the spirit of the remark. "I imagine God must've been in a good mood when He made them," she said in what she hoped was a neutral tone. She liked this young lady. She liked that she had come across the room to them as if no other response made any sense at all. She did not want to stop liking her. Still, she succumbed to her urge and reached as mildly as she could for her child.

"Oh," Lucy said, her arms light and empty, anxious she had caused offense. "They're wonderful," she said. "So dark and alert, as if nothing can escape her."

Julia's heart softened warily. She did not see one of the Chinamen rise and make his way toward her. She did, however, see Charlie appear quickly from the back room to intercept him with a gesture and several low words of Chinese. He did not look in her direction, and she was glad for the other boy's distraction. She knew Charlie well enough to read his countenance as that of a parent whose suspicions concerning a child have been suddenly borne out.

The boy's visage was familiar and she searched her mind's cupboards for his name. She could have searched for years, as this boy had been one of the group of workers most recently arrived in town, and she had not yet made his acquaintance. The familiarity she felt was due to the photos her husband had slid before her two nights prior. This boy's face had been on the top of the pile Sampson had discarded as irrelevant to the task at hand.

The boy said something to his foreman in return, and Julia had the distinct impression his comments concerned her, not because he glanced her way, but because of how assiduously he avoided doing so.

Charlie did not answer the boy, who stood there smiling and then made his way out of the room and closed the bunk room door behind him.

Now Charlie looked at her. His queue was gone, in its place a neat and Western cut. She remembered him telling her that without his queue, his homeland would no longer welcome him. The difference in his appearance was both drastic and not. How could she not have thought of him over the past days? Even when her husband's interrogations had been at their most vigorous, she had thought of him, when she had thought of him at all, as something that might eventually cease to exist. But, of course, here he was, alive and in front of her, wanting, she now understood, something very different.

The boy in the bunk room was Ah Chung Coon. He was a month shy of his twentieth birthday, fiercely dedicated to his mother, and embarrassed that he had so few memories of his father, who had died when Ah Chung was six. His eyes were wide-set, his ears large, his eyebrows oddly placed. His mouth held a natural downturn that made even his most passive expressions appear to be those of a judgmental elder. He was from a village less than half a day's walk from the foreman's, and upon his arrival the previous January, there had been talk between the two of them of the possibility that the branches of their family trees had crossed not too many generations ago. And they did indeed know people in common. The tailor in Charlie's village had originally come from Ah Chung's, and there were several women who had begun in one place only to marry into the other. Ah Chung had even sold cabbage at a stall next to Charlie's father's on more than one occasion, and he had attended one year of primary school with Second Brother. Then there was the fact that they shared one part of their birth names. But Ah Chung had been suspicious of assigning family status to anyone who would sacrifice his birth name for an English one.

Charlie had long ago learned it was best to find associations and loyalties where one could. Even fabricated ones were preferable to none at all. They made his job easier. So he had insisted that he knew Ah Chung to be a cousin. Three generations back, on their fathers' sides, he claimed, correctly guessing that the boy's ignorance of and shame about his father would prevent any further argument.

The boy had been in America only a fortnight before signing on with the Sampson Manufacturing Company. He had heard in San Francisco that the man was fair, the contract reliable, the living circumstances bearable. He spoke little English and had only a mild interest in learning more. A wife waited for him in his home village. She was not wealthy, but neither was she a step down for his family, and he felt his time in America to be something he did for her and her family as well as for his. He imagined himself at the head of a large village parade, the rest of the villagers fanned out behind him. He had bragged, before his departure, of the houses he would build when he returned. And he bragged to his present coworkers of the gold he had already sent home.

His coworkers were of split mind concerning him. The older men found him reckless and full of himself but not particularly worrisome. The younger agreed but treated him as a charismatic and demanding older brother, some-one whose wishes you would not deny even if you found yourself capable of doing so.

Nothing he had seen in this country had convinced him it had anything of substance to offer. Nothing made him more saddened than the sight of one of his countrymen sacrificing the Eastern ways for the Western. It was a sad-ness grounded in rage and righteousness, as if these were affronts against him and against all those countrymen walking proudly behind him at the head of his parade.

And so the foreman caused him particular dismay. There was his name, and his conversion to the foreigners' house of worship. There were the rumors of the recent contract negotiations and his underhanded dealing. Every aspect that allowed his white acquaintances to say of him, "He is more akin to us than not" was proof for Ah Chung of Charlie's true inadequacies as a Chinaman. And if he was not a Chinaman, what kind of man could he be?

There had been rumors in Ah Chung's home village about the circumstances of Charlie's brother's death. Only rumors, but still. And now there was the matter of Chain Kow's death and burial. The twenty-year-old had died less than a month after Ah Chung's arrival, succumbing to pneumonia. The foreman had consulted with no one about the burial, which took place in the village cemetery and was presided over by Reverend T. A. Griffin of the Methodist church. A not insubstantial number of the Chinese had gathered to try and do what they could to see their friend into the world of the dead. Improper funeral arrangements could wreak all manner of ill fortune on the family of the deceased, and even the most recently arrived understood that for now, in this place, their fellow workers were family, and the factory home.

They managed to remove all mirrors from their dormitory. They cleaned the corpse with a damp towel dusted with talcum powder and dressed him in a good silk tunic and pants embroidered with dragons.

The traditional Chinese coffin, rectangular with three interior rises for neck, back, and legs, proved to be beyond the carpentry abilities of the coffin maker, who instead offered up a simple pine box with an expression that dissuaded the Chinese from asking for anything else or more.

They broke the deceased's comb in two, placed one part in the open coffin, and granted the other to his closest friend.

They had hoped the coffin would not be carried directly to the funeral but placed on the side of the road outside the factory, where more prayers could be offered, more paper scattered. They had hoped that someone, perhaps the foreman, would have informed the deceased in the prescribed way that the funeral procession would have to cross a body of water, as an uninformed soul, it was said, would not be able to make such a crossing.

The mix of unhappiness, fear, emasculation, and rage that they felt as one by one none of these hopes came to be realized was furthered upon their arrival at the cemetery. The plot their foreman had procured was not in the most preferable position, high on a hillside, but in a hollow at the base of one of the cemetery's smallest rises. "He is burying us in a ditch," Ah Chung whispered to the boy on his left. Beyond that, the foreman did not inform any of the whites that ritual demanded that when the coffin was taken down from the hearse and lowered into the ground, all present must turn away. So when that time came, some turned, others didn't, and still others commenced to, then stopped, looking around like lost chickens.

After the passage of seven days, Ah Chung took it upon himself to make a red plaque and place it outside the dormitory door to ensure that Chain Kow's returning soul would not get lost.

Returning to the bunk room after his exchange with his foreman, Ah Chung discovered that plaque laid haphazard on his bunk. He glanced at the only other occupant of the room, a boy laid low with fever. The sick boy returned his regard.

When Ah Chung demanded to know who had treated the plaque with such indifference, the boy answered simply, "Charlie Sing." And when Ah Chung asked whether he did not find this the behavior of a foreigner's dog, the worker said nothing at first, and then, turning his slow, feverish eyes upon his fellow Chinaman, said, "Cousins, wasn't it?"

Ah Chung reddened and retreated to his bunk, turning his back to this world and its occupants who once again proved to be the sources of nothing but disappointment and dismay.

In the classroom, Julia was at a table, trying to instruct a new boy while simultaneously navigating the complexities of Charlie's questioning and keeping an eye on a squirming and decidedly awake little girl.

Charlie spoke to her in English, confident that the boy could not follow the conversation's thread. Such was Charlie's state that he failed to realize that they might be overheard by the nearby instructors, and he further failed to note Ida's intense study from her table across the room.

He said he was dismayed not to have learned of the child from Julia herself at perhaps an earlier date than the rest of the town.

She looked at him, her face unguarded. She seemed confused about why he should have expected such a thing.

He allowed her silence, continuing to stare at the tiny being between them.

"They say it is a Celestial child," he finally said, sadly regarding the basket.

"They will say what they will," she said, pointing at the new boy's slate and her rough drawing of a snowman. "Snow-man," she said to him with exaggerated emphasis.

"Snow-man," he repeated dutifully.

Charlie could not summon the voice to ask further questions. Perhaps it was not his child, though the idea that she had known another Celestial seemed beyond belief. So perhaps the knowledge that it was his child was merely a room Julia did not want him to enter. The sadness that possibility provoked filled his lungs like water.

"We must find a way to speak about this," he said. Her attention, he understood, was everywhere but on him, and this understanding filled him with a desolation that he thought he could not stand. He wanted to pull her hair from its combs until she yelped.

She tapped the slate and showed the boy, by placing her hand over his, that she meant for him to copy her letters. He set to the task.

She rested a hand on the baby's belly. Beneath it, the girl wriggled and turned.

"I don't see why we must do that," Julia said softly, looking at him fully for the first time all afternoon.

He thought his horizon of misery could not be pushed any farther. His mind was a marsh of despair. So when Ida made her way across the room—much later, she would tell him that she had not been able to stand seeing him in such a state any longer—he barely heard her inquire the child's name.

"Alice," Julia said. "Alice May Sampson."

And just like that, he watched his horizon recede even farther, beyond his most pessimistic imaginings. His heart was in the grip of a giant's fist, and he could not see how to unlock its grasp.

Years later, Julia would marvel at how little concern he had been to her. Before being with child, she would not have guessed it would have been so. Why had she not thought of the small circle as a circle of three? Why had this man whom she would've said she loved not entered her mind? Thinking of this disregard would never fail to make her neck color. She was not the person she had thought herself to be. But was it only curse to discover this about oneself? Might it not also be opportunity?

Chapter Thirteen

The town spent the opening weeks of August turning in on itself like a nest of hatchling snakes, and all relevant parties—Sampson, Julia, Charlie, Ah Chung, even Ida, Lucy, and Alfred—should have understood that their own pertinacity was going to serve as the source of further turmoil rather than less. It was as if they'd become boys with sticks, poking and prodding, their good sense overpowered by the spirit of inquiry.

Even if made aware of this understanding, such was their single-mindedness that it was likely their course would have been unswerving. After all, they might have declared, would anything in their short lives have been achieved without a staunchness of purpose, a blinkered tenacity? Each was sure of the virtue of his or her own aims.

Ah Chung and Alfred would have been especially dismayed to learn that their resolve was a shared resolve, as

Alfred set his stock in these ideals as American born and bred, something passed from native father to native son like brown eyes, wavy hair, a good hand with animals. Ah Chung would have found these opinions mildly comical. Heaven and Earth had begun in China. In the beginning had been a black egg inside of which a man larger than any other slept. In his hands he held hammer and chisel, and after eighteen thousand years of sleep, he awoke, splitting the egg in two. The top part, illuminated and unclouded, became Heaven, and the bottom, thick and dark, Earth.

To Ah Chung's Chinese eye, this country was but a fledgling place. Americans had perhaps adapted aspects of Heaven and Earth, but as far as he was concerned they were the tiny creatures on the bodies of tiny creatures, of consequence in only the most minuscule way.

In addition, there was the distraction of several tragic accidents on a single day. Donald McKay had been struck by the engine of the early evening train. He died in his son's house as the clock struck nine.

While bathing in the Hoosac River, A. M. Parsons dove violently against a rock and received injuries that bettered the best efforts of both local physicians.

Thomas Kearns in trying to lace a broken belt at the Glen Mill had the belt catch in his clothing and his arm was torn completely from his body leaving, witnesses said, the joint bare. He left a widow and six small children, and became the third death of the eleventh day of August 1873.

For many of the townspeople, Julia and Sampson and several of the Chinese workers included, this particular accident

returned from memory the one involving poor Miss Houle in the sewing room of Sampson's own factory less than two years prior. While cleaning her machine, the lovely Miss Houle had her flowing hair caught by a shaft. In a moment it had been wound up and torn from her head together with a portion of her scalp, making a frightening and terribly painful wound. If not for the remarkable presence of mind of Charlie Sing, who had instantly caught and dragged her from the machine, she would undoubtedly have died. It was this that had kept the town's minds away from the one question that eventually, once it was clear the poor girl would make an almost full recovery, pushed its way to the surface, bursting through like a grateful swimmer: What was the foreman doing on the women's floor at all? What possible task could the Celestial, so early in his own education in shoe manufactury, have been pursuing in the stitching room?

The direction of this cart had been furthered down its rattling path by sixteen-year-old Yu Lee, who claimed shortly after the accident that his foreman was courting the lovely Miss Houle. Perhaps because he was, in fact, enjoying a nascent flirtation with the young lady, Charlie made a vehement and self-righteous request for the immediate dismissal of the talkative worker. The young lady's father, also a Sampson employee, made the same request. Their sense of justice mattered more to Sampson than the opinions of a boy whose name continued, throughout the dispute, to elude him, and so he had granted the request.

It had been silly, the boys told one another after Yu Lee's dismissal, to think that Gold Mountain would be different in all ways. The shores of both places were, after all, lapped by the same ocean. The circle in which they were told to stand was much the same, no matter how different the dirt into which it was drawn.

And so it was no surprise when, two years later, in mid-June, Charlie and Sampson attempted to make short work of Yu Lee's return to town to share glowing accounts of his success in a Springfield needle factory. Some said that Sampson, perhaps at his foreman's request, had had the man driven from town. When the newspaper ran a small article about the return, Sampson gave the editor an unprompted interview in which he avoided all mention of the former employee but was quoted as saying, "The three years for which the workers engaged has just expired and with a very few exceptions they are reengaged, and we have yet to hear of any threatened strike among them, or of any desire on their part to leave their new home."

James T. Robinson, the *Transcript*'s editor, inquired of his son and partner as they fed the letterpress whether he had heard any speculation of a Celestial strike. Arthur Robinson assured his father that he had not, and the elder Mr. Robinson said that it was curious that Mr. Sampson felt it necessary to squelch hearsay that didn't seem to exist.

And when Arthur Robinson set the type concerning the three deaths in a single day, nearly two months after Sampson's comment, which Arthur had so easily dismissed, he found himself surprised at his certainty that the accidents would prove to be harbingers of further unhappiness. This was not his usual line of thought. Even his father scoffed at him, though he would eventually regard him with newfound respect and wariness when, by week's end, the Chinese would strike.

Sampson's determination arrived partnered with increased impatience. Never a forbearing man, he now seemed to be striding across previously unexplored expanses of restiveness. His request of his foreman had been humiliating enough. To have to now wait for something productive to come from that conversation seemed too much to be asked of any man.

It seemed to Charlie that his employer stuck his head into the bottoming room once an hour just to catch Charlie's eye and then raise his eyebrows in inquiry. To all of these intrusions, Charlie would respond with a slight shake of his head, his eyes closed to the other workers, who, he was sure, were taking note of these exchanges.

If he wasn't climbing the stairs to the bottoming room, Sampson was summoning Charlie to his office. Had nothing come of his inquiries of Mrs. Sampson? Whom had he interviewed thus far? What were his own hunches? A man's gut, Sampson told him, was often the best barometer in such a situation.

Charlie told him that his gut was undisturbed, and he'd never before been in such a situation. He must ask patience. He understood the difficulty of the circumstances. He understood Sampson's unrest. He would, as he had promised, do what was in his power to see a resolution come to fruition. Surely Mr. Sampson understood the delicacy of the inquiries he had to make. The turning over of the soil had begun. Sampson must give him time for further unearthing. Sampson had his employee's pledge that eventually, soon, he would discover all that Sampson wanted to know.

Charlie's gut had in fact been nothing but disturbed since he'd seen Julia. He had been unable to keep down even the mildest broth. Headaches accompanied those of the stomach. Even the dimmest of the boys had noted Charlie's excessive licorice consumption. Some of the boys trusted him. Many did not. The increased contact with Sampson was not a help in this regard.

But most importantly, he did not want what Sampson wanted. What Charlie wanted was to alter Sampson's attitude toward the information he could already produce. This he could not see how to manage.

As Sampson grew more restive, Julia found herself to be more and more an evergreen of extraordinary height and strength, with solid roots spreading in directions she had never imagined. The undeniable need of women to have child after child began to make a different kind of sense to her.

She was not insensitive to the stares and whispers, and she was, of course, exhausted and worn by her husband's daily pronouncements, but she felt all of it to be the insignificant circus acts of performers far below her. She and Alice stood amid the clouds, swaying in the breeze.

So on Wednesday, when her husband returned home announcing he had made a decision, she steeled herself to argue against it. She needed help with the child, he said. He had found someone to give it.

"Alice and I need nothing and no one save each other," she replied. She believed what she said so completely that she missed the hurt and sadness that her comment had conjured across her husband's face.

He stuck his hands in his back pockets and set his weight onto his heels. "You must let me give you this," he said quietly. "You have removed yourself from our life," he said. "I am trying to find my way back to you."

He could not look at her while he spoke. He had been inexplicably pleased to discover the girl he had noted during that first Sunday school lesson was the same Lucy Robinson who had suffered the infamous attack. He had been even more pleased when she had agreed to be taken on as a housegirl. Lucy's attack had cemented her in his mind as someone in need, so a request made of her did not further the humiliations he was suffering from all corners. When he had quoted the salary to her, her eyes had filled with surprised gratitude, and he was reminded in one stroke of how much he had been missing from his wife these past weeks. He was sure he could somehow explain this to Julia.

He stood there looking at his wife's large feet in her well-made boots, his sadness an iron band around his chest. When had they become a husband and wife who needed the explanations of polite strangers?

She regarded him. What it cost him to speak to her this way did not escape her. She swallowed what she had been saying to him in one way or another since her return, though she wanted nothing more than to tell him again that the one thing he could do for her was to welcome this baby as his own.

"Who is it?" she asked.

"It is someone you like," he said. "Young Lucy Robinson."

She felt like a cornered cat. She did like Lucy Robinson. She had told her husband so upon her return from last Sunday's Celestial class. "You are using my own feelings against me," she said.

He looked genuinely pained. He pulled his hands from his pockets and tugged at his hair as if to create more discomfort for himself. "I am never against you," he said. "I am always and already with you in body and spirit."

She looked unconvinced. Given the nature of their arguments since her return, she knew just what a divide existed between their particular desires. When had this happened? Was the responsibility for it hers alone? Not so long ago, she would have said there was no couple more in harmony. Almost every one of their days had ended with the two of them in their bed, their bodies fitting to each other like good silver in its velvet-lined case. It had been the source of her pity for the situations of other women.

Alice cried out from her bassinet at Julia's feet, and Julia bent to retrieve her. "What do you imagine she will do for us?" she asked.

Over the past days, Sampson had been struck each time by the way the baby in her arms turned the familiar shape of his wife into a foreign country, the contours of her borders faintly threatening. The resolve he had carried upon entering the room was slipping from his fingers like silt. "Whatever you require," he said vaguely.

Alice's scent filled Julia's nose and mouth. She could taste her at the back of her throat. "You know what I need," she said.

His eyes returned to the carpet she had felt an extravagance but he had purchased anyway. In one way or another, she had spent the time since her return asking him to turn his back on what the whole town knew, to carry on down this road on which she had embarked with not a word from her, his supposed partner on all roads. *Walk with me*, she was asking, *as father of this child*. And he had asked her in one way or another to request anything else of him, anything at all. "I cannot give you that," he said now.

Alice squirmed in Julia's arms, demanding attention. Julia gave her a finger to grip. "Are you absolutely sure?" she asked, looking at her child's round, healthy face. She was such an old mother. How would she give this child everything she needed? She felt suddenly depleted, a wool blanket wet and wrung out. All she wanted was for him to take her by the corners, shake her loose and spread her in the sun.

"I have spent my whole adult life loving you," she said.

Not all of it, he thought. "And I you," he said, still unable to meet her eyes.

"I know what I am asking," she said. "I know what an enormous and exceptional thing it is." She took a step toward him and then stopped, worried that if they came within too close a proximity of each other, she would lose her commitment. "But I am not asking it of you alone. I am asking it of us. Together."

Her heart was a gyroscope of determination and fear. She warned him to take his time before responding, to understand what it would mean for him to refuse them this. "Do you really want to stand before your wife of twenty-four years and tell her that despite all the obvious difficulties there is something inside of you that cannot allow the two of us to have and enjoy the one thing that has been missing from our otherwise healthy and blessed life?"

Sampson swayed on his stiff legs as if she had knocked him from side to side. She had conceived this child with another man. A Chinaman. He looked up quickly, regaining some of his familiar fortitude, and said, "Obvious difficulties? You are being either disingenuous or ignorant or both."

She went on as though he had said nothing. "I have always understood you to have sympathized with my grief and to have shared it as if it were your own. Was I so mistaken in my understandings?"

Sampson held on to the back of the nearest chair. Whatever familiar strength he had mustered was gone. How had his life come to this point? For what was he being punished?

"I want to do this for you," he said, his voice like nothing either of them had previously heard. "But I cannot see how." Despite everything, he wished to cross the room and take her hand in his, but if she were to refuse him, as he feared she would, he knew he could not stand it. Instead, he sank to the floor, his back against the chair leg, his knees pulled up.

She had not seen him like this since he was a young man. Her heart was a bird searching for a way out of a windowless room. She set Alice back into the bassinet and made her way to him. She knelt, her skirt covering his feet, and took his hands in hers. He had been betrayed, yet her touch made him dizzy with gratitude.

"If you knew," she whispered slowly, "would that be enough? Could you then go on?"

His head was a small spinning part, unclear of the larger machine's functions.

"If you had the knowledge, could you then deny it and continue with this life we thought we would not have the chance to inhabit?"

She wondered if he could do this, but she felt herself to be in a deep pit, and this the rope lowered to her from above. And so she placed her hands on his chest and leaned in to him. "Could you do that for me?" she asked, laying an emphasis on her final two words.

In the days since Charlie's encounter with Julia at Sunday lessons, he had spent what little spare time he had making his daughter a pair of shoes. Traditional stitch-soled, black cloth shoes. For the necessary materials, he deconstructed a pair of his own cloth shoes, the ones his mother had made for him, that he had worn on the ship to California, that he still wore at his workbench in the factory. He worked at night, by lamp, in a narrow field up the hill from the factory. He carried the required tools in a shoulder sack, a glass jar filled with tea, and a low stool upon which to sit. To his curious fellow Celestials, he explained that he was going to find a place of more quiet and calm to study his Bible. It was not an explanation that did anything to endear him to his charges, but it was an explanation that they regarded as true.

He used the palm of his hand to measure the white cotton soles. Between the soles and the black cotton uppers, he stitched a small ribbon of bright blue taken from the hem of one of his tunics. The sewing took longer than he expected, his missing thumb making him awkward with needle and thread, but he was happy to be working on a project such as this and felt no impatience with the time it was taking.

When he was done, he placed one of the shoes on his open palm and looked at it this way and that. He turned it over and saw his own patterns of wear on its sole. He slipped three fingers into the shoe and felt the depressions and dips of his own stride. Yes, he thought in his small circle of light, his daughter would walk in these shoes.

One of Lucy Robinson's first tasks was to arrange a meeting between Charlie Sing and Mrs. Sampson. This was on a Friday in the middle of a workday.

Lucy's hands, busy folding Alice's tiny necessities, stilled at her employer's request, but her expression remained unreadable. After a moment, she said, "The best time might be after the factory is down for the evening."

Later, Julia would chastise herself for making this request of Lucy so quickly. She would determine that if she had really cared for the girl, she would not have given her access to a matter so private. But at the time, Julia had very few wagons coursing about her mind except those containing her own needs, and so she experienced only thankfulness at having two heads rather than one to apply to the task at hand.

And Lucy's was a particularly efficient head. It was as if she had been asked to orchestrate the discreet and delicate every day of her young life. The Widow Allen's carriage barn, she informed Julia, had not been used in years and lay at the outermost edge of the widow's vast property in the dip of a high hill. One could approach it from field rather than road. She had somehow managed to get word to Charlie while calling just the right attention to herself by stopping in to Sampson's office to say that she was there to deliver a primer to the foreman for one of the new boys and she had thought Mr. Sampson might like to hear that his wife and child were passing a lovely, undisturbed morning.

Sampson had not asked for such reports, but was pleased enough at both the message and the messenger that he made no further inquiries.

She did indeed pass a primer to Charlie, in such a way that he was sure to see the small corner of Julia's stationery revealing itself from the leaves of the book. She attempted to quiet his alarm with a kind smile.

It seemed to her, as she returned to the Wilson House, that she was not of this world but gliding through it, touching its living inhabitants here and there, leaving warmth in her wake. It was a pleasure to think about herself in this unfamiliar way for a while, and it was the first time she had felt her alien nature as blessing rather than burden, and she resolved to speak to Alfred about staying in North Adams, at least for the time being.

Fannie Burlingame waited for a time when she knew there was no danger of finding Sampson at home to call on Julia. It was an awkward conversation for both women, but Fannie soldiered on, sure in her belief that often the most virtuous ends require the most difficult means.

Politely perched in two stiff chairs in the front room, the women faced each other, Alice in her basket on the floor between them making her infant sounds.

"I am not," Fannie reassured for the second time, "suggesting that any relationship at all is something of which to disapprove."

Julia nodded, refraining from saying that she wouldn't think that's what her dear cousin would be suggesting, given her own relationship with her own Celestial.

Fannie stood, suddenly impatient. "Please, Julia," she said. "You are married. To my cousin." She broke off as if dismayed at having to make things even this overt. "You cannot have *relations* with one of these boys."

Julia reddened, but said nothing.

"You cannot have a *child* fathered by one of them." Fannie looked at Alice. "Really, Julia. What were you thinking?" she asked.

And maybe because Fannie was unable to keep the scolding schoolmistress out of her voice, maybe because

Julia knew that if she was to weather the war, she must weather battles such as these one by one, over and over, she stood, gathered baby Alice to her chest like a shield, and told her cousin that she didn't know what Fannie thought she knew, but she found this visit insulting and beneath them both. Fannie's thoughts belonged to no one but herself, as did Julia's, and to share them was perhaps unwise for both of them.

The Widow Allen's husband had run a livery service but had been neither a horseman nor a businessman and the company had been an outright failure. The carriage barn held the vestiges of his defeat. Dry and cracked collars, hames, and harnesses hung haphazard from the tongues and shaves of coaches and surreys all inappropriately extravagant for such a business in such a town. Mr. Allen had suffered from delusions of his own grandeur, and the purchases he had made to stock his company had reflected these fantasies. His large team had pulled a carriage he had ordered from England that was said to be modeled on the one in which the king himself rode. There it stood, large and oafish as a dull child kept back in school, against the carriage house's far wall. Its paint was chipped; its leather thoroughbraces, trunk, and driver's boot as cracked as a creek bed during a drought. The steel spreader bar was dull and rusty, and the hand-painted eagle on the door a ghost image.

Charlie felt as if, within an already foreign world, he had turned a corner into something even more unknown. He wanted to run.

He had arrived early, positioning himself in a back corner where, between the boards of two walls, he had clear view over several approaches to the barn.

His ears pulsed with the strain of listening. Would he be able to tell Julia's footfall from another's? Just how much had she told this Lucy Robinson, and to whom else was she speaking? Because she had handed him nothing but silence in his further attempts to speak with her, it had not occurred to him that she might be sharing something different with others. He swallowed, coughed dryly, and swallowed again.

One jacket pocket held the portrait he had never presented, the other held the small shoes. His slim fingers returned to his tie and collar like an insect feeling its way. What kind of image would he cast in her eyes? From their first embrace in late spring 1872 to her departure for Florida in January, he had been unable to imagine what she saw when he stood before her. Once, when he had been feeling particularly cared for, he had asked. It had been evening, an early November chill in the air. They were in the spot they liked best, in the shadow of Balance Rock, the large blanket she had brought with them tucked tightly under their chins. They were both growing cold, but neither of them wanted to move to get fully dressed.

He tucked his nose beneath the blanket and inhaled.

"What are you doing?" she said, smiling.

"Smell you," he said.

She didn't know if he meant that was what he was doing or what she should do. Both made her blush.

He told her that when he saw her, he saw as well a memory that always gave him pleasure: his father swinging on the big gate to the far field at the end of another long workday. The sun had been low, his father's exhaustion clear, but as the fence made its big arc, his father balanced on one foot on the lowest rung, Charlie had also seen the happy boy beneath the tired man.

Her eyes had filled with tears of pleasure; she had placed a hand against his broad cheek, and he had felt enough out of harm's way to ask, what about her? What did she see?

She hesitated, and somewhere his heart told him to leave this particular line of inquiry where it was. He had spent his life in this country in continuous states of wariness about the answers to various forms of that question. And perhaps because of that, he continued to push at a place that if he had been honest, he knew would give way.

He flipped the blanket away, revealing his naked chest to the air and to her. Her face filled with anxiety. He asked her again to tell him what she saw.

She told him not to be silly and tried to cover him. Again, his heart gave him its warnings, and again he ignored it.

"I need to know," he said.

He wanted to know what she saw *of* him so that he could know what she saw *in* him. And in her hesitancy he had his answer, but he had spent the ensuing months convincing himself that it was within his power to change it. What other option did he have? Could the ability to be a chameleon, a trait so strong in him, really be equally strong in her?

She approached the barn from the far field, picking her way with small steps through the tall grass. It was the gait that came over her when she was nervous. And she wore the expression he had seen whenever he had asked something new or unfamiliar of her. The time he had pushed her on the swing they had discovered in a clearing miles away from any houses, hanging from a branch of a sturdy chestnut. The time he had made her close her eyes and taste his brew of ginger and chrysanthemum. On such occasions, her face was adorned with a mix of caution and optimism and it had filled his heart to tipping.

The baby swayed in its basket against her hip. When she neared the barn, she paused, rolled her shoulders back, and took on the look of a Temperance Society representative, and whatever hopes he had for this meeting jumped away like the grasshoppers escaping her footfall.

Lucy and Ida were being impatient with each other, and Alfred regarded them from his chair by the window the way you might watch two dogs threatening to disagree.

Even the few days Lucy had spent in the Sampsons' Wilson House rooms had been enough to make the tenement apartment smaller and more inadequate. She couldn't help but note the grime on the sills, the mold above the stove, the stains in the basin. The smell of vinegar did nothing to eliminate the lingering odors of the previous lives lived in these rooms.

And this particular Friday, she had the added affront of Mrs. Sampson sallying forth to a secret adventure. No matter that Lucy's role in arranging the adventure had brought her pleasure. Now all she saw was a life extraordinarily different from her own.

She wanted to tip Alfred from that seat that he seemed never to vacate and dump the soup Ida was skimming all over her leather boots. The room revealed at least a dozen other things with which to find fault.

Ida looked up and smiled. "You're late," she said.

The girls' intimacy made Alfred nervous, thankful as he was for it. Just yesterday, Daniel had asked, innocently enough, why neither Lucy nor Ida ever stepped out with any of the local boys. He added that some of the boys thought the girls might believe themselves to be better than regular folks. Alfred had used what he knew to be the tried-and-true technique of reminding others of the lingering effects of Lucy's attack. Daniel had blanched and stumbled to say he hadn't meant any offense.

"Is the Widow Allen not serving supper tonight?" Lucy asked as though in collusion with her brother's unspoken mind.

Ida reddened and studied the soup with great interest. "You're taking such care of that baby, I thought you might be able to use some help over here," she said, regaining herself.

Lucy straightened Alfred's work boots, which lay at odds with each other by the door. She picked up Ida's hat and gloves from the kitchen chair and laid them on the front table. "Thank you," she said as though she meant just the opposite.

Ida set the table with three bowls and poured three glasses of milk. "And how is that baby?"

Lucy ignored her. Ida had made no secret of her objections to Lucy's new position. She had argued that Lucy already had the solid and enjoyable work of dressmaking. She spoke of the flexibility of hours, the advantages of working for no one but oneself, but they both knew that what bothered her most was that the job took Lucy away from her. If Lucy no longer needed Ida's care, Ida was no longer needed at all by anyone. In Ida's mind, it was as if Lucy had dismissed her, and though Lucy would never admit it to herself, this had in actuality been part of the job's appeal. If asked, she would've insisted that Ida's new interests had caused her nothing but pain. She wouldn't know how to say that she had, in some part, begun to feel herself a tiny, caged thing, and Ida both fellow animal and eternal custodian. Her asthma had worsened as if Ida's hand were closing around her lungs. Sometimes when Ida was sitting especially near, Lucy could hear the small cracking sounds of delicate things breaking.

From the beginning, she had felt that the baby needed to be held away from her dear friend. It saddened her, but it also made her reckless, though she couldn't have explained how or why this was the case. And so she apologized to both her brother and her friend for her petulance, and included them warmly in her prayers preceding their meal, but they weren't halfway to the meal's end before she told them, relevant to nothing, that baby Alice was fine, currently, in fact, accompanying her mother on an errand of private purpose. She went on unbidden, laying bare the details as she knew them.

★

The baby regarded Charlie as he soldiered on, reaching into his satchel for the gifts he had been saving. He tucked the coins on their red string and the tiny peachwood arrow by her blanketed feet, and tried to place the rice-filled pillow beneath her head, but settled for next to her ear. He was saving the shoes and the portrait for last.

He explained each item's purpose while skepticism painted itself faintly across Julia's face. When he told her the arrow was for protection against demons who looked to steal children for the purpose of reinforcing the foundations of bridges, her skepticism blossomed into scorn.

"The foundations of bridges?" she repeated, and swept all three items expertly out of the basket and into her bag.

"The pillow is made from a scarf of my mother's," he said.

She buttoned the bag shut deftly with one hand and set it back on her arm. The basket hung from her other arm. She seemed unwilling to relieve herself of anything. Her hat remained on her head. Her hands remained gloved.

"I made those things," he said.

"They're lovely," she said. "We thank you."

It was the voice he'd heard her use with store clerks. His insides were expanses of ice forming across dark water. He touched a finger to the baby's forehead. Her eyes tried to follow it in that haphazard infant manner. She looked to him like a lunatic grandmother, and he wondered whether people were right about the consequences of mixing the races, but then the baby's eyes settled and he saw himself, his brothers, and grandparents. He leaned in to look closer, as if he might be able to see a miniature rendering of his entire village.

Julia pulled the basket and the baby slightly out of reach. "I know you are disappointed," she said in the manner of someone who has grown impatient with formalities. "I think I have some idea of what your hopes may have been, and I am sorry that they cannot be realized." She was speaking as though if she did not make haste, she might forget where she was going, and her voice had the determined fragility of a young girl arguing with her mother. "But I am counting on your good sense to help me do what is best for all involved." She readjusted the basket. "I am sure you will agree that Alice's well-being must be put above all else." And now the fragility won out, her voice breaking like dry kindling.

He cupped her neck with both his hands, and she stopped speaking.

"Why do you use this voice with me?" he said, putting his head close to hers.

She closed her eyes as if her head ached. The basket was wedged between their legs. Alice regarded the shadows that had fallen across her.

"This is me," he said. "I know you," he said.

She was crying. She put her bag and the basket down on the dirt floor uneven with the hardened ruts of old wheel tracks. Outside, the sun had fallen, but the cool wave of evening had yet to break over them. A disoriented bat swept above them in the rafters. In the house across the field, the Widow Allen began her lonely preparations for a supper for one. She kept her head bent to her kitchen tasks, her eyes away from the windows with a view of the hill. Even the thought of the barn filled her with a sense of all she had lost. She did not see Ida making her way up the road, which was just as well, as Ida was not heading for the house but for the shed at the crest of the hill, where she planned to wait and see what she would see. The sight of yet another receding back would have been too much for the widow to bear, and she would have skipped yet another meal.

Julia wiped her tears with Charlie's hand. "It is all too hard," she said. "I see only one way through." And then she explained what her husband had promised her. If she would just give him the name of the father, he would do nothing with it but tuck it away in a locked drawer. If she would just give him that, he would uphold the roof under which Alice could flourish.

Charlie's core thawed and rushed with the warmth of fear. His lungs filled with spring melt. He opened his mouth, but said nothing.

She said, "I cannot see how any other options are actual possibilities." She hooded her eyes with his hand and looked at his feet. "What *can* I do?" she asked, her voice stronger.

Her need for him made him feel as though he'd woken from the best kind of sleep, but he saw the two of them as if on a stage, an orderly and judgmental audience all around them.

Her eyes were filled with animal sentiment. "I cannot have this child taken from me," she said. "I would not survive it."

He found his voice, ready to offer what he was sure she was seeking. "We can be family," he said. He made a circle with their two hands, the nub where his thumb should've been against her palm, and reached into his pocket with his free hand for the shoes.

He felt the muscles tighten in her arm before he saw the cast of her face, but both told him that he had been mistaken. She was a performer; he was the audience of one who had been too rapt by the drama to see its inevitable conclusion. He could imagine her asking what exactly he expected could become of the two of them together. She would be right. So clear was his sudden understanding that he knew what she would say before she spoke. He was not even shocked at its magnitude.

She needed a name. "Please," she said, still holding his hand. Her eyes were full of fear and love, but not for him. He withdrew his hand from his pocket. His heart was a massive animal brought to its knees.

Chapter Fourteen

Ida did not wait at the shed as she had planned to. The sun had dropped completely behind the hills, the sky had dimmed and blued, and something about the leftover light and the busy work of the doves in the cornfield made her feel small and shamed. She imagined her father observing her and asking, his voice filled with disappointment and love, whether this was really the path she wanted to take. Knowing one thing about a person did not mean you needed to find out another. People deserved to live the delights and burdens of their lives in private.

She had until now found this attitude an excuse for his lack of curiosity. He could pass hours in his workshop figuring out the mechanism of a spring, the weights and pulleys of a clock, but ask one question of him about the whys and wherefores of a sister or a teacher, a friend or a cousin, and he would pinch the top of his nose with his slater's hands and shake his head as if a dog he had always thought well of had misbehaved. But now she saw his inclination as kind and generous, something simple but of certain value.

So she returned to her room in the widow's home, but sitting there in her small attic chamber, the heat like wool against her skin, she found herself thinking of the mix of sadness and rage in her brothers, the solitude of her father, the excessive busyness of her mother. Each thing she embraced here was like brick after brick in the wall she was building between them and her. Her father was a kind, good man, but there were things about herself she would never be able to share with him.

She understood her interest in Charlie to be the latest of these bricks. His eyes were level and slow and she'd never seen him in anything but a reasonable state of calm. He was more like a woman than any man she'd known and it was hard, therefore, not to think more highly of him than perhaps he deserved.

In her attic room, her mind went this way and that along these routes, and got so lost that she dozed fully clothed, one foot off her single bed. When she woke, an owl called from a distant tree and received no response. The boards creaked as the Widow Allen made her way downstairs, enduring another sleepless night.

Ida made no attempts to disrobe or even remove her boots. She examined the six squares of night sky mottled by her window glass and found herself wishing she knew more than she did about the constellations. She turned the night's dinner conversation over and imagined the information Lucy had offered and what Ida herself already suspected as stars in that black sky, the heavenly body they made fractured and unclear.

Appearances aside, who could know the completeness of what had passed between Mrs. Sampson and the foreman? And what right did any of them have to prod in a pond whose only obvious qualities were its depth and murk? Lucy and Alfred had decided to stay in town for the foreseeable future. She knew what mischief someone like Alfred could get up to. She would not do damage here. In the morning she must convince Alfred of the same. Her father would be pleased by her decision and the reasons for it.

But the full truth was at that point in her life beyond her understanding. Her mind, in its wandering that night, kept returning to speculation of what might have passed between the Celestial and the white woman. And to a fascination of such pull that she could no more turn away from it and its implications than a child could from an open door through which she was not meant to be looking.

Given how the rest of their evening had gone, Alfred thought it best to vacate the apartment well before his sister rose the next morning.

He had quizzed her as much as she would stand for the rest of the night. Her loss of patience had been to his mind so mean-spirited that he had felt forced to point out that if she had not wanted to reveal any more, she should have revealed nothing at all. And anyway, he had added, he didn't need her information. Had she forgotten that he'd been at the depot the day of Mrs. Sampson's return? He'd seen that rat eater concealing himself like a thief. She hadn't seen the expression on his face.

Ida had been as dismissive as he'd ever seen her be with him. She couldn't imagine what exactly he thought he knew, but there were any number of things beyond his conception that the foreman and Mrs. Sampson could be meeting about, and he had no idea where that baby had come from. As a matter of fact, it might not have been born from Mrs. Sampson at all; she might've gone away to purchase her very own Celestial child. As she spoke, she began to believe in the possibility of her own arguments. None of them had the faintest idea what lengths a woman of Mrs. Sampson's means would go to to find herself a baby after all these years. No, she'd said before gathering her hat and gloves, she would not sit around listening to this drivel, and he would do best to refrain from speaking any more of it.

Once Ida had left, his sister announced that she regretted ever sharing the tiniest crumb of the tiniest crumb with her thick and doltish brother and that she would certainly not do so again, and then she retired to her sleeping area, making more noise than necessary in her preparations for bed.

He now had no idea what to think, though he felt what he almost always felt: resentful and hurt. He had not even wanted to risk heating his morning coffee, and so had taken a tin cupful of what was left in the pot with him. He drained that before he reached the corner of Pearl and Main, and tossed the cup into the shrubs behind the Murphy house.

His only goal was to head toward the Sampson factory with no clear aim about what he would do upon arrival. He felt as he had as a boy when he'd secretly known Lucy to be lying to their parents. He hadn't wanted to reveal her lie; he'd just wanted to watch her perform it. How or whether that situation bore on this one was not clear to him; one had merely conjured for him the other, and so when he saw Homer Handley heading to the factory, he fell into step alongside, asking cheerily what Homer knew on this fine morning.

Homer was made wary by young Alfred, warier still by the last week's whisperings. But even prior to that, Homer had found the boy shifty and too needy to fully trust. His looks were not reassuring. He had the face of a rich man demoted to a farmer's life. And he was Southern. Homer's ancestors were Massachusetts-born a hundred years back. He found himself bothered by the way the boy said, "Nice to see you," instead of "Nice to meet you." He didn't like his accent. It made the boy sound ignorant. He knew that when he returned home that evening and related these sentiments to his wife, she would remind him that this past week had been hard on a lot of folks, and that surely the one solution here was more charity, not less.

He imagined her fingers plucking burrs from his trouser leg and felt a calm settle over him. He could stand anything for a short time, and so he kept the judgment out of his voice and answered as his most convivial self, "Not much." He could not think what else to add.

Alfred had his hands in his pockets, shrugged his shoulders up to his ears, and then dropped them again.

Homer comforted himself with the thought that in a few yards they would reach the gate of the factory, through which Homer had all rights to pass and Alfred none.

"Sounds like things inside these walls have been up one hill and down another," the boy said, indicating the factory.

Homer's gut hardened against the clumsy investigating. He wanted to cuff the boy lightly and remind him of all he didn't know. "Shoes and boots," he said. "Still and always, I imagine."

Alfred seemed especially pleased by this, as if he'd been administering a quiz and Homer had finally performed up to expectation. "Maybe not," he said, drawing his hands from his pockets and circling them into an overhead stretch.

Homer did not have a chance to ask what the boy thought he was talking about, though even without the commencement of the strike that interrupted them, Homer would not have put that question to him, not wanting to give the fool the satisfaction.

The Sampsons would not learn about the strike until early evening, as they had been taken over the mountain by Mr. Gavitt with a six-in-hand to picnic at the cascade near the eastern portal of the tunnel. They had been invited by Dr. Anable and his brother, with their wives, of course. Also joining the party were George and Susanna Butler, Everett and Caroline Southwick, and Elias S. and Rose T. Wilkinson.

Sampson had felt they should absent themselves from the plans. He had an assortment of reasons, all of which he felt too obvious to have to outline, although he did say he must conclude that the invitation had been extended out of something other than courtesy.

Julia, who had been sleepless with nerves the previous night, her conversation with Charlie stampeding through her heart, busied herself with packing several baskets' worth of infant needs and pretended not to have heard. Perhaps because of her meeting with Charlie, she felt even more acutely the need to make her public way in the world, Alice and her husband at her side. Whereas prior to the conversation she had felt herself to be forging ahead into a moonless night, she now felt she'd been handed a torch and a small, lucid map. She understood this to be a rational way to feel. When, after all, had Charlie refused her anything? Her mind held tight to this fact, letting loose its grip on the equal certainties that this was a request that pitted him against his own and one designed to help her secure a life from which he was to be excluded.

Her husband stood in his usual office dress, unable to have discovered anything in his wardrobe appropriate to picnicking. She thought to say that if he was really to keep to his promise, he must become familiar with traveling as three. "I think," she said, quietly, "that a lovely, unencumbered day at the cascade would be just the remedy for me."

His objections faded, as she knew they would. How had she managed to surround herself with two men wanting so badly to please her? How had she managed to be grateful enough for neither?

The group that poured out of the factory was a most unusual sight. Led by Ah Chung, some carrying their peg rasps, their shirtsleeves rolled above the elbows, the dozen or so men strode quickly into the factory's side yard as if they had suddenly remembered something of dire import await-ing their attention. They constituted barely one-sixteenth of the total number in Sampson's employ, yet they walked as though a mob of two hundred. In the early morning August sun, it was as if a group of sleepwalking children came to from a dream, disoriented and uncertain.

They flocked near the back stoop and watched Ah Chung pace across the yard.

And while the white workers and the remaining Chinese hovered in the doorway, watching the peculiarities of the day unfold the way one sibling keeps his eye peeled to the pun-ishment of another, Charlie made his way into the group and stopped. "Where are you going?" he called to Ah Chung in Chinese, trying to fill his voice with offhanded curiosity.

The group turned toward Ah Chung and Charlie knew that when the boy looked around, he would see a dozen men aligned with Charlie at their center.

Continuing to overestimate his own power would be one of his mistakes in the months and years to come. He should not have, just an hour ago in the dining quarters, brought up the subject of the baby. He should not have pursued his questioning about paternity. He should not have offered bonus pay for relevant information. He should certainly, at any rate, have noted the changing atmosphere of the room. He should have taken more complete note of Ah Chung's countenance, and he should have done the same now as the boy turned to regard his foreman.

Ah Chung smiled. "Hello, Cousin," he said, and then asked if Charlie wanted to ask more questions.

Charlie asked again where the boy thought he was going. The others in the group watched as if they, too, were curious.

Ah Chung said he was going to talk to Sampson. He said maybe Charlie should ask himself some questions.

Charlie told him to behave.

"Behave?" the boy said. He addressed the group. He was not the one, he said, who had pledged his loyalty to a white man. He was not the one whose bundle of gold coins at the end of every week was so much weightier than the rest. He was not the one making funeral arrangements and employment decisions. He was not the one dining in white homes, buying the white man's turkeys for the white man's holidays.

He gestured for the group to join him on the grass. He waited for the boys to settle around him and then suggested that perhaps Charlie had left more than his brother on that boat. He put voice to what they all felt: the only brothers they had in this strange country were each other. Would the foreman treat them the way he had treated his own relations?

Ah Chung turned to Charlie. "I hear from my village that your mother still grieves the loss of her youngest son."

Charlie said nothing, though he knew it was a damaging silence to hold.

By this point, even the girls in the sewing room were sitting on sills, trying to ascertain meaning from their aerial views. Some of the white men asked the Chinese boys near them to translate. All they could manage with their limited English was to shake their heads and offer, "Very bad."

"I've never gone to meet Mrs. Sampson in her house," Ah Chung said, scanning the group. "You?" he asked the youngest boy.

Charlie knew what was required of him if he wanted to regain any of the ground slipping away. He must speak of the mixing of the races the way these peasant boys thought of it. He must speak of the baby as the perversion they thought her to be. He must infer about Julia the same thing. And this was where his mind shut down. Though he had spent the night wounded and sick with sadness, even rage, at her, he could not share that with these boys. So he continued to say nothing, and Ah Chung took his hesitancy and held it up to them as more evidence of the foreman's misplaced loyalties. Charlie understood that he might be right. The vessel Charlie had been sailing since his arrival in this country, to carry him to a safe place, began to rock beneath him. Those with him began to leap away, taking their chances in the surrounding waters. He wanted nothing more than to join them. Instead, he turned and made his way through the crowd at the door back into the building.

It was Homer Handley who convinced Ah Chung to return the boys to the factory. Who knew when Sampson would agree to meet with them, if at all? What aim would it accomplish for the group to sit out in the unforgiving sun?

"We not work," Ah Chung said to him.

Homer shrugged. "Do what you want," he said. "Just seems wiser to do it inside."

And so, even with Alfred Robinson's eyewitness account, it was a difficult strike for the *Transcript* editors to describe in the following Thursday's paper. It resembled not at all the strikes they were familiar with reporting. There was no threatening of the sort the newspapermen were accustomed to. What seemed to be occupying most of the Celestials' time was a kind of well-mannered refusal. They refused to leave their quarters. They refused to ascend to the bottoming room, where the number of tables at work was reduced by only four. When the time came, they ate and drank and laughed with those who chose to continue working. Sampson had supplied them with room and board and they did not see reason to deny themselves what they had been contractually promised. They made no speeches. What discussion there was took place in small circles of wooden stools pulled close enough to speak with no question of being heard.

Flummoxed, father and son Robinson resorted to a six-line story on page three of a four-page newspaper.

Mr. Sampson's Chinese Workmen

As false and exagerated stories are afloat concerning a temporary trouble in Mr. Sampson's establishment, we are prompted to state the facts. A portion of the old workmen had a dispute amongst themselves, not with Mr. Sampson. This trouble lasted for a day or so, but was settled, and on Tuesday they all went to work and everything is proceeding as before. This is all there was of the "strike."

On Thursday morning, her coffee cold and her daughter growing impatient, Julia read the article and was bothered by it in ways she couldn't fully fathom. Her mind faltered at the word *settled* and again at the phrase *proceeding as before*. Somehow, she felt the editors had missed the point. She believed, without knowing why, that the events of the last few days suggested that these boys were not going to be held within rooms of her husband's making anymore. Perhaps even Charlie would not have the sway over them that he had enjoyed. And she discovered that these apprehensions on her part prompted concern not for her husband, or for Charlie, or even for the boys themselves. Her own situation, after all, allowed for a certain sympathy with their desire to break free of the fences behind which they had been instructed to live. She wanted only to know what the heavens had in store for herself and her child and who could help her avoid it.

Chapter Fifteen

Sunday the seventeenth of August was filled with thunderstorms, the skies a slate gray, the leaves under assault by wind and water. Alfred's boots were wet through, his skin white and puckered within his wool stockings. If it had not been Ida doing the asking, he would not have found himself in the street's muddy ruts on an evening such as this heading toward church, for him the most unlikely of destinations.

The Reverend Mr. Bartlett of Lowell and a Professor Hitchcock of Amherst, both agents of the Massachusetts Total Abstinence Society, were to address the public. When Ida had arrived at the apartment after supper, Alfred tried to raise the topic of the strike and what it might mean in terms of his suspicions about Charlie, but Ida had cut him off with news of the Society's meeting. All were welcome, Ida had assured him. It would please her if he would come along. When she saw his face, she asked whether he really so much preferred his beer to her, and he flushed and reached for his hat.

The Baptist church was filled, the inside air close and humid. They were able to secure two seats halfway down the aisle, but the pews were overcrowded and Alfred found himself pressed damply between Ida and a large bearded man who seemed unwashed by anything save the rain. Alfred moved closer to Ida, and though she did not object, neither did she yield any more space to him, so he sat, miserable, and tried to make his frame narrower than God had seen fit for it to be.

Julia was in the front row, the baby sleeping against her shoulder. Even those standing restlessly behind the church's last pews could see the child's spray of black hair against her white bonnet. Mrs. Vera Pendleton suggested to her husband that it was as if Mrs. Sampson had chosen the bonnet for the express purpose of making a show of the hair's color, and her husband, who did not like to agree with his wife unless offered no other path, had to concur that it did indeed seem that she was bent on flaunting the child in ways that did not strike him as completely necessary.

Lucy and Sampson, who had arrived late, sat a row behind the Pendletons, and Lucy held out hope that either her employer had not been attuned to their talk or that he had not been dealt too hard a blow by it. In her few weeks of work for the man, she had found herself with more and more goodwill toward him. Some of this had to do with the fact that he was under strain both at home and at work, and she discovered easy sympathy for the public nature of his troubles. Some of her compassion had its source in a kind of selfishness: it was a relief to have the town's tongues wagging about scandals other than her own. Ida had told her years ago that the time would come when people would return to thinking of her simply as Lucy Robinson, rather than placing that ubiquitous *poor* in front of her name. They would find other troubles to toss around. There were always more balls in trouble's basket. But Lucy had not been able to imagine such things coming to pass, and still felt as a person laid low with illness feels about those moving about her in health. How did they manage it?

So since these weeks with the Sampsons, she was enjoying the vigor of comparative good health. She found him gruff and clumsy and full of nerves about appearance and reputation, but rather than wincing at his displays, she discovered herself to be smiling at them and occasionally succumbing to the urge to pat him on his thick, sloped shoulder or even once to tug painlessly at his graying beard, astonished at her forwardness and the pleasure it brought her.

In those moments, he had stiffened and allowed the girl's exuberance to pass without comment, as he did not know what words to put to use in such a situation. He would, however, have been able to say that her presence in their rooms brought to mind cups filled to the rim. He felt every day upon his return to the apartment that he was encountering a large table, well set for ten happy guests.

He had, of course, heard the Pendletons as well as she had, but had not been particularly struck by their comments, since they articulated his own sentiments. Regarding the tilt of his wife's head, the particular line of her neck, he could tell that she would soon be suffering from one of her headaches. He knew, too, that she would not, in public, minister to herself. The brown bottle of Dodd's Nervine would remain in her bag until her return home. In such cases, he knew, it offered her some small solace to have him within reach.

He glanced at Lucy and was struck by the thought that she had once been a child no larger than the one in Julia's arms. Winging its way behind that as if in migratory formation was the notion that baby Alice would one day take the form of a young woman. These were ordinary thoughts, comprehensible by the dullest of half-wits, yet they filled his mind with astonishment.

"What is it?" Lucy asked. "Are you overheated?"

"Do you realize that you were once a tiny infant?" he asked.

She regarded him as if for signs of heatstroke or brain fever. "I do," she said.

He sat back in the pew and placed his hands on his thighs as if having just completed school exams. "That's a remarkable thing, isn't it?" he said.

She sat back as well and watched the Reverend Mr. Bartlett take the pulpit. "It is," she said.

There was a brief delay, as there seemed to be some discussion as to the order of the speakers.

"You know," Sampson said. "I built most of this church." He gestured around them.

Lucy followed the gesture. The building was, in fact, much like him: squat, of sturdy brick, filled with New England history and pride. It was nearly as wide as it was long and, without the spire added the previous year, would've appeared even less like a church and more like a factory. Indeed, she felt that the enthusiasm about the recent expansion, especially the construction of the spire, the tallest in town and the second-tallest in the state, as more than one congregant had mentioned to her, had most to do with attaching some lift of alleluia to an edifice that seemed much more comfortable squatting.

"It is a lovely building," she said.

Sampson took perhaps more pride than he should have in the church, if not in the goings-on within its walls then at least in the walls themselves. He had certainly been instrumental in the fund-raising and construction, though perhaps his role had not been as crucial as he imagined. As his world in the factory grew more and more under siege, the importance of his church and his other civic contributions increased, and in this last week, he had found himself going out of his way to pass by these buildings as often as possible on his daily constitutionals.

In two years' time, Lucy, still in his employ, would hear of the fire in the church, and she would think of him, his disappointments and disasters held before her as suddenly and clearly as her own hand.

"The spire is the second-tallest in the state," he said.

"I have heard that," she said.

At the podium, Reverend Anable seemed to be successfully mediating the disagreement between the two speakers. Lucy and Sampson sat and watched.

"Would you like to sit with your wife and child?" she asked quietly, for reasons she didn't fully understand.

He looked again at the back of his wife's head. "I think there is no room for me there," he said, and the room quieted, as if in response to his observation, as Mr. Bartlett did, finally, commence to speak.

Alfred had no hopes for the man's preaching, except for its duration, as he looked forward to an hour or more in Ida's company. He tried to ignore that she seemed to have forgotten he was there.

Bartlett opened with the society motto and then asked the gathered group to recite the society pledge. He referred those on their inaugural visit to the pamphlets beneath the pews.

The group stood. Ida spoke from memory. Alfred read along silently with the logic that not speaking the words aloud made his whole participation less hypocritical.

They were told to sit.

Mr. Bartlett went on to say that Old King Alcohol was the great enemy of the human race. Temperance was the only way to throw him from his throne. He didn't have to remind this gathering that temperance was the moderate and proper use of things beneficial and the abstinence from things hurtful.

"See?" Ida whispered.

"What?" Alfred whispered back.

The bearded man told them to quiet themselves.

Alfred sat back, so perplexed by Ida's comment that he missed much of what both speakers said. He was doomed, he thought, to be in the position of trying to make sense of Ida V. Wilburn.

Professor Hitchcock drew the meeting to a close by reminding the group that temperance was not merely an issue of physical well-being but also one of morals and ethics. Theirs was the first society to do full justice to women, for example. As women had suffered more terribly than any other class from the evils of intemperance, it was felt that they should have a voice and a vote in all measures designed to overthrow this monster foe of the race. The wisdom of man and the love of woman should always be conjoined to accomplish the best results.

Alfred wondered if this was what Ida had meant for him to take from this evening, another lesson in her long struggle to get him to admit that boys were, by and large, foolish and wild.

"I'm no simpleton," Alfred whispered.

Ida regarded him. "Of course you're not," she said.

He waited for something else, some qualifying comment, but it never came.

Hitchcock went on, "Our Order knows no distinction on account of the color of a person's skin any more than it does the color of his hair or eyes. I believe that here in North Adams, with your proud tradition of welcoming all races, you must know this more clearly than elsewhere."

It was as if he had reached down from the pulpit and pulled Julia and the baby up there with him. She felt the room's attention on her bare neck like hands. She tucked Alice's blanket more securely around her and reaffirmed her grip on the child.

"Could he know about the child?" Alfred asked Ida.

"That's not the point," Ida said.

"It's not?" he said, hoping she would explain.

"Ssh," she said, putting a hand on his knee. "Just listen."

But he could scarcely listen with his knee bearing the weight of her hand, and Hitchcock seemed at the end of his wisdoms, and after an explanation of membership, which apparently involved the signing of the pledge along with the payment of one dollar to be a year's member, ten for a lifetime, and the singing of "The Teetotalers Are Coming" and "The Drunkard's Dream," the meeting was dissolved.

Charlie did not know how to stop the train that seemed to be steaming its way toward his delicately constructed life, yet simultaneously he felt it impossible that the train was actually coming or could do any real damage. He understood these to be insights in conflict, but felt them equally nonetheless, the effect being a constant state of inner argument. He was, by the middle of August, pummeled and exhausted by himself.

For all of Sampson's reassuring talk to the newspapers, both he and Charlie knew that as strange in appearance as the strike was, it was still a strike, and as such was summons and provocation to both employer and his trusted man. Even the phlegmatic George Chase was ruffled, stopping in to his employer's office twice as often as before to ask Sampson about his plan of response.

There were still workers doing their jobs so it was not that Charlie had such a difficult time keeping the boxes of product trundling out the back door. That was mostly a matter of gently pushing those workers who had remained at their machines to stay a little longer, work a little harder. But the beginning and end of each day, when Charlie had need to pass through the living quarters and encounter Ah Chung and his pack, were insult of the sort most difficult to stand. Each sight of them was humiliation and a blow to the reputation that he had spent so many years cultivating. He was gripped by the conviction that his damaged reputation was the sole obstacle to a life with Julia. How could she imagine a life with someone who could not even manage his own? He could take pride neither in the man he had been nor in the man he might be. He held Ah Chung centrally responsible.

Yet his disbelief that any of this ruin could actually come to pass and his unshakeable conviction that he was capable of working his way out of the tightest grip allowed him to continue to countenance the reassurances he gave Sampson, about both the operation of the factory and the procurement of the identity of the child's father, and to continue to act as though the workers' respect and admiration was a given. He even treated Ah Chung's dozen as though he was the best kind of father with mischief-making sons. He inquired after the eating habits of one and made a medicinal brew for another. If they smirked or exchanged looks

with one another in response, he chose not to see. Some days he was more successful than others. Most of his nights were sleepless. His appetite was poor, his work habits careless, his mind filled with images of Julia and Alice: torment and consolation in equal parts.

It was Sampson, finally, whose impatience overflowed. On a Tuesday evening in late August, he called Charlie to the Wilson House apartment and announced that he was sending for new Chinese from San Francisco. "The market is turned down, and still we are having trouble filling orders," he said. "If these boys here will not fill their berths, I will fill them with others like them."

Charlie nodded, yet he knew with certainty that this violation of their contract would only further enrage Ah Chung and the rest, even the ones who had for the moment chosen not to strike. But his ears were attuned to the sounds of Julia and the baby coming from behind the thick oak door over Sampson's shoulder. The sitting room was filled with evidence of the child and the care Julia was taking with her. Tiny towers of small clothes were in various states of construction on the sewing table. Baskets filled with the baby's pleasures and necessities rested in handy places throughout the room. The air was suffused with the smell of talc and milk. There was no sign of the gifts he had offered.

Behind the door, Julia was talking to the child as if to a grown woman. What if the door opened and he stood in her full view? What would she see? So, while nodding, he found himself challenging aloud his employer's instructions. It was polite and circumspect, but challenge nonetheless. Did Mr. Sampson not think that perhaps just the threat of calling in new workers might be enough to persuade the strikers back to their tables? Since one of the strikers' complaints was what they believed to be their oppression, might it not be better to make clear their options to them, but allow them the power of choice?

Sampson furrowed his brow and waved a hand as if clearing the air of something unpleasant. "I am not engaged in courtship with them," he said impatiently. "They are not objects of my affection. Tell them it is within my rights to replace them all, idle or not."

Charlie remained silent, yet Sampson looked up as if his foreman had said something reasonable and right. "Yes," he said. "As a matter of fact, tell them all that I am ready to exercise that right."

Charlie's neck tingled with minute warnings.

"Don't your people hold stock in group responsibility for the individual act and all that?"

Charlie didn't answer. It didn't seem to matter.

"If they do not offer up the father of the child for replacement," Sampson said, lowering his voice, "I will replace them all." He gestured toward the closed door behind him and his voice softened. "I cannot go on like this," he said.

Charlie said nothing.

Sampson's voice returned to its usual tenor. "So, there you are. The choice is theirs," he said. "As you suggested."

Charlie stared with such blankness that Sampson asked if he had heard. Charlie bent his head in his usual bow. Had his eyes been open, he might have seen the catchall basket on the floor containing spare buttons, some old receipts, a small carved dragon, and a Chinese hairpin. But he didn't, and in truth, the only questions he had were for himself. How had he ended up companion to Sampson on one side of a door with Julia and Alice on the other? Who must he hold responsible for that?

"We boys are not as dim as you think," Alfred said quietly to Ida on their way home.

"Not all," she said. "This is true."

It did not seem to him a comment necessary to address. His stride suffered and he appeared to gently lose his way for a moment.

She righted him with a hand to his arm. "Was I too late bringing you to the meeting?" she teased. "Has the hard cider already found its way around you?"

They had taken the long way home, Ida suggesting that they could do with as much of the breeze off the river as possible, and he was quiet and breathed through his mouth as they picked their way past the horse manure outside J. M. Avery's livery stable at the river end of Summer Street. The horses stood in the shade, their impossibly large heads hanging in the late summer heat. Flies gathered in the corners of their heavily lidded eyes. They leaned into each other like tired lovers, one rear fetlock cocked to relieve themselves of some of their own formidable weight.

Ida had never been able to resist a horse, and she slowed, removing a glove to place her palm between forehead and muzzle at the face's broadest part, like an agent of God distributing blessings. She paused at a well-formed chest-nut larger even than the rest. "Hello, good pony," she said.

Alfred did not take to horses, but the sight of her draw-ing pleasure from something that gave her so much of it brought back memories of their childhoods. Though they had not always had the other directly in sight, they had spent their childhoods side by side, running in the same pack of children, scolded by the same adults. She had once dared him to ride the Wilburn ponies in the Rappahan-nock River. He had not wanted to, but he had. The ponies were short, stocky Shetlands, and even ten-year-old Ida and Alfred could easily flatten their feet on the ground as they sat astride them. His pony was black, but beneath the Virginia sun he could see mottled rings of dark brown like a leopard's spots. Ida led the way down the short muddy embankment into the wide river, the horses wearing noth-ing but halter and lead rope, and he was not prepared for the feel of the small animal under him as it took flight within the water. It was as if the sturdy, warm animal on the dry ground had become a creature of the sea, slippery as a scaled thing. He had not been able to see a way to stay astride such a beast, and so he had not; each time he tried entering the river, he slipped quickly from the pony's back. And so he had settled, finally, for watching her. She had laughed with joy at the swimming pony and the clumsiness of her friend and the goodness of the life they found them-selves living, and she had brought to mind the illustrations in his book of myths and legends of strange and marvelous sea women riding the backs of dolphins and whales.

Now, she regloved her hand and rubbed her nose against the chestnut's muzzle one last time.

"Why're you so rough with me?" Alfred asked.

She looked as if she wished she could tether herself to the line of horses.

"I don't mean to be," she said, wiping her gloves on her skirts.

"But you are," he said.

She joined him at the end of the street, dust clouding their boots, and took his arm to continue down to the river. "I know," she said, and then fell silent.

Although above them were the rear lots of J. Boyles's newly built house and the Bloom hostel and R. Hartwick's livery, down in the hollow of the bank, picking their way across the shore's mix of sand and mud and river rocks, both of them felt as though the town and its inhabitants were many hills away.

He stopped at a small sandy outcropping shaded with birches and maples of the most unnatural bent. She walked on a few steps and then stopped to face him.

He said nothing, but she did not turn away. Small fish schooled together in the shallows. Somewhere, a bullfrog made his sounds.

"I like you," Alfred said, thunder and lightning striking between his ears. "Why do you find me so lacking?"

She did not remove her eyes from him. Her heart was filled with concern at what it had required of him to say such a thing.

"Our lives've been rooted together from the start," he said. "My mother always said that the best wife is also a best friend." He looked at the trees. Their shadows spotted his face. "Maybe we're not best friends, but I guess we might be."

A cardinal pair swept past and landed on a thin huckleberry branch bent almost to the water. They regarded the humans and took off in different directions.

Ida knew everything he said to be true. She hadn't realized until that moment how much she had counted on him never saying any of this out loud. Because she knew that the obstacle to her love for Alfred was something he could do nothing about and something she could never share.

"Is it just that I am too familiar?" he ventured. His voice was now breaking and the small boy inside was terrible to see. She wished she could take him by the hands, the way his mother did when he was in the grips of his most boyish upset, put her face to his, and tell the truth. It was that he was not familiar enough. No matter what he did or said, he would never be the girl who bricked the path upon which she wished to travel. What exactly was the nature of her love for Lucy? She would've been unable to say. All she knew was that she was her best self in the company of Lucy Robinson.

As headstrong as she was, she could not bring herself to that level of honesty with him. And because her original intent had been to extract his promise to do no damage when it came to Charlie and Mrs. Sampson and that baby, she found herself doing much worse. She did take him by the hands, and she did put her face to his, in order to tell him that all he said was true, and although she did not love him now, she might yet learn to love him.

Although the relief on his face was not complete, when he gave her a brief, shy smile and said, "Well, then," Ida knew herself to be a hateful person, something heartless clothed in human guise.

Ah Chung and the striking workers voted to return to their machines upon hearing Charlie's news that they were to be replaced. Although Ah Chung himself was for continued defiance, the others were made nervous by this news. They had signed contracts, after all. They had families who were counting on the regular arrival of their sons' earnings. They did not like to imagine their mothers bearing the burdens of village life, or believing their boys to be anything but good and upright sons. And Ah Chung, savvy enough to know when to push and when to align, concurred. He did, however, point out that it was Charlie who had delivered this message, and not just Sampson who benefited from their return to work.

Reading the boys' faces as they took their supper after their vote, Charlie knew that although Sampson had gotten what he desired, there was nothing to celebrate here. Even the cooks dished his food to him in silence.

Perhaps because of his shame, he could not bring himself to relate the second part of Sampson's message. How could he announce to this group that unless a father was named, all of them would be sent away?

In his bunk that night, unhappy boys all around him, sleep eluded him again, and he lay awake astonished at the position in which he found himself. How could he name a father? How could he not? Was it not better to sacrifice one to save the rest?

He thought of Third Brother. Had it not been better for one of them, at least, to have made a successful arrival on Gold Mountain? What good would it have done to align himself with someone so clearly in the grip of death's long fingers?

From across the aisle Ah Chung's voice rose above the surrounding noises of sleep and dream. "Another sleepless night, Cousin?"

Charlie didn't answer, shame and rage at this young upstart mixing in his gut.

The boy above Ah Chung said, "Who are you talking to?"

"Mr. Foreman is troubled," Ah Chung answered. "I have a family member in need."

The boy snorted. "He is not your family."

"But he says he is." Ah Chung leaned out of his bunk toward Charlie's. "Cousin. He says you and I are not family. You must set him straight. You must make your authority clear."

"He's asleep," the boy said.

Ah Chung settled back down on his bunk. "He is not asleep," he said.

Charlie could tell both of them were smiling. He remained silent. Had he been in their position, he would have felt the same way. And so, in two days' time, when even the nonstriking workers voted to remove him from control of their finances, he would know the futility of argument. He too would no longer have looked to him as

their best possible delegate, their one-man migrant associ-
ation. So when they chose a new foreman, he would retreat
sadly to his bunk in the middle of the day and say aloud to
the empty room, "I have made a mess of things. I am sorry
to have shamed us all."

It would fail to occur to him that this was the position
his brother had been in on that boat, and also one with
which Julia was more than familiar, the position commonly
occupied by most people in this world: voicing their sadnesses into empty rooms, the only consolation the echoes
of their own articulations bouncing off the walls. It would
fail to occur to him that even Ah Chung lay on this same
pallet. So he would grasp no consolation in the apprehen-
sion that his misery was a shared one. It would seem to him
on that hot August afternoon that he was a solitary man,
lost between past and future. For the first time in days, he
would sleep.

Chapter Sixteen

By mid-September 1873, the total United States debt was $2,270,000,000. What few green apples embellished the orchards of Hampshire and Franklin Counties had been generally preempted by the worms, and the apple harvest of that locality would prove almost a dead failure.

Boston newspapers reported that soup for the poor in their fair city cost $4,000 the previous year, while refreshments for the city government topped $41,000.

North Adams's water was almost entirely drawn from the Clarksburg Reservoir, and the levels in the north branch of the Hoosac were barely sufficient to drive the mills more than one day in the week at full head.

The *Transcript* of September 11, 1873, ran a front-page article titled "The Age of Suicide," which claimed that "the habits of the period tend peculiarly to self destruction." Further articles instructed the paper's readers on "How to be Rich" and the "Treatment of Old Horses."

At seven in the evening on that night, a terrific explosion of nitroglycerin occurred near the central shaft of the Hoosac Tunnel, resulting in the death of David Bourdon, assistant blaster. The *Transcript* the following week reported that the explosion had been felt in Pittsfield. Bourdon's body was removed the day after death to Canada, his former home, where his family awaited it for proper burial.

And Ah Chung reminded his fellow workers that even the French Canadians took care of their own.

By September 18, they had been back to work for some weeks, though the mood within the bottoming room was as careful as if fox and house cat suddenly found themselves lapping from the same puddle.

Ah Chung was waiting for Charlie to offer some further example of misplaced loyalties and Charlie was determined not to offer anything at all. He turned more and more inward, his shoulders sloped with the effort.

Julia wanted a name. Sampson wanted a name. The Sunday school teachers, who knew practically nothing of the particulars of Charlie's position, seemed to stare at him with open pity. Merchants endeavored to give him his change without touching his hand. The minister at his Methodist church pulled him aside after services to say that he imagined the situation at the factory to be rough and wondered if Charlie would like to unburden himself. Dogs avoided him. He began to feel that if he could manage to allow day to run into day, he could, in the manner of a spirit returning to the Celestial world, disappear almost entirely.

He had been given a deadline of September 22 by his employer. "The father's name, or I hand them all tickets back to San Francisco," Sampson had said.

Shortly after that, Julia had managed to get a note to him through Lucy Robinson. *Are you really, after all, not going to help me?*

And so when the town awoke on Friday, September 19, to the news of the failure of the great banking house of Jay Cooke and Company, Charlie may have been the only person to welcome the information. He would be further pleased to learn that several other businesses would follow in its footsteps, making the nineteenth of September forever known as Black Friday, the beginning of a financial panic that would last for sixty-five months, the longest nationwide depression the country would see for decades to come. Charlie thought not about hungry children or despondent or ruined families. He thought instead that this news might be distracting, and he was glad.

And for one or two days, he was correct. Sampson tracked the news from New York with the relief that a subject other than baby and wife, strikers and paternity could provide. What a respite to be able to stay Julia or George Chase, both no doubt bringing further anxiety to his doorstep, with a raised hand and say, "Apologies all around, but I must attend to this."

During Friday and Saturday, he had much to track, as Wall Street was in the wildest excitement of terror. Jay Cooke was a firm of continental relations and immense business, and its fall carried with it some of the strongest banking firms of the city. Failure after failure was announced until it seemed as if the whole street would go under. By Saturday night, some forty-one leading houses had failed in New York alone, and railroad values had fallen six percent, other stocks as much as ten. Wall Street was filled with crowds of men mad with alarm and despair. Suicides were expected, and by Sunday, expectations had been met.

And so Charlie's Monday deadline passed unnoticed by his employer. In fact, Charlie saw nothing of Sampson for several days, and he began to hope for further grim news from New York as a blanket over the fire of his own local troubles.

But by Thursday, Sampson's thoughts had begun to hold both the faraway and the local in the same frame, mostly because of a remark of his wife's.

"It seems to me," he said loudly enough for her to hear him from the nursery, where she had been busying herself in ways he found inexplicable for a time he found impossibly long, "that the depreciated paper currency is at the bottom of this all."

She said nothing. Rattling sounds commenced and then ceased.

"And the cause of that is the prolonged financial debauch we have indulged in. We have been living wrong, and now comes the punishment and retribution," he went on.

Her voice when it finally did make its way out the nursery door was filled with impatience. She said, "'Accumulation and speculation are the team to which business should yoke itself.' Isn't that what you used to say?"

He wondered whether the time would ever come when he would find the precision of his wife's memory blessing rather than burden. "Speculation, yes," he said, "but wise specula-tion. Not this willy-nilly kind of exploration that entails the abandonment of all that we know to be sound practice."

Julia stood at the door with Alice in her arms, and once again he had the impression of being ganged up on.

"So no experimenting," she said. "No unprecedented acts of business the consequences of which would not be clear until delivered upon us?"

He frowned at her, stood, and then sat again, taking enormous interest in the arms of his chair. "All right, all right," he said. "I am not an idiot."

"I did not say that you were," she said, swaying lightly from one widely planted foot to the other. She had taken to per-forming this action whether or not she held Alice in her arms, and he found it disquieting, as if some spirit had taken up residence in her body and was busy exploring her inner rooms.

"All I am saying is that it seems you may have started speaking on one subject and found yourself on another," she said, the impatience drained from her tone.

He picked at the brocade of the chair.

"Stop that," she said gently.

"No matter," he said, standing again. "Perhaps we all have gone too far astray. Perhaps the answer on Wall Street and here is the same: a return to prudence and honesty."

It was the closest he'd come to admitting to her what an extreme betrayal he felt her behavior to be. Until now, they had spoken of their problem almost only as if it were made exclusively of the baby and the paternity, and not also of her trampling on their vows, their love, their twenty-four years of life together. It was as if they'd chosen to stand on and discuss the tip of an iceberg, ignoring the underwater mass beneath them.

The thought of the small of her back guided through a doorway by another's hand, her mouth coaxed into laughter by way of another's words, brought pressure to his eyes and bile to his throat. He could not allow his imagination to go farther. She was still rocking Alice.

The sight of someone he loved holding someone he didn't was strange and unpleasant.

Another man had known her. This was something he would have to live with. His deadly and impossible task. "Oh, Julia. The oldest of them is close to half your age."

Her eyes flashed with surprise and alarm and, he hoped, shame.

"I know," she said plainly.

He was crying, and he screwed his eyes shut to put a stop to it.

"Look at me," she said.

He did.

"I did not intend to hurt you," she said.

He regarded her. How could someone he had presumed to know so well have surprised him so fully? He had taken such pleasure in his familiarity with her ways. It was a pleasure that even in retrospect he could no longer enjoy.

She was still rocking. "Stop that," he said, giving his face one final determined swipe. And she did, and Lucy Robinson, listening from the apartment's kitchen, heard the floorboards cease their creaking, and inside, all was still.

★

Other than what she'd told Ida and Alfred about the meeting between Mrs. Sampson and the foreman, Lucy had kept what information she knew buttoned safe to her chest, and she wished she had not shared what she had. That incaution had caused her much shame. She prided herself on her discretion, on her ability to be the quietest voice in a room. As a child, she had been the one who had consistently been brought into adult confidence. Her mother especially had found that the sharing of secrets with her offered a particular kind of consolation, and although she often felt guilty about using her child for selfish purposes, the relief it allowed her was too large to resist. For Lucy, the effect had been to make her feel even less of a child. Until she grew to be friends with Ida, she had not been a girl to like the rough-and-tumble play of youngsters on a farm. She did not like tromping down creeks or slipping into rivers; the odor of barns and the animals within them made her feel as if many hands were being held firmly over her mouth and nose. But neither was she a bookworm, a good girl who excelled at chores and who would never consider letting her bonnet go untied. She was not a child as her family or friends understood a child to be. And so she had found herself thinking, *Why not embrace the adult world?* Perhaps there would be more for her there. She had therefore become the model of maturity and poise, an adult who operated with the caution of someone in a foreign land.

The only place she had not felt herself to be an inter-
loper was in the presence of Ida. They'd been a country of
two. "Thank goodness you have found someone to be your
natural self with," her mother used to say. "Your particulars
seem to suit each other." Their brothers teased them about
it, and other acquaintances steered clear.

And so her reaction to Ida's behavior on the following
Sunday came as a surprise. They were spending the week's
end as planned, at the opening day of the Cattle Show and
Fair of the Hoosac Valley Agricultural Society at the North
Adams Fairgrounds just outside the town proper.

After several days of perfect weather, the clouds had begun
to gather, and Sunday had opened with a drizzling rain. The
livestock were beginning to make an appearance; the Exhibition Hall was filling with tables and booths. The roundabout
was on hand but not yet up. By early afternoon, when they
found themselves investigating the fair's main thoroughfare,
some half-dozen booths were ready and anxious. Lucy suggested the Grand Arena for the matched carriage horses, always her own favorite. Free-ranging animals made her nervous;
those under yoke or harness seemed to her dignified and secure.

Ida wrinkled her nose. "No," she said. "Let's not." She
looked around as if searching for, but not expecting to find,
an alternative.

Lucy registered surprise and a little hurt at the speed
with which her friend had disregarded what she knew to
be Lucy's preference.

"The weather is miserable," Ida said and then fell silent, as
if this were Lucy's fault.

From the pens came the sounds of cattle and poultry, sheep and swine. Lucy imagined jaws sliding over hay, dirty tails taking desultory swipes at insects. In the rain, the smell was sure to be overwhelming. "Do you want to see the animals?" she offered.

"You don't like animals," Ida said.

"But you do," Lucy persisted.

"Don't do anything just for me," Ida said, her voice smoked with sarcasm.

Lucy was baffled. Her mind sorted through possible offenses she might have inflicted and landed on the even less pleasant possibility that Ida's recent sour moods had nothing to do with Lucy.

Ida looked around as if waiting for someone she was sure would never arrive. "Everyone likes autumn," she said. She scanned the hillsides. "Just something that comes after summer and before winter, if you ask me."

"What's gotten under your bonnet?" Lucy asked.

Ida regarded her. "Nothing," she finally said. "Just wore out."

"You should rest," Lucy said.

Her friend snorted and suggested they get out of the weather in the Exhibition Hall.

In years past, they had tended to avoid the hall. Filled with its garden vegetables and floral arrangements, its works aspiring to art and its infinitude of cushions, scarves, and tidies, it was the one place certain to make both girls feel most foreign. But they made their way through the humid, crowded tent. They stopped to handle Mrs. Lamphier's Peerless potatoes, weighing a pound each. Ida held up a basket bouquet of star of scarlet geraniums on a ground of purple ageratum, turning it this way and that. "It's pretty," she said.

Lucy raised her eyebrows. Last year they would've rolled their eyes together at such a thing.

Ida proceeded to the wax anchor, cross, and crown by Mrs. J. J. Pratt of Williamstown, and several pictures in worsted by Mrs. O. D. Titus. Lucy followed, lost in her own thoughts about Ida's current mood and what Lucy might have done to put her there.

Charlie's portrait was almost hidden among the other photographs and paintings of Lucius Hurd. Hurd had arranged it between a view of the Taj Mahal and another of the pyramids of Egypt. Ida plucked it from the row, resettling it with the other portraits. "Embarrassing," she said. "As if he's some sort of exotic landscape." She searched the vicinity of the table, and Lucy feared she was looking for Hurd himself to give him a thick slice of her mind.

Lucy took her by the arm, hoping to prompt her into proceeding away, but Ida seemed not to feel her hand. "I would buy this if I could," she said.

"What for?" Lucy asked with a little too much surprise. They had both received *cartes de visite* from the Chinese workers, but that novelty had passed. Lucy wasn't even sure where her copies were anymore.

"Not everything has a practical use," Ida said. "I'd buy it because I like it. I like him."

This last comment, and the way Ida said it, as though trying unsuccessfully to toss it off, sent a tremor through the small of Lucy's back. Since she was not predisposed to engage in such an understanding, she did not identify it as jealousy. She did not admit that Ida's comment upset what she had come to rely on as the natural order of their relationship. Even if she felt caged and trapped by Ida's attentions, she had come to rely on their presence. And both women remained so locked against themselves and the world around them that they missed word of the excitement transpiring at the Grand Arena, where the team of William S. Blackinton, a pair of remarkable large and handsome horses, became frightened by striking their feet against the whippletrees and started on a run, their driver powerless to hold them.

The track was occupied by matched horses on exhibition and by many other conveyances and the dangers of a disastrous collision were imminent, but the horses turned from the track and started across the uneven field. They passed in front of the judges' stand and finally regained the track and only after two further circuits did they, panting and white with foam, slow to a walk and allow themselves to be driven home without injury.

Upon their return to the Robinson apartment, the girls were told about the episode by Alfred, who at first expressed worry as to their well-being and then shock. "How could you have missed such a thing?" he asked. "Are you deaf, blind, and dumb?"

Ida assured him that they were not, and Lucy said that they had been otherwise occupied, and both stood there nursing their mutual sense that the other was most to blame for the miseries of the day.

*

Charlie spent the afternoon within the scaffolded Methodist church. The old building had been removed in April 1872 to make way for the new, which was meant to be ready for occupancy by the middle of the upcoming November, and which from certain angles, interior and exterior, could be imagined as already fully completed and constructed.

Perhaps its most impressive feature, besides its $85,000 cost to subscribers, was its massiveness. It boasted not one but two towers, both of which competed in size with the main part of the edifice, which seemed to loom over the street like a house cat over a fishbowl. The workmen were absent on Sundays, and the signs on all three entrances read: NO ONE MUST ENTER, so Charlie found himself alone.

He sat gingerly on one of the new seats of the horseshoe gallery at the western end and knew immediately that whatever peace he had hoped to claim would not be found in this place. The seats were chestnut trimmed with black walnut, much more elaborate than the oak benches in the old church.

He found the interior plan more than vaguely discomforting, rooms branching off halls in ways that were impossible to track. Studies and libraries tucked under double stairways. Pocket doors disappearing into walls. The whole thing struck him as more animal's den than sacred space. So why had he sought solace here?

"There you are, my Celestial," a voice from behind him said.

His heart lurched at Julia's pet phrase.

It was Sampson. "I hope you don't mind my having hunted you down," he said, and Charlie understood that his employer's attentions were returned to him. He gestured to the pew, and Sampson removed his hat to sit.

They regarded the choir gallery.

"Did you know the organ is to be at a cost of $4,500?" Sampson asked.

Charlie shook his head and told Sampson that he was not consulted on the church's daily operations.

"Well, perhaps you should be. This preacher of yours is a very loose accountant and has proven to have very imperfect talents for the disbursement of money." He glanced at Charlie. "Your boys' decision about removing you from the care of their finances aside, I find you most expert in this arena." He seemed to be trying to ascertain if any offense had been taken.

Charlie remained silent. His employer's kindness incited shame.

"Methodists," Sampson added.

Charlie knew about the Sampsons' conversion. He had often bothered himself imagining the occasion of their dual baptism, building on the few facts Julia had given him. It had been a Sunday afternoon in late March, the river water still frigid with winter melt. He imagined singing and prayerful shouting. He imagined they had held hands, Sampson's assertiveness giving strength to the normally reserved Julia. He imagined the minister pulling them forward and back beneath the service of the water.

Both men were silent. The late afternoon light fell through the open windows on the west side, and dust motes floated like snow in its beams. For several moments, Charlie felt it to be a pleasant site to pass the afternoon and pleasant company with whom to pass it.

"One branch of Julia's family was Methodist," Sampson said. "Joseph Hayden, machinist for Giles Tinker. Helped form that small class in the Notch."

"I think sometimes to convert to Baptist," Charlie said, picking quietly at the pew's trim with his thumbnail.

"Well, you'd be better off than you are here," Sampson said. "Eighty-five thousand dollars for a place to pray," he added, shaking his head.

Julia had never been able to make the differences between his Methodists and her Baptists plain to Charlie, and he had asserted that it seemed to him that all Western churches turned their congregants' faces to an interior circle, whereas Eastern worship lifted faces up and back to the shared space of history and memory. He had tried to explain the experiences of kneeling to the family altar, or sweeping the ancestors' graves. But the inadequacies of his English frustrated him and he worried that he was making no part of what he wanted her to know visible. For this reason, he had once found himself presenting his thoughts on the matter to her in Chinese. When she had not seemed disconcerted, he had gone on. He explained that when he prayed in the Chinese way, he saw all who had preceded his own family and he understood upon whose backs he now knelt. And he saw all future generations, on whom Charlie could rely to honor him. Thus a man's life became both more important and less. The line could not be formed without the one man, but the one man was powerless without the strength of the others before and behind him.

Julia had loved the fluid cadences of the Chinese and had repeated some of her most favorite sounds. But despite the pleasure her pleasure brought him, he knew that he had been unable to make himself clear, and that this might always be the way between them.

Now, as he sat next to her husband, his thoughts sailed from Baptist conversion to pursuit of yet another livelihood, from applying for citizenship to quick accumulation of large sums of money, each a potential way to persuade her that he was the kind of man any woman should want to make father to her child and husband to her self.

"We were married in the Union Church in Stamford, Vermont, you know," Sampson said.

Charlie wanted both to run from the building and to listen more attentively. "I did not," he said carefully, as though each word were a glass in a tall tower of glasses.

"It was the only church in Stamford for years. You weren't going to get more than one from a group of settlers who had left Massachusetts to escape long sermons." He gestured around them. "You could have fit three of that church in this one," he said.

Charlie gave him a small smile.

"In the summer months, by the time we villagers made the walk to it, our stockings were covered in dust. In winter we kept warm by filling our foot warmers with coals donated from the fireplaces of the Wilmarth House. It was my job to fetch the coals from the inn and distribute the warmers through the pews. My first sight of Julia was from the ankles down."

Charlie had peeled stockings from those same ankles. She had told him she had always found her feet to embarrass her more than any other aspect of her body and so he had lavished particular attentions upon them.

Sampson said, "Now there are two churches up there. Hard-shelled Baptists and shouting Methodists."

He glanced at Charlie, who nodded and said, "I see."

"She wore shell combs in her hair. Her nose was dusted with rice powder." He smiled sadly. "Did you know we have been husband and wife for over twenty-four years?"

"It is a long time," Charlie said with equal sadness.

"Thank you for saying so," Sampson said, though Charlie did not know what he had said that merited gratitude.

Sampson leaned forward, his elbows on his thighs, his hands clasped between his knees. "I have told her that if I know the man's name, I will not harm his person or livelihood." He straightened his shoes against the seams of the carpet. "I have promised her that with the name lodged in my mind, I can go forward. I have promised her my role in the life she desires."

He turned his head without raising it and regarded Charlie. "Could you do such a thing, Mr. Foreman?"

Charlie could feel the dampness between his shoulder blades. He had spent the last three years determining his own course by using this man as sextant. One night shortly after Julia and Sampson had departed for Florida, he had haunted Sampson's office. He had opened and closed the man's books. He had straightened the rug. He had even slipped into the extra pair of boots always kept by the door. It had been silly, yet thrilling.

And now this man sat before him at a loss. Charlie sympathized with the disorientation, and answered with honesty. "I don't know," he said. And then he apologized, aloud for his ignorance, and in his mind for his betrayals.

Ida passed her Sunday evening as she usually did, at the Celestial Sunday school, but since the strike, there had been more agitation and less focused study. Boys now clumped around Ah Chung and his clan more than they looked to their teachers. The small gifts for teachers had not been presented in several weeks, private lessons had taken a downturn, dinner invitations from the volunteers had been politely refused.

All this made it hard for the teachers to keep their own focus, and Ida found herself deaf to her two students as she strained to make sense of the gathering around Ah Chung's table. Finally, able to stand it no longer, she arranged to trade tables with their elderly volunteer teacher. The poor Mrs. Slattery was only too happy to remove herself from this inattentive and unsettled group.

Ida sat beside Ah Chung. "Speak English," she commanded.

He smiled at her. This boy had always struck her as unpleasant. Too sure of himself from the moment he had stepped off the train. Whereas the other new arrivals spent their energies on steadying the boat, his attitude had from the outset been more like that of a dog bored with play. It had taken longer for her to understand whether he took this stance in order to improve the situation for his fellow workers or merely for himself. Even after the strike, her mind was not made on this issue, and her uncertainty resulted in further impatience.

"You and yours seem to be complaining," she said.

"You want us complain in English, Miss Wilburn?" he asked, still smiling.

She wished to slap him as she used to slap her brothers. She took a breath and attempted her best Sunday school voice. "I am your teacher. I am interested in your complaints. I am interested in you," she said.

"You not my teacher," he said. He pointed across the room at Mrs. Slattery. "She my teacher."

She chose to ignore him. "If you have a problem, perhaps I can help."

He said something in Chinese to the group. They laughed, some of them glancing at her awkwardly.

"English," she said again.

"My English bad," he said, a low whine invading his voice. "I guess my teacher not so good."

More laughter, though Low Yuen, one of the youngest, looked stricken.

Ah Chung was now addressing the group more than her. "Maybe that our big problem," he said. "Okay, Miss Wilburn. That our complaining. We need better teacher."

Against her judgment, she said, "So first you replace your foreman, and now your teachers? Perhaps you would like to do the teaching? Perhaps you could handle the finances and the education of these boys." She gestured at the group, most of whom had lost comprehension of her, or had never had it in the first place. They looked at one another, wondering what was required of them.

He spoke to the boys around him. They stood, their benches scraping, gathered their hats from the wall pegs, and with bows in her general direction, took their leave. The young one, Low Yuen, turned back and moved as if to speak, but then chose to walk on without doing so.

After the last had removed himself to their living quarters, Ah Chung stood, settling his own hat on his head. "I not speak English. You not speak Chinese," he said, as if explaining not only how they had arrived at this place but also where and how they should move forward from it. Ida flushed. He shrugged at her, turned, and took his leave.

She remained on the bench. And she was still there when Charlie returned from the church to find her the sole occupant of the dark and otherwise empty schoolroom. Her confrontation had made her feel as she had during a childhood encounter with a black bear in the woods. *Make yourself big*, her father had always told her. *Make yourself a bigger animal than he*. And so she had, her arms aloft, her feet wide in the spring growth. She had yelled; she had waved her hands and arms as if ridding herself of insects, and the bear had been dissuaded, dropping to all fours and retreating into the deeper woods, twigs and branches snapping under his lumbering weight.

And so when Charlie approached her table and inquired as to her well-being, she decided on honesty and said, "You have your hands full with that Ah Chung and his boys."

Charlie lightly tapped the table's edge. He turned his hands palm up as if he might find those boys nestled there like baby squirrels.

She smiled. She had always liked his hands. "What I meant was that they are a troublesome group, are they not?"

Charlie did not like to speak ill of his own with the Americans; no good could come of it, but Ida Wilburn had always struck him as a straightforward young woman, upright and sure. He knew others thought her too brittle, too strong, a little mirthless. Once he had heard another Sunday school teacher refer to her as a battle-axe. He had grasped the sentiment if not the meaning of the term. But he was tired of constant watchfulness. It had been a decade of relentless attention to the shifting weather of the Americans around him. He was tired of it. She had filled the months of Julia's absence with distraction and attentiveness. She seemed to find him appealing because of his differences rather than despite them. She was kind.

And so he answered her directness with more of his own. "I think on them too often," he said. As he spoke, he was astonished at the extent of his exhaustion. He sank to the bench opposite her, too tired to keep his back straight.

Her eyes were filled with benevolence. It made him want to put his head on the table.

They sat for a moment, the night sounds coming in through the windows closed against the fall chill. She asked if he was familiar with the story of Antaeus, and when he responded that he was not, she told him it was a story he must know, an ancient story with relevance, she was sure, to their own situation here in this modern village.

It occurred to him that even before Julia's departure from town, indeed since his arrival in town, Ida had treated him with a respect and admiration that he had appreciated, even given his own inattention to anyone other than a certain few.

She explained that whenever Antaeus, the earth-born, was thrown to the earth, he received new strength and was in consequence able to overcome all his antagonists, until Hercules one day held him aloft in his arms and strangled him in the air.

It was not clear to Charlie what to make of this tale. He could see no relevance to his own life. But he nodded and told her that it was a most interesting story.

She nodded in return, pleased, and said that although she was a Baptist, it seemed to her that Christian strength was not the only path to spiritual strength. The spirit of God moved her when she least expected it, in the most unlikely of places. Spiritual strength accrued when one rested one's strength on the immediate fact of things.

She stared at him, and he worried that once again, in his failure to comprehend, he was disappointing her.

She leaned forward and did the most astonishing thing of covering one of his hands with hers. Her hands were rougher than Julia's, but not unpleasantly so. Her fingers were the same width at their tips as they were at their base. She brought back for him a memory of his mother's way of holding his hand when they took wagon rides with his father to sell their rice and vegetables. They would lie in the back of the wagon on quilts spread over sacks of rice and baskets of cabbage. They would stare up at the sky and she would braid one of his fingers over another, add a third, undo them, and start over. In this way, they would pass the whole ride.

And so he relaxed his hand beneath hers and pretended that to be sitting thus was an ordinary part of an ordinary day.

She told him that she had been sure that as a Celestial, he would find the tale interesting and perhaps even helpful to understanding the current situation among the other boys.

He turned the story over in his mind. What possible course of action could she be suggesting, if any at all?

She patted his hand and withdrew hers, standing and readying herself for departure. "Whatever help I can offer you may have," she said.

He was mystified, but already missed the weight of another's hand. "Thank you," he said. "Very much."

Later, he would ask her what she had meant by telling him that story, and she would not recall having done so. He would try to set the scene for her, the hour, the disagreeable conversation she had had with Ah Chung, her hand on his.

"I don't remember," she would say in such a way to convince him that further interrogation would turn up nothing. And then she would say with simple plainness, "I remember your hand."

On Wednesday the first of October, Sampson, miserable, informed his wife that a name had been procured. He wished for the source to have been his wife, but one could not always achieve one's wishes. Instead, he had been forced to rely on Mr. Sing, a man whom he now had one more reason to admire and trust.

Julia nodded, turning around the fact that Charlie had given Sampson, rather than her, the name like a jeweler searching for flaws. Had he thought the discomfort of her husband announcing the news to her would be less than that of her announcing the same to him? Was he in some way announcing a loyalty to her husband rather than her? Or merely doing his best to achieve what she most desired?

She wondered what name and had to rein herself back from inquiry.

They were in the bedroom, where she was resting, a sleeping Alice in the bassinet beside her.

Sampson sat ineptly on the edge of the high bed. He found her quilts too stuffed, her bed pillows too numerous. "It is a horror to know," he said, avoiding her eyes.

It pained her to know how much he was suffering and how little she could ease it. "I'm sorry," she said. But she could not keep from adding, "You will keep your promise to me, will you not?"

As she spoke, she understood that from now on, not only would she be unable to ease his suffering, she would continue to add to it. She understood as well that the pain this would cause her was tolerable.

He scanned the room like a beast ranging his cage with his eyes and took her hands in his and bent his forehead to hers. "How can I do this?" he pleaded. He rolled his brow back and forth against hers. "How can you ask it of me?"

She was crying, but she gestured toward Alice. "This is how," she said through her tears. "Please," she added.

He lay down beside her and she wrapped herself around him. He knew that in the morning, he would hand the boy a week's pay and a ticket on the afternoon train. Both were already in the drawer of his desk. But for now, he tucked his wife's hand beneath his resting face and hoped that the baby would never wake.

Chapter Seventeen

On Thursday, October 2, 1873, a four-pound toadstool was discovered in Lee. Peter Galligan paid the police court $250 and was sentenced to six months in the house of correction for liquor selling, while on the charge of keeping a nuisance he was fined $20 and received three months' imprisonment. The *Transcript*, speaking on the country's financial crisis, opined that if the businessmen of North Adams stood by the local banks, deposited as usual, and drew only for the regular purposes of trade, then the fury of the storm in New York would not have serious effect in local terms.

The day was crisp and bright and all God's objects appeared as if spit-polished by earnest young boys in uniforms of well-pressed cloth.

It was hard for those who had been, in one way or another, waiting for the identity of the father for so long not to think that today would bring some relief. Even those townsfolk who did not know the particulars of the Sampsons' unresolved situation had felt the anxieties of the past months. And certainly the recent lives of the Chinese workers had been filled with unrest. It might even be argued that the town entire, alien and native, wealthy and wanting, had been living as a herd of horses, noses to the air of an oncoming disturbance of weather. It would be solace to be able to relax their attentive ears and drop their heads to the grass.

But the realization of desire is often dissimilar to the fantasy, and almost as soon as Sampson had handed the young Low Yuen his ticket, his final pay, and his measured thanks, those divergences commenced to roll through the town like thunder.

First off, the boy's reaction offered Sampson no satisfaction. Whereas Sampson had secretly hoped for a moment of unspoken yet complete understanding between the two of them, the boy's eyes were filled with nothing but confusion. He was enough of a boy and enough aware of his position in this world to keep his questions to himself, but they started to make their way into the world soon after he left the office.

The news of his dismissal traveled through the factory at a rapid pace. His fellow workers had watched him being summoned from the bottoming floor, and when he didn't return, they began one by one to quit their tables and make their way down to their living quarters, and Homer Handley and the other white workers took note from their

own stations that here was yet another day of compromised work and diminished product.

Despite what Julia had believed, Charlie was not surprised to hear of Low Yuen's dismissal. She had, he thought, been naïve, and Sampson, he knew, understood himself to be a right and moral person, inclined, even obligated, to bring what he understood as injustice to public light. Charlie had known, as he had offered Low Yuen's name, what would come of his action. What he chose to believe was that Julia knew as well, and that what she was asking was not just for Charlie to build her a door out of the trap in which she found herself, but for him to pass through that door with her. So great was his need for this truth that he did not examine its illogic.

He remained at his pegging machine until he realized it would be the wiser move to follow his brethren downstairs. He reminded himself that he should be as curious as they; their reactions should be his reactions, and it struck him that he had become someone who had to play the role of a Celestial rather than be one. He was saddened.

The Chinese were gathered in the bunk room, as if even their own dining quarters were too public for such a day. There were too many of them for the available open space, and he was reminded of the journey that had brought them all to this country. Perhaps their lot in life was to go from one cramped room to another.

At the center was Low Yuen, who had rarely been the center of anything. He still clutched his train ticket. He asked one of his coworkers if he would mind reaching his bag from beneath his bunk. Ah Chung stilled the coworker with a gesture. "He's not going anywhere," he said, pulling a stool over with his foot and indicating that Low Yuen should take a seat, which the boy did.

Ah Chung asked him to recount the scene in the office. "Leave nothing out," he said. But before the boy could speak, could explain that, no, Mr. Sampson had offered no explanation for the dismissal, before the boy could be made to feel the small sting of shame at not having asked for one, Ah Chung glanced Charlie's way and said the houseboys of foreign devils were not welcome there.

Charlie removed himself without argument, as he believed that this too would go the way he expected. Ah Chung would use the dismissal to reincite his band of supporters. Whether or not a reason for the dismissal was discovered, he himself would be blamed for it. This would not be a miscarriage of justice. He would be further isolated from the group, further pushed beyond the outer walls of their small imitation of home. As he passed through the dining quarters and let himself quietly out of the factory's side door, pausing on the bottom step to look first left and then right, he reminded himself with the stubbornness of a child that this was what he had wanted.

Although not making use of the train ticket had been Ah Chung's idea, Low Yuen himself had been at a loss to imagine crossing the country on his own, returning to San Francisco alone and unemployed. It was a city he found filled with nothing but chaos, inciting in his body nothing but fear.

He could not return home until he had stored away enough money to pay his debts and the cost of the trip, and even if he found his finances in such a state, he could not imagine returning to his village, to his overworked mother and stern father, as essentially the same boy he had been when he left.

So instead, he returned to his work station. He kept his head bent to the task of attaching one part of a shoe to another. Who knew why Americans did the things they did? It was best not to question their behavior, but to stay out of its way.

Because Sampson chose to avoid the bottoming room in the days after the dismissal, and because the room's white foreman had more trouble than he liked to admit telling one Celestial from another, it was several days before Low Yuen's continued presence moved into the frame of Sampson's vision. And even when it did, his mind was slow to wrap itself around the implications, occupied as he was, and had been, by Julia and his fear that she would, through some channel he had not gated or dammed, discover that he had not kept his word to her.

In the days after the dismissal, as Ah Chung and his group quietly investigated the reasons for it, Sampson felt the torment of anticipation for the thing he least wanted to come to pass. It was of no consequence that Julia was happier than she'd been since her return, or that she seemed to have taken and let go a certain clutch on life. It was as if she had stood for a long while at the shore of a lake and had now decided that despite the temperature of the water, she would, after all, venture forward.

His belief that his betrayal had been sired by hers did not bring him any solace. Everywhere he turned, he anticipated and imagined her wide face filled with sadness and hurt and, worst of all, a lack of surprise.

Of course, the way she found out did not occur, and would not have occurred, to her husband. He had complete trust in Charlie Sing, more now than ever. It was the trust between man and dog or preacher and congregant. The lack of equality had been embraced by both parties so well and for so long that any resentment was not even a whisper from disharmony's corner.

Charlie did not tell her in order to betray Sampson, though he understood and regretted that particular consequence. He told her for the reason that he had done everything since her return. For her, for their child, for the possibility of family in this still strange world.

They had arranged, with the help of Lucy Robinson, who still had not arrived at an understanding as to why she continued to help two people whom she knew barely at all, to meet at Natural Bridge. There, beneath the giant boulder where he had just months before gone to read Julia's last letter from Michigan, she listened to what he had to say.

Blue jays argued in the shrubbery. The birches stood already bare, while, other than the hue of their leaves, the maples stood in mantles of full summer. Had either Charlie or Julia bent to lay a hand to the ground, they would have felt the oncoming winter seeping up through the earth like a snowfall in reverse.

"I expected as much," she said. She looked at Charlie sadly. "How could I expect more from him than I offered myself?"

It was not the sadness in her eyes that laid fist to his stomach—it was the way her face, her body, everything about her was already steeled against it. This was not, he knew, an auspicious direction for the conversation to take.

"Low Yuen is very young," he said.

Her face stilled and hardened further. "He will make do," she said. "Why should he be any different from the rest of us?"

His concern for the boy was overshadowed by his concern for himself, and so despite her hardness of feeling and his own guilt, he asked, "Now what happens?"

Inside, his heart and mind made bargains with each other. If she looked at him, he had a chance. If she took his hand, even better. With nearly anything else, he should prepare for defeat.

She put a hand to the side of his head, covering his ear, part of a cheek. "How can we know?" she said. "None of us would have foreseen what has so far taken place."

Her face was still determined, and whatever thrill his heart had enjoyed at her touch began to settle. She was touching him the way an aunt touches a nephew, wondering at the boy's growth while she hasn't been looking. It was the intimacy of strangers, and he felt as if his heart had been pushed into the dirt beneath them. At least it was her hands doing the burying. His rage at his own inadequacies tumbled through him, and to keep from slapping his own face, he cupped her neck with both of his hands and suggested they quit this place. "It is a big country," he said, as though an agent for transcontinental tours. "She is my child too," he added.

"You and I will always know that," Julia said, the sadness finally overtaking her face.

He understood this to be the beginning of a farewell, and he interrupted her, sure that if he stopped her speech he could stop the sentiment behind it and its consequences. "And Alice," he added. "She will know who she came from, what she is."

"She must be a Sampson," Julia said.

He shook his head slightly. "We'll find somewhere where she can be ours."

She took his hands and held them between them as if they were children at a dance. He stared at the white of her skin and the workings of her throat and thought he might be ill.

"There's no place like that," she said, as if explaining to a child that sugared treats do not fall from the heavens.

"Why not?" he said. "Who says that?"

She secured the ties of her bonnet and smoothed the bodice of her dress. "I say," she answered. She touched a finger to his lower lip and then she left. He watched her recede, her squared shoulders, her skirts washing evenly against her legs. Her resolve and fortitude were long delicate needles through his heart. She did not look back. Had she done so, he would have seen a face set and determined, agony pulsing beneath the skin.

★

Lucy Robinson would spend some part of the remainder of her long life turning over the decision she made that late October of 1873. The unrest at the factory among the Chinese had bothered her the first time around, and bothered her more when they struck for the second time. Perhaps this was because there was more open agitation, and despite drawing attention farther away from her own scandal, unrest was still unrest, and any turbulence that threw itself out into the world made it impossible for her to live under the pretense that her own attack was something of the past. Her anger with herself and her anxieties grew. Was she to be forever in that man's thrall? Even the Sampsons had learned without instruction how to move around her slowly, as if all behaviors need be performed with hands open and in full view.

It angered her that all these people felt the need to protect her. It angered her further, as the years passed, that their instincts were correct.

So for a while that October, she kept what she knew to herself. She and Ida witnessed the growing dissatisfaction among Ah Chung and his band at their Sunday school sessions. The strike this time around more closely resembled the agitation of the Crispins that the town well remembered. The thirty or forty Chinese supporting Ah Chung protested. They made signs. They worked to get others to join them. They presented a list of demands. Low Yuen must be reinstated. Charlie must be dismissed in his place, as it was Charlie who was to blame for the wrongs perpetrated against them, Charlie who was working for some selfish design of his own. They must have higher pay, better job security, better living quarters. Why should they be paid less than the native workers? Which race was producing the better quality shoe in the shorter amount of time?

"Where was this spirit when the Crispins needed it?" Alfred grumped to Lucy and Ida one night. He had been unemployed for months.

Ida said, "As if you would do anything with a Chinaman, even stand on a picket line with him."

Lucy said nothing, taking note that although the Robinsons were the closest thing to family Ida had in this small village, and they had not returned to Virginia partly out of loyalty to their strange community of three, she was, once again, siding against them.

At certain points in her life, Lucy would tell herself that she had been motivated by a sense of justice. She determined that she had felt the need for justice more acutely because it had eluded her own situation. And she did genuinely believe that setting things right in one arena might help relieve the burdens of the other. Though later, she would have the wisdom to admit that something less altruistic had been at work in her young heart.

She could have worked to settle the unrest without damage to Charlie. She could have tried to persuade Mr. Sampson that his usual gruffness and inflexibility might not best serve his interests when dealing with these particular Celestials in this particular case. She might have appealed to Mrs. Sampson's sense of justice and morality; she might have asked her whether she could stand watching one boy field the consequences of another man's actions. She did none of those things, a fact that, in the years to come, would roost solidly in her mind.

On the twenty-fifth of October, an overcast and damp Saturday, Sampson dismissed Ah Chung and the ten other Chinese who had most annoyed him by their complaints. Their protestations, he said, were groundless and they had a seeming determination to do all in their power to prejudice their comrades against their employer and those other workers who saw fit to remain loyal to him.

On Saturday evening, upon returning to his apartment at the Wilson House, Sampson told Lucy and Julia that the dismissed men had accused Charlie Sing of causing their discharge. A bitter hatred of the good man had grown, Sampson told them. It would be two days before the dismissed workers could be put on a train. He worried for Sing's safety.

On Saturday night, Alfred out with Daniel, Lucy related the news to Ida over dinner. The apartment already held the chill of winter despite the closed windows, their seals lined with cotton scraps. Lucy warmed her hands around her stew bowl. "It is a terrible situation," she said, genuinely troubled by the unhappiness that had rolled in like a mist. "Poor Low Yuen," she said, thinking of the meetings she'd arranged between Mrs. Sampson and Charlie. It was not, she supposed, impossible that the boy was the father. Mr. Sing and Mrs. Sampson might not have been meeting about their own relationship after all. But this was not, she figured, the likeliest truth. The likeliest truth, she had come to believe, was usually the one that stepped forward from the crowd, and when she thought of all she knew, there Charlie was, front and center.

She wondered what else he could've done. She wondered what she would've done in his position. She found it impossible to imagine herself standing in his shoes. She looked at Ida as if the solution might be found with her.

Ida sliced a carrot with the edge of her spoon and blew on it briskly. "Well, I have compassion for Low Yuen, to be sure, for all involved, really, but I care most about you." She glanced at her friend over her raised spoon. "You seem unwell. I don't like others if they tax you."

Perhaps because it seemed to Lucy that it had been so long since her friend's attentions had been turned on her so directly, and perhaps because she had spent her life in denial about the degree to which those attentions made the difference between a full or poor day for her, Lucy found herself telling Ida all that she knew. Maybe Ida could fix things. It was, after all, what Ida was best at. For a moment or two, Ida's face allowed her to question why she had ever kept a thing from her.

The boy was not the father. Charlie Sing was the father.

Ida made a sound of disbelief. Ida told her friend not to be ridiculous. She was acting like her brother. There was no way for anyone to know the truth of this situation. It was, from every angle, the most unlikely of situations. To try to grab and hold the truth here would be like trying to grasp an eel barehanded.

In all of Lucy's unhappy imaginings of what Ida might present her with, disbelief had made no appearance. Skepticism was the purview of the first officer to the scene of her attack. But Lucy had always relied on the hard truth that she would speak and Ida would believe, and here Ida was, repudiating and rejecting. This perhaps accounted for the briskness with which she answered, "I know because I have seen and heard what I have seen and heard."

"What have you seen and heard?" Ida asked.

Lucy set her spoon down and put her hands in her lap. "I think the details will cause you pain," she said with a simple authority that achieved what she had hoped. Ida's spirit dropped like a kite on a windless day. She stared into her bowl as though something other than carrot and potato would be found within it.

"But surely," she said, "they do not love each other."

She did not attempt to temper the importance of the question for her, and Lucy understood that it wasn't that her friend didn't believe Lucy's explanation; it was that she had come to the same conclusions herself but was not willing to say them aloud. Lucy's certain knowledge of what and who mattered most to her oldest friend hit her like the concussive waves of a blast.

The unhappiness the knowledge incited sat across Lucy's chest. After a moment, she said, "Oh, but they do. I have seen evidence of the strongest feeling between them."

Ida was stricken.

"It is most genuine," Lucy added.

Later that night, Ida would request that she not speak of her ridiculous theories to anyone else. She would insist on Lucy's word on this matter, but for now, she sat at her place, speaking of other concerns.

Lucy kept her spoon in constant and easy motion, but in the years to come it would be this moment to which she returned. The simplicity of Ida's feelings for the Celestial and the way concern for him took priority over all else, even her own suffering. The surprise of the hurt this inflicted on Lucy. Ida had been the only one who after the attack had known how to care for the wounds and then the scars in such a way as to ease suffering rather than increase it. She had not, as others had, told Lucy that everything would be better; she had told her that some things would improve, and others she could stand. Lucy had loved her for that.

The next day at lessons, Lucy slipped a short, unsigned note into Ah Chung's primer making clear what Low Yuen was accused of and who had done the accusing. It would be of no solace that she had kept her promise to Ida and had kept her silence with all others, abstaining from mentioning Charlie's name even in her conversations with God.

On that Monday morning, Ah Chung threatened Charlie Sing with the ex-foreman's own gun. Sing would withdraw the accusations he'd made. A formal apology would be offered. He must quit the factory or be shot. Charlie's sadness was still so overwhelming that he watched the action as if from above, a monkey in a tall tree, briefly curious about the odd creatures below.

He was surprised at Ah Chung's antics. He understood the boy to be opportunistic but had the misguided sense that, as a result, he could rely on him for a certain degree of pragmatism. He had perceived a calculated bluster and not the extremity he now witnessed.

Ah Chung and five of his most devout followers stood between Charlie and the bunk room exit. Charlie held his hands palm up. He avoided eye contact. Ah Chung took small, bouncing steps toward him, and Charlie moved back until he hit the far wall. Another forty or fifty workers were gathered outside the door. He understood that although they might not engage in whatever happened next, neither would he receive aid from their quarter. In his faraway manner, he felt this too to be fair.

His voice was calm when he suggested they summon Mr. Sampson or Mr. Chase. All could be resolved, he said. Nothing was yet beyond repair.

The group moved in on him. Later, he would recall his vague understanding that together these boys fashioned something quite different than they did when apart. He had the sensation he'd once had as a boy swimming in the sea when a cloud had passed before the sun and the underwater world had turned sinister in one smooth stroke.

Ah Chung stood close to him, the toes of his black cloth shoes nearly touching Charlie's leather boots. "You have behaved in a way that shames us all," he said. He listed the fates that the man deserved: May he never return to his homeland. May his family hear of his behavior and close their doors to him. May he have no descendents to sweep his grave.

Charlie wept in silence. It was a detail he would never share with Ida.

Something in the group relaxed, and in that moment, Constable Hunter made his way into the room, Sampson close behind.

"Nothing can justify the brutality," the *Transcript* would declare on the following Thursday. And the town would, for years, be ashamed of what had been uncovered beneath the surface of the village and its occupants.

Ah Chung was arrested, the pistol removed from him. All the while, he made his accusations: Charlie Sing had accused an innocent man. Charlie Sing had, once again, sacrificed another to save himself. Sampson kept the implications of the boy's claims at bay. That afternoon, and for all following days, months, years, it was as if the implications existed not at all.

Constable Hunter escorted the boy to the town lockup accompanied by forty agitated Celestials. By the time they reached the building, a large crowd of all classes had gathered.

The sight of their leader being locked in the cell sent the Celestials to his rescue. They surrounded Officer Quinn at the outer door, trying with the physicality of boys to remove him from their path, jockeying and shoving and throwing the occasional inexpert clout. The two officers endeavored to keep the Celestials from the building, dealing out blows only when, they later argued, absolutely necessary. But the Chinese aggression was too much and, the onlookers argued, too unfamiliar. The Celestials, whom the town had come to embrace, had undergone some astonishing transformation. These were not the boys the town had called their own, and the officers were compelled to call on the crowd for assistance.

Alfred was at the front of that crowd. *Finally*, he remembered thinking.

"The blows fell without mercy upon the heads of the bewildered and half-crazed Chinamen," reported the *Transcript*. The fists, clubs, and stones used were "unmerciful and uncalled for." It was "a shocking scene of wanton cruelty."

Charlie and Sampson remained in the factory, sitting in each other's company in the Celestial bunk room. They could hear the disturbance, and still they did not move. Once, Sampson cleared his throat and Charlie looked over at him, but Sampson said nothing and Charlie looked away again.

He remained against the back wall. Sampson sat on a stool, and this is where they were found when the two most seriously injured Celestials were carried in for care.

Ah Chung was fined five dollars and costs, amounting to nearly a month's wages. He paid the fine on Wednesday morning and, effectively bankrupted, was forced to quit town.

For several days, Charlie was given an armed guard until the rebellious Celestials were discharged and removed themselves from town.

The following Tuesday morning a new importation of fifteen Chinamen arrived from California. They lived with the orderly ones already employed in quarters separate from those engaged in Monday's events. Sampson instructed that there was to be no suspension of business and there was not, and he announced to the papers his hope that the usually quiet life of the Celestial American would not again be interrupted.

But in the privacy of conversation with his wife, he outlined in ferocious detail the particulars of the riot that he had gathered from various sources. He spoke plainly, refusing to cease even when her eyes would no longer hold his.

The baby was not safe there, he said.

Julia was sitting in the large wingback by the fire. Alice lay on her back along the length of Julia's lap. Sampson crossed the room and stood above them, cupping the baby's head with his short, wide hand.

"It has been made clear to me that the recent unrest is linked to your Alice," he said quietly.

Julia offered her fingers to her baby's curling fists and said nothing. Alice arched her neck to take in Sampson's face behind her.

"People were hurt," he said. "On both sides."

Julia swiped at her eyes.

"I think we must make some hard decisions," he said.

He promised they would be temporary. He promised to find a way for the three of them to have the life she desired. Perhaps another town, another business. He repeated that it would be temporary, but he did not see any other way for the immediate future. They must, he finally said, find a temporary place for the child. For her own sake.

For several moments, Julia wept, and then she gathered herself and told her husband that if he feared for his daughter's safety, then he must fear for his wife's as well, and so both daughter and wife would quit this town for as long as he felt it necessary.

It took Sampson several seconds to comprehend her meaning. Her clarity of vision, and the determination to see that vision attained, was not something he had expected. For her to say something like that was not in any way to his advantage, and so his ears refused for a moment to hear her.

And, astonishingly, he had not predicted this reaction. He had just assumed that his way would be had. The distances that had been laid between them in the previous months had been nearly unbearable. To imagine them enlarged was impossible. His anger and frustration swelled inside of him like dammed river water.

"She is not my daughter," he said. "You, on the other hand, are my wife." His voice was mean and small, and Julia stiffened as if bearing up under its blow.

"I am her mother before I am anything else to anyone else," she said, knowing that her words were inflicting the sharpest kind of pain on the man she had pledged herself to, in this life and the next.

The Saturday before Thanksgiving, the thin November sun occasionally made an appearance from behind the low clouds, but its warmth was imagined more than felt by the holiday travelers on the station platform. The morning train west was to be nearly at capacity, as so many were quitting the village for annual visits to far-flung family. Julia and Sampson had delicately agreed on this as a departure date, implying without saying aloud that her departure might be less noticeable as a result.

Julia tucked Alice's fur blanket around her in her basket and pulled her woolen bonnet lower over her brow with two expert tugs. Sampson and Charlie watched. The luggage was stowed in the baggage car, the tickets checked twice. Sampson had that morning in their apartment seen her make secure her purse of coins within her skirts. He had cleared his throat and said that of course whatever further funds she needed, he would wire immediately to her sister's bank in Cassopolis.

So now on the platform, all three of them turned against the wind and stamping their feet like pastured horses were at a loss.

Charlie held no understanding of why Sampson had asked him to accompany them, but he had been unable to resist the opportunity. It was how he had felt about Julia from the very beginning: that no matter what their destinations would be, he wanted the chance to speak with her one more time along the way. He had passed the previous few weeks in various forms of argument with her, privately overt and publicly covert. And even now, when she had made herself abundantly clear, he had to resist the urge to grab her arm and run.

He pulled the small black shoes from his coat pocket. Still wrapped in muslin, they made an odd, lumpy bundle.

He held them out to her in one hand, and unwrapped them with the other.

"For Alice," he said. He gestured at the frayed cloth. "Made from my own shoes," he explained.

She made no move to take them.

"These shoes were made for the Chinese military thousands of years ago," he said. "Very strong. Very comfortable."

She glanced at her husband. "How kind of you, Mr. Sing," she said, rewrapping the muslin and tucking the shoes into Alice's basket. "They are too big for her now, of course," she said. "But it is a most thoughtful gift."

How kind, he thought. *How thoughtful*. The politeness of strangers.

"They will fit her someday, I think," he said.

Every one of his arguments had come back to the simple premise that he wanted to make a family with her and her husband did not. And every one of her responses had been equally plain: she would rather be on her own with Alice than with him.

Each time she had made this apparent, he had understood it but not believed it. Even now he waited for her to turn, one foot on the train's first step, and offer herself to him with a small beckoning wave. This was why he had accepted Sampson's invitation: because if she were to make the offer, he must be there to receive it.

Sampson, too, had no understanding as to why he had asked for the man's company, though he found himself vaguely comforted by his presence. Ah Chung's accusations still rose through his mind like steam, but he liked Charlie, he had trusted Charlie from the outset. He had made an investment in the man, and he did not like to think he had been so wrong about so many things. His wife's straight back, her face turned away from him, toward the train that would take her miles away, was reminder enough of what had come of his instincts and aspirations.

Even this morning, watching her pack the last of Alice's things, folding them into the most extraordinarily tiny bundles, securing them in the carryall as though executing a difficult jigsaw puzzle, he had thought: *I could fix this.* And yet he had known he would not. Had all that had passed between them fashioned him into a different man, or had his genuine form been revealed? He imagined it was a question that circled her as well, and he took some small solace in that.

The first whistle sounded, and most of the travelers hurried aboard, eager to be out of the damp and wind.

He touched Julia on the elbow, and when she turned, said, "Stay."

She glanced at Charlie, and he took a few delicate steps away. He could give her at least that, he thought, his heart breaking.

She turned back to her husband, her eyes filled with tears, and held gloved fingers to his chapped lips. "When you can convince me that you are asking that of Alice as much as of me, I will," she said. "On the first train."

Charlie had not stepped far enough away to keep her words from his ears. *I am asking that of you*, he wanted to scream. *That is what* I *am saying*. He imagined throwing himself around her heavily skirted legs. He imagined announcing his love in his best English. He, too, had not expected any of what had come to pass, but here it was, here they were. *This is* my *child*, he imagined saying to the other travelers.

He had not expected to fall in love with a pale, blue-eyed American woman, but here it was, here they were, and what he feared she might have already forgotten was: *The child is ours. There was you and then there was me and now there is this, and she is ours.*

But he said nothing, which was completely characteristic, surprising no one, least of all himself.

Julia shook his hand and then embraced her husband, hefting Alice in her basket, waving their offers of assistance away. As she climbed the train's steps and found her compartment, settling her hand luggage above her seat, her breathing settled for the first time in weeks. Of course, there was much about which to fret; she was not naïve about the worries ahead. She felt sure she would return, later if not sooner. How, after all, could a single woman with such a baby make her way in this world? An hour into the trip, the train's compartment would seem large and bullying, and her mind would fill with the ways things could go wrong. She would recheck the bag of coins secured in her skirt and rewrap the bread and cheese in her basket. She had never done anything of this enormity. She had never been brave enough to try. Suppose she was not saving Alice, but destroying her best chance for happiness? She would think of Abraham and Lot's wife and Noah and Job, all those difficult choices with all those possible outcomes, so many of them dire.

But for now, the train still at the platform, she lifted Alice out of the basket and held her to the window, waving her tiny fist at Sampson and Charlie standing shoulder to shoulder.

Sampson returned the wave as if in a parade, and Charlie gave the baby a bow.

"Say good-bye, Alice," Julia whispered into the pucker of her daughter's perfect ear. "That's my good girl. That's my own good girl."

27 September 1893

Chapter Eighteen

On Wednesday the twenty-seventh of September 1893, Charlie Sing descended the metal steps of the 6:15 from New York City. The sun was low, its light a pale mix of summer and the promise of winter. Its heat was pushed aside by the briefest of breezes and he wished he had carried a warmer coat. He had not expected to return to North Adams in this lifetime and felt the wary anticipation of a disobedient dog returning to an owner's outstretched hand.

Sampson was dying. Charlie and Ida had known for weeks, since Lucy Robinson's letter. But a second, more recent, missive contained the unexpected news that Julia, too, was ill. From the shock of her husband's failing health and the fatigue of caring for him, the doctors were saying. Neither was expected to survive the week. Ida read aloud, standing at their kitchen window on Third Avenue in New York City. She had been his wife for over fifteen years. They had married in the United Baptist Church, Richardsville, Virginia, before God and Ida's wary mother, grim father, and six angry brothers on the twenty-third of July 1878. She was the mother of their five surviving children, whose sounds in the small apartment filled him with pleasure. Each time Ida had carried a child, the adjustments to her figure had amazed them both. Having missed this experience with Julia, he had found the incremental changes riveting and tremendous, as if he'd been allowed to glimpse the busy life of an underwater world. Watching her negotiate the maneuvers of daily life, he had been filled with warmth and gratitude, and had often crossed the room to take her hand and press it to his mouth.

Lucy's second letter did not mention Alice, and they did not speak direct of her either, but Ida looked up from the small, neat pages and said, "You must go."

On September 27, Alice May Sampson woke before light. She was two months beyond her twentieth birthday and lying in her childhood bed, surrounded by the detritus of her early life, felt herself ill-equipped to manage what needed managing. Though the Wilson House apartment had been busy with strangers and friends, clergy and physicians, she felt, as she often did, that what was of relevant concern to those around her did not bear on her own province.

In late June, her father's health had showed some improvement, and the Sampson family had returned to North Adams from their home of the last three years, Washington, DC, with wary hopes and cautious optimism. Her father's meetings with friends were cheery, and she grew impatient with the length of time the short walk through the lobby of the Wilson House and down only a block of Main Street took, halted as they were by well-wishers of all shapes and sizes, people at whom she smiled and nodded whether she recalled them or not.

She resented this as she always resented time with her father taken from her. She had spent most of her young life feeling as though she were in competition for his attentions. On one side of the field stood clergy and bankers, hospital builders and school fund-raisers, sadness and regret, missionary societies and worthy individuals, bravado and pride. On the other, Alice. She had felt more guilt than usual about this resentment when, by late August, his health had taken one turn for the worse after another, and the family left for Saratoga in search of some relief. Less than a month later, a week prior, they had returned to North Adams, none of them relieved of their sufferings. It had been necessary to have her father transported in a chair from carriage to apartment, which Alice found both saddening and mortifying.

Of her mother's affections, Alice had always had an overabundance, now more than ever. Her mother could not pass by her without laying a hand on her head or shoulder. She kissed her when she sat to eat. She embraced her when she left the house. Such gestures made Alice feel as if her mother were an extra cloak, a feeling that was equal parts care and suffocation.

Perhaps because of such ministrations, her mother's own failure had not occurred to Alice as a possibility, so when

Dr. Carr had informed her on the evening of Friday last that her mother had been stricken with a kind of shock, most likely brought on by her concern over her husband, Alice had stared at him pleasantly for a moment. There must be an error in his figuring. But by the next morning, when both Doctors Carr and May concurred that her mother suffered from Bright's disease, an ailment of the kidneys, and Alice had gone to her mother's chambers and seen her face, she would not have been surprised to learn that by week's end she would lose both parents.

She could not stand to be in either's room. She felt that between the professional and capable hands of the doctors and Lucy and the hotel staff, there was nothing she could offer. She was impatient with their presence, but lived in fear that everyone would quit the apartment, leaving her the only person to ease the suffering. She found herself spending what she hoped was not an unduly noticeable amount of time sitting at the window of the front room. There she could make a pretense of keeping watch, of greeting visitors. She tried to strike a pose that suggested she was available for help.

Charlie had come to Ida when there was nowhere else to go. Ida had known that even then. Julia and Alice had returned to North Adams early in 1874, after less than six months away, responding, as she had always said she would, to Sampson's assurances that he was ready to be father as well as husband. He had written her on paper torn from a ledger book, which had instantly endeared him to her, as had the fact of the letter itself, knowing as she did how rarely he undertook that particular endeavor. He had written, *It is true that my knowledge of that other man is hideous torment to me. But it is also true that without you, I am a man alone at the bottom of a vast mountain, my face lifted to the sheer expanse above me. Without you, I am this man for time eternal.* She had held the letter up for baby Alice and had said, "You see. He is our own Calvin Sampson after all."

After their return to North Adams, after Julia and Sampson, Alice between them, had settled into life in all their wary ways, after the town's interest in all of them had faded away like a footprint in sand, to Charlie it had seemed as though he were watching three children playing house on a wide expanse of thin ice, melt already slick across its surface. Everything he did communicated his determination to present himself as a viable alternative to the choice Julia had made. He quit the factory. He made a declaration for citizenship.

He abandoned the Methodists and, on a chilly day in March 1875, was received into the Sampsons' Baptist church. The Sampsons attended the baptism, as did Ida and Lucy, gathering with the other congregants around the baptistery and reciting Matthew 28:19 in one voice before Charlie was lowered backward beneath the water while Ida stole an appraising look at Julia.

His citizenship was granted by Chief Justice Horace Gray after an examination before the judge in September of 1876. In the same year, regular service commenced through the Hoosac Tunnel, California Democrats staged an anti-Chinese rally that attracted a crowd of twenty-five thousand, and less than one percent of the Chinese in America were citizens.

He opened his own wholesale and retail store, funded in small part by an investment from the Sampsons. He specialized in Chinese curios, coffees, and teas, and the *Transcript* praised his latest endeavor for its very large stock of heavy groceries, consisting of flour, syrups, molasses, etc., selling at extremely low prices for cash. Sing's motto in business, the *Transcript* revealed, was "Pay for what you get, and be sure and get what you pay for." He was, in the minds of the townsfolk, if not one of their own, certainly one their own could now wholeheartedly embrace. They frequented his shop. They inquired after his health. They prayed alongside his kneeling form.

Shortly before Christmas of 1877, Alice appeared in the store, her four-year-old head barely clearing the counter. She had maintained the sober demeanor of her infancy, and Charlie, staring down at her from behind the cash register, felt as if beholding a grown woman from a land of diminutive people.

If he was surprised to see her unattended, he did not show it. "Can I help you?" he asked.

She wanted to buy a gift for her mother. "I have money," she said, opening a small purse and showing him the several coins within.

He nodded solemnly.

And so he found himself treating his daughter as he would have treated any customer. He displayed his wares with respect and circumspection. He selected a wide array of items that he thought her mother might like, his heart in a state of exquisite misery, and then he stepped back in his usual way, allowing the final election to be the customer's alone.

While Alice decided between a spray of silk flowers and a small carving of a dog, he studied her. Her hair was as black as his own. As she concentrated, her mouth turned down slightly, her eyebrows gathered toward each other. Her lips moved in small ways, as if in quiet discussion with herself. She handled the objects with excessive care. How could he stand encounters such as these? How could he not?

"They are both very nice," he offered.

She regarded him, her brow still knit. "You are very tall for a Chinaman," she said.

"Yes," he said. "I am."

"*I* am very tall," she said and returned her attentions to the items before her.

He waited. He had spent so much time over the last few years catching glimpses of his daughter, trying to discern himself in her, that it had not occurred to him that those similarities might someday present themselves to her. He imagined her holding him in her attention and announcing that they looked very much alike.

But she flipped the dog upside down and examined its underside. She held the flowers out at arm's length and then pulled them in, holding them by her waist.

He suggested the flowers. "Your mother likes flowers," he said.

She eyed him, then pushed the dog across the counter and opened her purse.

"A good choice," he said, wrapping the gift and pressing it into her tiny gloved hand.

The front door opened and a flustered Julia swept in. She folded Alice into her arms and chided her for running off on her own. Her face was very near the girl's and he remembered how whenever Julia had discussed something she felt of great importance, she had moved her face closer to his.

Here we are, he thought. *Mother, daughter, and father.*

Julia looked up at him. "I'm so sorry," she said. "I hope she was not too much of a disturbance."

She turned to Alice. "Apologize to Mr. Sing," she prompted.

"I'm sorry, Mr. Sing," Alice said.

Mr. Sing, he thought.

"Apologies not necessary," he said to both of them. "No disturbance at all."

Shortly after that visit, Charlie Sing sat for one last portrait. It was notable for several reasons, not the least of which was the wry upward tilt of his mouth, as if he and the viewer shared some secret knowledge. He presented himself as the wise elder, his hands on the shoulders of two seated younger charges—two Celestials still at work in Sampson's bottoming room. All of them were in Western suits, the gold chain of a pocket watch like Sampson's draped casually across a worsted vest. One wore a straw hat. The backdrop and props worked to suggest the outdoors. He imagined standing before Julia in such a way as to appear an appropriate and even desirable partner. He hoped the photograph would communicate force and staying power. He hoped she would look at it and see a man who had conquered strikebreaking and shoemaking and was now turning his eye to further successes. He hoped she would see an American. But she was, apparently, unwilling to entertain him alone, and so the door to the Sampson apartment was opened by Sampson himself, and Charlie found himself politely greeting husband and wife, little Alice peering at them all from the settee upon which she was occupied with an oversized picture book.

His aspirations for this visit had been so high that he refused at first to see the scope of his failure, refused to see husband and wife exchange a quick glance after viewing the print, refused to hear the bemusement in Sampson's voice as he exclaimed at the most unusual way the photographer had brought leaves and twigs into the scene. He chose instead to offer the photograph as a gift to both of them, to accept Sampson's offers of tea as well as biscuits, and to smile and make conversation with his former employer. He wished Julia had studied the photograph longer. He wished she had entered the conversation. He wished to be able to join her on the hearth rug with Alice and her wooden blocks. He anticipated with dread having to take his leave.

For a time, he displayed his copy of the photograph at one end of his store's front counter.

Ida had remained in North Adams, working at Lucy's former sewing business, continuing the occasional English lesson with Mr. Sing. She watched him despair over the question of how someone could make do when on the other side of the road there was the possibility of so much more, until she could stand it no longer. His desire for Julia and their child was for Ida an animal too large for this world. It would have been easier if feelings such as these did not exist at all. As it was, seeing them but being unable to touch them herself was a torment. So she had left, returning in late 1877 to Virginia and her father, her ailing mother, and her brothers.

Alfred was already returned, working as a slater for the Wilburns, and it was by way of him that she finally came to understand those feelings of Charlie's by her own example. Shortly after her return, Alfred spent several weeks reslating their barn. He spent much of his time on the steeply pitched roof watching her move around below. His attentions caused her shame. It was no longer necessary to curry his favor, but to avoid her fear that she was the kind of person who took what she needed and then moved on, she gave him more attention than she might have. He endured her brothers' teasing and her impatience, and his stoicism made her think that perhaps she had underestimated him. During those weeks of slating, she stopped one day and tilted her face up to him, and he smiled, surprised and pleased to be noticed, and gave her a little wave. And she saw that he was a good man, but not a good man for her.

★

From the depot, Charlie set out for Lucy Robinson's place, but he knew she was spending most of her days at the Sampson apartment, and the thought of entering empty rooms not his own brushed him with sadness, so he turned in the other direction and headed for the factory.

The last of the Chinese workers had quit the business and the town over thirteen years previous, and most likely he was the only Celestial now walking the streets. He recalled bits from the *Transcript* article that Lucy had mailed to him. The headline read, "Departure of the Chinese." The workers were called "almond-eyed children of the Sun," and their ten-year stay described as "an orderly and unmolested life, quiet to an extreme degree." One phrase he had turned over in his mind in the years since came to him again as he stood before the familiar fence and red brick of the wide south wall: "And so as the time of the Chinese expired . . ." As if someone had known when they'd arrived that their time would be limited in advance by forces other than themselves. He remembered telling Ida when he first read the article that it was as if he had died but had not known it.

She had told him that he was more alive than he had ever been while in that factory. And he believed her, and did not share his lingering worries that perhaps to have given up his first people, his first world, was to have given up too much.

Shortly after the New Year in 1878, Julia took Alice on an afternoon excursion. They took the stage to Pittsfield, then walked several blocks to the unassuming studio of a fledgling photographer named Whitmore. Alice was accustomed to being her mother's near-constant companion on all assortments of outings, but they had never sat for a photograph before, and her mother had taken even more care with their attire than she usually did. Julia wore her most somber dress of black silk. Her collar was white, the bow at her neck a dark green velvet. The dress's sleeves were gathered in tight pleats at the wrist, the rest of the sleeve draping so as to leave the shape of her arms to the imagination. The dress's skirt was wide and full, obscuring the upholstered chair upon which she sat.

Alice sat in her mother's lap, wearing a white eyelet dress trimmed in white lace, polished black boots, and a plain white bonnet. She had not wanted to be held on her mother's lap, maintaining that she was big enough to stand, or even to have her own chair, but her mother had insisted and Alice would rarely be the kind of daughter to refuse her mother direct. She was by this point an uncommonly serious child, and though she had no idea why she had been brought to a place such as this one, she trusted her mother, and so she sat as told, still as the sky, watching the man disappear behind his giant machine that looked, she told her mother on the return stage, like a bug. She liked bugs.

In the photo, Alice's eyes appeared as black as they were in life. Julia's eyes appeared, as blue eyes always did in those early days of photography, white, and had Mr. Whitmore not colored the irises blue, her appearance would've been startling. The child regarded her mother, and although

Julia looked toward the camera, there was something in her expression that suggested the strain of holding her eyes where they least wanted to be.

The print, which she had delivered to Charlie, snapped his heart like brittle bone, suggesting as it did that although Julia was holding the viewer in her gaze, she was not holding him in her heart or mind. As a response to the portrait he had made for her, it was, for Charlie, a devastation. It made clear, once and for all, that her eyes would always and forever be in motion, seeking out those of her daughter, with neither the attention nor the inclination for any other pursuit.

He had therefore, at Lucy's suggestion, turned to Virginia. There was mining to be done in Virginia—hadn't he done that long ago in California? Ida's aunt ran an affordable boardinghouse with clean rooms and good food. He might not know the place, but he knew someone in it. He had even discussed the matter with Sampson, who had urged him to go. Had Charlie thought that he would remain in North Adams for all his days? It was time for him to make his way in the world like a true American. Sampson bade him well.

By February of 1878, Charlie had gone, and by midsummer, he and Ida had wed. He did not feel her to be a consolation prize. He felt, as he tried to make clear to her, that someone had taken his face between soft hands, turned it from the window through which he had been looking for so long, and said, merely, *Look. Over here. There is much to be seen.* The fact that he had not looked in this direction before, he told her on the night before their wedding, was the fault of the viewer, not the view.

At the small Baptist church that she had first attended as an infant in her mother's arms, she and Charlie stood before God and her family, and Ida marveled at her lack of nerves. Truly, she thought, she had never known a man like this one.

Alfred was witness to the marriage. He stood in the last row of the airless one-room church barely able to contain his gall at her choice. And so Charlie was glad, when he and Ida decided to move back North—to escape her still-angry family for what they hoped would be the more tolerant anonymity of New York—to be leaving Alfred behind.

Lucy, too, had been to the wedding, and seeing her there sharing space with Charlie in God's small room had settled something for Ida, and she had felt lucky to have them both in the world.

In the early going, Charlie had been so sensitive to Ida's anxieties that he had imagined his feelings for Julia written in bold characters on a long scroll and rolled tight, tied in red thread, and sealed with wax. It had given Ida and him enough space to find the materials to build their own kind of happiness, and although in the structure they made, Julia's absence was always for him like a boarded-up window, it was nonetheless a place of sturdiness, filled with both warmth and breezes and many clean rooms.

It was only after Ida and he had been confident of each other for many years, after they had been able to speak of North Adams and their time there, that he had relaxed his vigil, and the scroll began to unroll as if someone's large hand had given it a small push down a long table, and Julia came leaping from the paper as if she had never left. And he imagined both women in the same crowded room, pushing against whatever pushed back. He told Ida almost everything. He did not say he was the girl's father, but he did not feel he had to say such a thing for it to be the truth between them. He did not tell her how often he continued to think of Julia and Alice. These thoughts, he knew, did not detract from his strong feelings for Ida and their own children. Because he could not explain this phenomenon fully to himself, he chose not to attempt to explain it to her.

Alice had, of course, been there throughout. She had, according to bits and pieces from Lucy's letters, turned out to be a straightforward and reserved child. She had a tendency toward moodiness, and was sometimes dramatic in unexpected ways. Once, Lucy had written, as a nine-year-old, the child had cried when they replaced one carriage with a new one. A mention in one of Lucy's letters of something she had said or done could buoy him for days, and omissions of such details left him bereft and irritated, and on days such as those, Ida and their children had learned to move with the quiet of spiders, making their own happinesses. Though he near constantly considered asking Ida to seek news of the girl from Lucy, he considered it more strongly at times such as these, but the pain he knew such a request would cause kept him from making his deliberations a reality.

He wondered as to Alice's developing appearance. He imagined he could predict her passions and sadnesses. He flew on fantasies such as these until his wings tired with the knowledge that all these things would never be his to see. How could he know what made her smile when he could not even know her smile? And then he would plague himself with questions: Were her teeth small or gapped? What were the lengths of her fingers? Did she suffer from headaches? Did she suffer at all? And most of all, what did she know of her father? He imagined Julia storing her secrets away, doling them out piece by piece, or saving them up to hand to her daughter at some point in one spectacular flourish. His largest fear was that there would be no doling or flourish, just year after year of silence.

The factory's windows were dark and empty. The doors were bolted. He climbed over the fence and walked the gravel path to what had been their entrance. The temperature had dropped. He put his face to the nearest window, but all was dark, and he could not see what now went on in those rooms.

On Wednesday evening, Fannie Burlingame arrived at the Wilson House apartment to pay her respects and say her farewells to Cousin Calvin. When she reappeared from Sampson's chambers, she was dry-eyed and brisk, and Alice rose from the window seat to escort her aged cousin to the door.

Alice had never felt comfortable around Fannie. There was nothing she could point to as hard evidence of her cousin's disapproval, but she felt it nonetheless, the same way she felt small dips in conversation sometimes, as if a soft spot had been discovered, the ground almost giving way. The town thought Fannie an odd duck. She had adopted a Celestial boy. She had never married.

Alice held the door open and waited for Fannie to pull on her gloves. The old woman regarded her. "This has been hard on you, I imagine," Fannie said.

Alice had heard something similar from just about every visitor to the Wilson House that week. "It is harder, I'm sure, on my parents," she said. "I am trying to be a help. And, of course, we have Lucy. She's been quite wonderful."

Fannie fastened her cloak at her neck. "What word do you have from your father?" she asked.

Alice stared at her, confused. "So sorry," she said, "but I'm not sure what you mean. You yourself have just seen my father."

Fannie looked neither surprised nor chagrined. In fact, Alice could not remember her studying her with more kindness. Fannie patted Alice's hand and apologized. She was old, she said. Alice must forgive her, she added, and then she kissed Alice on the forehead and left.

At seven, twelve, sixteen, Alice had been much the same person as she had been at one, three, and five. Likewise, at twenty, what she knew, she knew because she had been told, not because she had inquired. If she had made a written record of what she knew about her parents, it would read like an index or endnotes. She knew, of course, of her father's Chinese Experiment. She had the sense, even as a child, that any subsequent failures or successes were measured against that first unprecedented event. The Chinese had left and Sampson had persevered, yet he had lost significant monies in other business ventures. Alice remembered hushed, anxious conversations between her parents behind closed doors. When she was fourteen, the Millard factory sole stitchers staged a walkout, the first shoe strike since the Celestials' arrival seventeen years previous. That same year, her father retired, the business sold to Chase. Her father had been melancholy for weeks after his retirement, and Julia had told Alice that they must do what they could to cheer him. Alice had been unable to think of what talents she might possess that her father would find worthwhile, and so she had spent some hours sitting across from him doing her lessons, occasionally asking him for help though she needed none.

So it was unlike her now, as a twenty-year-old, to edge into her mother's dressing room, open the armoire, and draw from the bottom shelf the leather valise that accompanied her mother wherever she went. Alice had spent her life watching this valise be moved from carriage to train, train to carriage, one bottom shelf to another, but until now, it had never occurred to her to ask about its contents let alone see for herself.

She took the case into her own room and locked the door behind her. The leather was worn, lovely to the touch, and as the lock sprang open, Alice noted how easy behavior such as this was and marveled at her never having engaged in it before.

Having had no expectations for the contents of the case, she was equally and pleasantly surprised at it all. A handkerchief clumsily embroidered with her mother's initials and her wedding date. Letters from the Baptist church that Alice didn't bother to read. A rock with a white band around it. Mementos of Alice's life: a lock from her first haircut, her first tooth, a portrait of mother and daughter that Alice remembered sitting for. A carved wooden dragon. A mahogany hairpin. Tucked into one corner, wrapped in muslin, a small pair of black cloth baby shoes. Her own, Alice assumed, but she didn't remember wearing them.

At the sounds of Lucy moving past her bedroom door, Alice shut the case and slipped it under her bed. No one would miss it now, and she resolved to return to it later when she had more time.

As night fell, Charlie stood across from the Wilson House, looking up at the Sampsons' windows. He was three months shy of his forty-sixth year. His eldest son, Herbert Hallen Sing, was fourteen, his youngest, Robert Edward Lee Sing, seven. He lived at 2722 Third Avenue in New York City and was in the employ of the Chinese firm of Sun Hung Lo at 196 Park Row, "catering to Chinese residents and the curious."

His eldest child, his daughter, was up there, behind those windows. He waited.

By 1893, Stephen Grover Cleveland had succeeded Benjamin Harrison as president, and the small town of Pomeroy, Iowa, had been nearly destroyed by a tornado, seventy-one killed, two hundred injured. The first public zoo in the

United States had opened in Philadelphia, and Madison Square Garden was home to the first artificial ice rink in North America. The discovery of saccharin had been announced, and in Menlo Park, New Jersey, Thomas Edison had demonstrated incandescent lighting to the public for the first time, while within a span of less than a week, Asaph Hall had discovered Deimos and Phobos, outer and inner moons of Mars.

The 1893 World's Fair opened in Chicago in May, displaying a map of the United States made entirely of pickles, and in the same month, the Supreme Court legally declared the tomato to be a vegetable.

Kwang-su was emperor of China, and the Kong Chow Company in San Francisco had shipped 1,002 sets of bones back to China as a way for the deceased's clan members to avoid the displeasure of the spirits and the condemnation of society at large.

California labor leaders had introduced a MADE WITH WHITE LABOR label that winemakers were forced to put on their bottles, true or not. Twenty-eight Chinese were murdered in the mining town of Rock Springs, Wyoming, eleven burned alive in their cabins. At the Treadwell Mine in Alaska, all but one of the eighty Chinese miners—the well-liked China Joe—were forced aboard small boats and cast adrift. Thirty-one Chinese were massacred on the Snake River in eastern Oregon. In Tacoma, Washington, three thousand Chinese were given twenty-four hours' notice to quit town, and for decades, no Chinese would be allowed back.

The Chinese Exclusion Act was eleven years old. It would be five decades before repeal.

That September the weather in North Adams was brilliant, as though God's angels were singing in sharp tones. Oren David had returned from visiting the World's Fair and Niagara Falls. Miles Bracewell had, as usual, sung in the Baptist church on Sunday, and on the twenty-seventh of the month, in separate rooms in their Wilson House apartment, both Julia and Calvin Sampson passed particularly difficult nights.

Alice was at a loss. There had been now, for nearly an hour, a man standing in front of White's Jeweler and Silversmith across Main Street. He seemed to have noticed her, sitting there in the window seat, though she couldn't be sure. She decided that they were engaged in a game, though she wasn't clear on its rules. Finally, when she grew bored, she turned to Lucy as she passed through the room, clean head rags and a tin bowl of fresh ice on a tray, and told her there was a man down in the street.

"How strange," Lucy said, unable to keep her impatience out of her voice. She took Julia's shawl off the settee and headed for the back rooms.

"He is a Chinaman," Alice said evenly, and Lucy stopped, her hand on the door's knob.

This was the reaction Alice had often received when she spoke in any way of China or the Chinese. She had always registered the response. Once, a teacher had asked if she was part Indian, and Alice had said no, and that had been that. Although her lack of curiosity may have been more than mildly surprising to those around her, it was not a conversation any of them wanted to have, and so they allowed her lack of inquiry to maintain itself, the way one allows a crack in the ceiling to go unattended. *Perhaps this will not need attending to at all*, one thinks in such situations, at least until the moment, and sometimes beyond, when God's weather comes pouring through.

Because it was the familiar thing to do—and during a night when both one's parents were on the downward path the familiar seemed to offer the most solace—Alice merely said, "He must be acquainted with my father."

And Lucy merely answered, "Yes, he must," before opening the door, passing through it, and closing it with her foot.

While Sampson was not afraid to die, it was also clear that he wanted to live. He was impatient with doctors and clergy, and before she fell ill, only Julia could calm him enough to remind him that everyone wanted what he wanted. Everyone was doing what could be done to make him well. He was like a boy in the midst of a tantrum, unable to articulate even to himself what he wanted, but clear that his desires were large and crucial. Julia was the only medicine that worked. So soothing was she that he found himself extending his fits so she would not leave his side. "Stay," he said to her again and again so he could take pleasure in watching her do so.

But by that Wednesday, she had been missing from his chambers for several days, and his body had begun to accept the small ways in which parts of it were shutting down like gas lamps being dimmed for the night. Except for the effect of opiates, he would be conscious until the end came and science retired in defeat, and those witnesses to his body's failure would later say that he had faced death as he had faced life, with composure, and with the anticipations of the faithful, but he would have been the first to tell them in his brisk way that appearances were almost always deceiving.

Julia was ill, he had been told, and he could not bear that his body would not allow him to tend to her.

"Is she alone?" he asked Lucy once and again, though each time she assured him that she was not.

"Don't worry," she said, tugging at his bedsheets and pillows, bringing him at least momentary relief. "I won't allow such a thing."

And he would smile and close his eyes, reassured, and then open them, panic written across his face in a clear hand. "Is she alone?" he would ask.

"I must see her," he would say, and Lucy would tell him that she would do what she could.

"I made a mess of things," he said once on that Wednesday, the late afternoon sun warming his pale face.

Lucy did not know how to answer.

"Is she alone?" he asked, and she sent hushes at him, her hands ministering to him like expert witnesses.

When she wasn't with him, she was good to her word, attending with devotion to Julia. She would not have predicted that she would have stayed in their employ for so long and with such happiness, but she had. Years ago, when

Alfred had made ready to quit the village, sick up to his ears with Yankees and their Celestial friends, he had assumed she would make the journey with him, and she had had to tell him gently that her life was there. She had hated to see his solitary figure, clothed in his Sunday best, disappear into the dark of the passenger car, but she had known her choice to be the right one.

By the night of Wednesday, September 27, Julia was disoriented and in extraordinary pain, but clearly wanted to be in the company of her husband. Her dreams from that middle country between this world and the next were restless and energetic, and punctuated by a sudden lucidity, his name on her dry lips. This was something no one would have predicted, Sampson's name where everyone would have expected Alice's, but once heard, this wife calling for her husband made perfect sense.

Her hallucinations were filled with gifts given and taken away. In some, she was blamed for things of which she was innocent. In others, she dodged responsibilities that were hers and hers alone. They were populated with curious and prodigious characters, or filled with the most ordinary of passersby. In some, she was alone. In others, Alice accompanied her. In none did Sampson appear. In her delirium, her torment at this was tenfold.

Take pity, she begged, but to whom she was not sure. Alice had been all. Julia had lived her life by this belief. But here, on God's threshold, she held what she had gained and what she had lost in both hands at the same time.

She had not seen her husband for what seemed to her like days. Drinking and eating were beyond her. The pain was a wall against which she threw herself. She had no idea of the time, but she reached out with a sudden energy and came up with Lucy's hand.

"I must see him," she said.

"I know," Lucy said. "I know," the words like a distant train pulling into a faraway station.

The obituaries of Calvin T. and Julia H. Sampson took up two full pages of the eight-page *Transcript*. The editors reported that Mr. Sampson had died at six o'clock in the morning of Thursday, September 28, four days shy of his sixty-seventh year. His wife of forty-four years had followed him to their Lord's Celestial Kingdom at two the following morning, her sixty-seventh birthday. The paper reported his indomitable will and her kind heart and generous impulse. When it came to Calvin Sampson, the paper reported, all was definite, concrete, and substantial. Those he did not like had amplest knowledge of his feeling, and those he did were lifelong beneficiaries of his goodwill and fierce loyalty. Mrs. Sampson had not been specially prominent in the social life of the town, devoting herself to her daughter, and to her reserved ways and retiring life. The coffins of husband and wife were to be laid side by side in a single grave.

The papers did not report that in the loneliest hours between Wednesday night and Thursday morning, Lucy and Alice had helped Sampson into a movable chair, had wheeled him into Julia's chambers, had made sure that husband and wife were within reach of each other, and had quit the room. For a moment, the two women had stood in the parlor, but even that had seemed unseemly, and they had each retreated to their own bedrooms, as if on this night Calvin and Julia should be the only people allowed the company of one another.

Neither woman ever spoke about that night. In the years to come, especially when her husband's arms gentled and held her, when her children gathered around her like birds, their love allowing her to feel that she was capable of stepping off a cliff into flight, Alice liked to think that the time in that room had been a solace for her parents. That they had found a way to tell each other the things they had needed to say. She wished for them the life as they wished it rather than as it had been. From her life of abundance and blessing, she wished that she could have given them more.

After a time, she had returned to the parlor, to her window perch, and though she made no sound, Lucy soon joined her, sitting in her customary chair by the fire.

"We should take him back to his room," Lucy said.

"He is still there," Alice said.

For a moment, Lucy misunderstood, but then she joined Alice at the window, and both women regarded the man below through the bubbles and waves of the window glass. He was standing in the dim light of the gas street lamp, his face to them, as if he'd known that if he waited long enough they would appear.

It was well past two. The night was dark, the sky's stars and moon hidden with a solid wash of clouds. The glass was cold to the touch. Inside and out, all was stillness and quiet.

"He is someone your mother would want you to meet," Lucy said after a time.

Alice had kept her curiosity at bay for so long that the strength of her desire to know was like sudden pain. She felt as if she'd been lowered into water too hot to stand.

The year was 1893, and Alice May Sampson tried to decide what she wanted to know from that man beneath the street lamp, and whether she had the force to ask. She felt as though God had swept His hand across the world's terrain, filled His palm with her parents, herself, and the stranger on the street, and all the shards and stones of man's small business on this earth, and was now, after years of holding them in the hollow of His hand, going to cast them to the skies. In the far distance, there was the whistle of an approaching train. All three of them attended to it. Who knew what was possible? They lifted their faces and waited for what from His hand would be ordinary and what would be singular. Either would be welcomed. Both would be astonishment, for them and for us all.

Bibliography

The following sources helped in ways large and small:

Land Without Ghosts: Chinese Impressions of America from the Mid-Nineteenth Century to the Present, R. David Arkush and Leo O. Lee, eds.

Their Lives and Numbers: The Condition of Working People in Massachusetts, 1870–1900, Henry F. Bedford

The Crispins, Calvin, and the Chinese, Senior Thesis, Richard V. Bennett

Baptist Life and Thought, 1600–1980: A Source Book, William H. Brackney, ed.

The North Adams Shoe Manufacturers: How They Created a Successful Industry Only to Abandon It, Senior Thesis, Matthew S. Bryson

Images of America: North Adams, Robert Campanile

The Chinese in America, Iris Chang

The Chinese of America, Jack Chen

A Son of China, Sheng Cheng

History of the Temperance Reform in Massachusetts 1813–1883, George Faber Clark

The Forging of a New Mill Town: North and South Adams, Massachusetts, 1780–1860, Dissertation, Timothy Christopher Coogan II

Berkshire County, Rollin Hillyer Cooke, ed.

History of the Hoosac Tunnel, Orson Dalrymple

Recollections, Washington Gladden

Women's Letters: America from the Revolutionary War to the Present, Lisa Grunwald and Steven J. Adler, eds.

Closing the Gate: Race, Politics, and the Chinese Exclusion Act, Andrew Gyory

Berkshire: Two Hundred Years in Pictures, 1761–1961, Richard V. Happel, Robert B. Kimball, and William H. Tague

The American Note-books, Nathaniel Hawthorne

A Gazetteer of Massachusetts, John Hayward

The Organization of the Boot and Shoe Industry in Massachusetts Before 1875, Blanche Evans Hazard

The Life Stories of Undistinguished Americans as Told by Themselves, Hamilton Holt

The Chinese American Family Album, Dorothy and Thomas Hoobler

Stories from Our Hills, Jean Jarvie

A Shopkeeper's Millennium: Society and Revivals in Rochester, New York, 1815–1837, Paul E. Johnson

Chinese America: The Untold Story of America's Oldest New Community, Peter Kwong and Dušanka Miščević

A New England Girlhood, Lucy Larcom

An Early Vermont Sampler, Marion B. Lawrence

A Shoemaker's Story: Being Chiefly about French Canadian Immigrants, Enterprising Photographers, Rascal Yankees, and Chinese Cobblers in a Nineteenth-Century Factory Town, Anthony W. Lee

The Knights of St. Crispin, 1867–1874, Don D. Lescohier

The Chinatown Trunk Mystery: Murder, Miscegenation, and Other Dangerous Encounters in Turn-of-the-Century New York City, Mary Ting Yi Lui

Clarksburg, Massachusetts, Then and Now, 1749–1962, Ethel Mae Marsden

An Illustrated History of the Chinese in America, Ruthanne Lum McCunn

Chinese American Portraits: Personal Histories 1828–1988, Ruthanne Lum McCunn

"Celestials" in a Shoe Factory: Middle Class, Labor, and the Chinese in North Adams, Massachusetts, 1870–1880, Senior Thesis, Benjamin T. Metcalf

The Unwelcome Immigrant: The American Image of the Chinese, 1785–1882, Stuart Creighton Miller

Plant Wizard: The Life of Lue Gim Gong, Marian Murray

History of the North Adams Baptist Church, 1808–1878, A. C. Osborn

Old-World Questions and New-World Answers, Daniel Pidgeon

North Adams and Vicinity, Illustrated, H. G. Rowe and C. T. Fairfield, eds.

Cradle of the Middle Class: The Family in Oneida County, New York, 1790–1865, Mary P. Ryan

A Candlestick in this Place: History of the First Baptist Church, North Adams, Massachusetts, Doris M. Sanford

Telling Travels: Selected Writings by Nineteenth-Century American Women Abroad, Mary Suzanne Schriber, ed.

History of Massachusetts Industries: Their Inception, Growth, and Success, Orra L. Stone

Strangers from a Different Shore: A History of Asian Americans, Ronald Takaki

Iron Cages: Race and Culture in 19th-Century America, Ronald Takaki

A Different Mirror: A History of Multicultural America, Ronald Takaki

New York before Chinatown: Orientalism and the Shaping of American Culture, 1776–1882, John Kuo Wei Tchen

The Path to Mechanized Shoe Production in the United States, Ross Thomson

America in 1876: The Way We Were, Lally Weymouth

The Gunpowder Mills of Maine, Maurice M. Whitten

The Silent Traveller in London, Chiang Yee

History of Berkshire County, Massachusetts: With Biographical Sketches of its Prominent Men, Thomas Cushing

"Calvin Sampson's Chinese Experiment," *Yankee*, Brent Filson

"The Knights of St. Crispin in Massachusetts, 1869–1878," *The Journal of Economic History*, John Philip Hall

"The Shaping of Values in Nineteenth-Century Massachusetts: The Case of Henry L. Dawes," *Historical Journal of Massachusetts*, Fred H. Nicklason

"Asian Pioneers in the Eastern United States: Chinese Cutlery Workers in Beaver Falls, Pennsylvania, in the 1870s," *Journal of Asian American Studies*, Edward J. M. Rhoads

"Chinamen in Yankeedom: Anti-Unionism in Massachusetts in 1870," *The American Historical Review*, Frederick Rudolph

"Calvin T. Sampson," *New England Manufacturers and Manufactories*, J. D. Van Slyck

"The Sampson Family," *The Giles Memorial*, John Adams Vinton

North Adams, Mass. Troy Daily Times Presses

North Adams: Old Home Week, 1909

Early Life and Customs of Berkshire County from Collections of the Berkshire Historical and Scientific Society, 1892

1753–1953: Commemorating the 200th Anniversary of the Founding of Stamford, Vermont

The Berkshire Hills, Federal Writer's Project of the WPA for Massachusetts, 1939

Records of the Bureau of Statistics of Labor, 1870

Interrogation Transcript of Charles T. Sing

Interrogation Transcript of George D. Sing

Many local and national newspapers of the time, especially the *Adams Transcript* (now the *North Adams Transcript*) and the *Hoosac Valley News*.

Acknowledgements

For all kinds of assistance at all kinds of times: Talia Mailman and Payap Padkeelao; Kacy Westwood and Jason Clark; Kevin Scott Wong; Barbara Lane and Erica Mae Peterson; Justin Adkins; Barry Goldstein; George and Nancy Parrino. And especially Anthony W. Lee.

Any historical inaccuracies are my responsibility, as are, of course, the historical liberties I've taken in the name of fiction.

For early and crucial readings: Andrea Barrett, Sandra Leong, Marsha Recknagel, and Eric Simonoff.

For rigorous and generous later help: all the folks at Tin House Books, but especially Lee Montgomery, Nanci McCloskey, Rob Spillman, and Meg Storey.

For my children: Aidan, Emmett, and Lucy.

And, as always and for everything: my husband, Jim Shepard.